L

The Powerful One was attired in a corset. It clasped around her narrow waist and exaggerated the curves of her hips and the rise of her succulent breasts. Her long nipples had giant pearls at their tips.

Adam watched as a muscular youth caressed her. He became erect at the vision despite the torturous cock-ring which encircled his penis. Adam groaned and writhed in frustration. After half an hour, the youth was dragged from the room and The Powerful One turned her attentions to Adam.

'Bring him to me,' she ordered one of her hooded guards. Adam's heart sank.

Lake of Lost Love

MERCEDES KELLY

First published in 1997 by
Black Lace
332 Ladbroke Grove
London W10 5AH

Typeset by SetSystems Ltd, Saffron Walden, Essex
Printed and bound by Mackays of Chatham PLC

ISBN 0 352 33220 4

Chapter One
Monkey Tricks

*O*n Monkey Island the air was full of music. Drums rattled and the melodies of lutes, flutes and banjos rose in a crescendo of sound. On a large bamboo platform, a metre above the sand, two figures writhed in a sinuosity of erotic dance. Kelila, dark-skinned and shining with perspiration, was naked except for a white, silk plaited rope which wound around her athletic body, touching her curves and hollows and accentuating her round, firm buttocks and proud breasts. She wore gold rings in her nipples, ears and navel, as well as anklets of gold and a wide gold collar, inlaid with diamonds. Attached to the collar was a short, plaited silk leash. Holding the other end of the leash between her strong white teeth was the redheaded Isadora, American exotic dancer supreme, lover of Kelila. Isadora wore black-dyed animal skins, soft and shiny, which clung to her elegant body like a second skin. Her elbows, shoulders, breasts, buttocks and knees were left visible, and the white flesh shone through the black leather like fire burning on a dark night.

Suddenly, Isadora drew the native Kelila closer to her in an erotic gesture of power, pulling the silken rope

1

ever tighter, drawing her towards her. Kelila pretended to fight the rope, and she whirled around, entangling herself in the plaited threads. Isadora, her blue eyes gleaming, placed her leather-clad hands on the native girl's heaving breasts and tugged on the nipple rings. Both women swung together like one black and white creature, one bending backward to touch her head on the ground, her legs braced, her pubis thrust forward. Then the other would appear to give in to the other's strength and fall back passively. But the dominatrix, Isadora, was inevitably the winner in the dance of sexuality. Finally, she wrapped her prize in the rope and kissed her on the lips. Kelila sunk to her knees and bowed her head to the ground, where she kissed the leather-clad feet of her mistress.

The roll of drums came to an end and the audience of natives applauded. Isadora and Kelila bowed and ran off to change.

The Kelidora Dancing Academy of Monkey Island was, for Isadora and Kelila, a solution to their problem of how to make a living and stay together. They had been lovers for several years, ever since Isadora was shipwrecked with Angeline Bijoux on the Isle de Paradis, and Kelila had helped Isadora nurse Angeline back to health. Isadora and Kelila had a mutual love in dance; Kelila came from the dancing tradition of Monkey Island and Isadora had been an exotic dancer and actress in America. Together they formed a wonderful partnership, made more successful by the fact that they were lovers. Kelila had always taken the passive role in the relationship, while Isadora was the dominatrix.

Now they taught females the intricacies of dance. Girls came to them from other islands, too, attracted by the reputation of the renowned Kelidora Dance Academy.

'Kelila, my darling, how about a nice long swim?' Isadora asked her partner one morning.

2

'Yes, Isadora, if you want,' said the softly spoken, almond-eyed beauty.

They changed into light cotton sarongs, long to their ankles but tied around their waists so their breasts swung proudly free. They walked arm in arm to the beach, and found the little rock-strewn cove deserted. They threw off the sarongs and hung them on a rock. Kelila ran into the water, her firm buttocks bouncing like rubber. The two women kept in shape by swimming and dancing every day. Their bodies were the tools of their trade and they took care of them assiduously. Isadora took her time following her companion into the clear, turquoise water. She waded in, relishing the cool water on her hot thighs, and the lapping of the little waves on her bottom. Her strong legs thrust through the water until she was waist deep, then she dived forward and swam. Kelila came back to her, her black plaited hair wet and glistening with diamond drops of water. They held each other in the cool, refreshing sea, their hands knowing where to cling, where to fondle, where to stroke. They caressed each other tenderly and pressed together in the watery bed. They had been together for several years and their mutual ardour was still not quenched. Isadora loved her passive slave even when she was whipping her. Kelila adored her mistress even when she inflicted pain. The two were ideally suited. Their fingers fluttered and danced in each other's salty sex while they murmured sweet nothings in each other's ears.

'Will Angeline come to see us, do you think?' said Kelila, when they were stepping out of the water.

'I do hope so. Angeline always wanted to be a dancer,' said Isadora, lifting her heavy red hair and letting it dry in the sun. 'I just hope Prince Hari allows her to visit us. We haven't seen her for a year.'

'It would be a good advertisement for the academy, to have royal patronage,' said Kelila. 'We could do with some rich pupils.'

3

'Why, Kelila, I do believe you are becoming greedy. What do we want for? Nothing! Our days are spent dancing and swimming, eating and sleeping in the best and kindest climate in the world. Our health is good and we have each other. What more could we possibly need?'

'Darling, you are right, as always, but I think we should have a little something put by, for our old age.' Kelila shook her youthful, healthy limbs and walked up the beach to their home, a makuti-roofed hut on tall bamboo stilts, with a deck all around, over which were festoons of orange and pink bougainvillaea. There was a view through coconut palms of the sparkling sea. Weaver birds hung their nests over the hut and fluttered in and out of them in a fury of domesticity. The air was sweet with the scent of exotic blooms. Music came from the waves crashing on the distant reef, and insects, birds, monkeys and tree frogs who inhabited Monkey Island.

'You do realise that if Angeline comes to stay we will have to teach her for nothing, you know. We can't expect even royalty to pay when they are friends and we have specifically invited her.' Isadora shook a finger at her lover.

'Oh, Issy, you are so impractical. Of course they will pay us to look after her! They are aware of our circumstances. We have no family to look after us when we are ill and old.' Kelila walked off in a huff, knowing that disagreeing with Isadora would bring punishment later. But she always looked forward to the erotic chastisement that her lover would give her.

Sure enough, that night, Isadora wore her second skin of leather. She wielded a long whippy cane and stood, arms akimbo, waiting for Kelila to finish her ablutions.

Kelila, on all fours, crawled in to her lover's presence. Her body was naked except for gold anklets, bracelets and a collar of bondage. She licked Isadora's feet and

4

then stood passively, waiting for Isadora to clamp her to the wall chains that they had fixed in their bedchamber. Isadora did the necessary locking of metal bands, then stood back to admire her captive slave. Kelila's hair was tied in tiny plaits interwoven with seashells and coral. Her head was held high by the wide metal collar, to which a leather leash was attached. She stood, arms out and above her head, legs wide apart, her belly and breasts pressed to the woven wall, her bare buttocks glistening from a generous supply of coconut oil. Her bottom was pushed out, as if she was offering it to the cane.

'Yes, you are ready for it, my love, are you not?' Isadora whispered.

'Please punish me, Isadora, for I was wrong to question your judgement.'

Thwack! Thwack! The cane sang as it split the air and found its target. The chestnut-brown skin turned fiery. Kelila curved her spine more to meet the cane as it fell, but did not make a sound. After a dozen blows Isadora rested her arm. She bent forward and squeezed the inflamed flesh, and her lover flinched.

Next Isadora took up a long plaited whip and took aim. The knotted end of the snake-like weapon licked the flesh in a subtle flicker, faster than the eye could see. It happened again and again, until Isadora's arm was in constant movement. Back, up and forward to deliver the assault on the beloved flesh. Sometimes the whip was directed at Kelila's thighs or her flaring hips; sometimes it was aimed at her sex pouch which was visibly reddening and swelling under the erotic punishment. Kelila's head hung sideways on to one shoulder, and tears ran down her face. When Isadora saw this, she put the whip down and caressed her lover, covering her with passionate kisses. She left her attached to the wall chains but touched her lovingly on the face, stroking the tears from her cheeks and chin. She kissed her neck and

5

shoulders then her underarms, held open by the chains. She murmured love words into her ears and stroked the reddened flesh, then placed her leather-clad fingers between Kelila's legs and brushed the swollen flesh of her sex.

Kelila caught her breath at this delicate, lambent touch. Her head was drawn back by her mistress's hand on the leash and her face was held while she was kissed on the lips. Isadora's leather garment was soft on her flesh and it clung to her. Her sex lips were parted by a wide strap which also drew her buttocks apart. Her body was mostly hidden except for her elbows, shoulders, underarms and buttocks. It held her in and restricted her movements but exposed her in unusual places, making those parts of her body more erotic than ever. Her sex hair was pale ginger; fine curls that did not hide her sex but enhanced its pink colour. Suddenly she placed the whip between the slave's thighs and rubbed it firmly between her sex lips. Kelila moaned lightly as the whip's caress became more rhythmic. Isadora rubbed her leather-encased body up against her victim and opened her legs to feel her sex meet the reddened buttocks. The whip was between both women's thighs, and they writhed on it and cried out together.

Isle de Paradis, The Palace, May 1902

Hello darlings! I hope this letter finds you well, as we are. Thank you very much for your kind and very generous invitation. I would love to stay with you. I will definitely make some arrangements soon and let you know when to expect me.

My best love,
Angeline.

PS I will, of course, pay you for Angeline's dancing lessons. I remember very well your displays of exotic dancing here in the early days of your time here. It will give me great pleasure to

6

hand over my wife to your care and expertise for the duration
of three months.

    Yours very sincerely and with great affection,
    Hari, Prince of Paradis.

'It's wonderful news!' shouted Kelila, as Isadora read out the letter to her. 'But when is she coming?'

'They don't say, but I'm sure it will be soon.' Isadora folded the letter and tapped her lover lightly on the buttocks. 'Come on, honey, we have work to do.'

Chapter Two
Forbidden Apple

Jezebel's establishment, known as the Forbidden Apple, was in fact little more than a glorified hut. Like the other habitations on Isle de Paradis, it was raised on sturdy bamboo poles and constructed of woven coconut palm leaves – makuti – built around wooden floors. Unglazed windows looked out on to a jungle of palms, fruit trees, bougainvillaea and other glossy leafed, highly scented bushes and trees, whose vibrant flowers shouted with intense colour. Weaver birds made their little ball-like nests on the ends of palm fronds which hung low over the hut. Enormous, brilliantly patterned, fan-like butterflies flapped slowly through the jungle trees. The scent of frangipani filled the still air. There was a smell of sex, too, hanging over this simple hut.

Inside there were three chambers. One had a large mat on the floor, on which sat many unwashed half coconuts, containing the dregs of last night's banana wine. The other chambers contained beds, stools, cushions and chests and were for the main business of the establishment – copulation. Above the dark doorway, which was curtained by many strings of wooden beads, swung a two-dimensional model apple, made of wood, painted in bright red and green and with a huge bite out of it.

Outside the hut, lounging by the doorway, was the owner and madame of the establishment, Jezebel. She was a fleshy, olive-skinned young woman with a creased cotton sarong wrapped around her hips. Her large breasts would have hung almost to her waist, but were held up with a complicated arrangement of straps which pushed her bosom upward, yet allowed the large nipples to remain exposed. The effect was not unpleasing, it seemed, as a large native man who leaned there with her was obviously enjoying her buxom charms.

'Samson, suck my nipples harder, will you! You are not putting enough heart into it,' she complained to the handsome black man, whose loincloth bulged with his straining member.

'Ah, Jezebel, you never tire, my poppet! Where do you get the energy from?' The giant of a man eased his body over her so he could better reach her breasts. He played with her sex, pushing his large hand up between her legs so the sarong was lifted free of her round belly and her hirsute triangle was exposed. She lay down on the hard-packed, sandy earth and pulled him on top of her. His cock was released from its cotton bandage with a quick flick of her wrist and she pressed it into her. They knew how to please each other. Jezebel preferred to make love in public. She needed the excitement of being in a place where, at any moment. someone might come upon the sight of her naked flesh. She was and always had been an exhibitionist.

This brothel on the Isle de Paradis was the first and only establishment of its kind. She ruled over it and her girls with a rod of velvet rather than iron. Her own sexual appetite was the presiding factor, rather than a greed for riches. She had always had her own retinue of men who pleasured her, and she sometimes involved other younger men in the erotic games she invented.

This morning, however, she simply needed a good fuck, and Samson could be relied on to provide a long-lasting erection.

They humped and writhed together for several minutes and then it was suddenly over.

'Go and wake those lazy girls, Samson.' She slapped him playfully on his taut buttocks and her consort rose, grumbling, scratched his arse and farted.

Jezebel went to wash in the little waterfall in the forest clearing. Monkeys chattered in a loofah tree and large black crows cawed.

'Good morning, madame,' said Sylva, joining her, rubbing the sleep from her slanting eyes and undoing her sarong. She stepped into the flow of icy water with a shiver and a giggle and let the stream run down between her ripe breasts on to her tummy and down between her thighs. She turned and enjoyed the trickle of refreshing water on her straight back and flaring buttocks, raising her rounded arms to the clear blue sky.

'Hello, girlie,' Jezebel slapped the girl on her tempting buttocks. 'What's this?'

'Nothing! Only where Lana was too enthusiastic with her whipping last night.'

'I'll talk to her about it. You shouldn't bruise like that; it is not attractive.' Jezebel had had much practice in the art of gentle flagellation and erotic punishment. Lana was not yet adept at correction.

The other girls soon joined them, having dragged themselves from their beds to prepare for the early morning rush. Petite Gigi jumped about in the deep pool and washed her long, dark, wavy hair. Her blue-black skin shone and glistened with rainbowed drops of water. Her high little breasts bounced on her narrow ribcage. Her beautifully defined spinal muscles rippled under the glossy skin. 'Good morning, madame!' she shouted cheerfully.

Cherry-Ripe was also a native of Isle de Paradis and

10

had the same high breasts and slender shape as Petite
Gigi. Lana was made of different stuff. She came from
another island and was as tall, if not taller, than most of
Isle de Paradis' male population. She was statuesque
and her demeanour was haughty and proud. Her skin
was pale olive; almost yellow in certain light. Her hair
was a dark foxy red, thick and coarse. It fell in heavy
curtains on either side of her sharp-featured face. Her
lips, however, belied the sternness of her features. They
were wide and generous, though she tried hard to flatten
them to a thin line of controlled anger to please her
sexual 'victims'. She was Jezebel's latest find, and her
particular skills were in demand with certain customers.
All the girls were well treated by Jezebel and had their
wages paid regularly, which they usually sent home to
their families, because they needed for nothing at the
Forbidden Apple. They also took one day off every
week.

Bartolem, Jezebel's blond consort, a broad-shouldered,
well-muscled man in his thirties, called the group to
breakfast by banging a wooden spoon on a frying pan.
He had come, with Jezebel and Samson, to Isle de
Paradis a couple of years ago and had helped build the
Forbidden Apple. He had discovered that he had a talent
for cooking, and he now he prepared the meals for staff
and customers alike.

This morning was very like most other mornings. A
dozen or so men arrived and ate breakfast of pawpaw
and coconut mash or a bowl of rice moistened with
coconut milk, paid for the meal and any extras they
wanted, then disappeared into the gloomy interior of the
hut to fulfil their needs.

Once morning rush was over, Samson cleared away
the dirty dishes and the girls bathed and washed again,
and spent time doing each other's hair in intricate knots
and braids intertwined with exotic blooms.

'Cherry-Ripe, who was that man you were with this

11

morning?' The high, piping voice belonged to Petite Gigi. Her face was a moon-penny, round and flat, with a small, pert nose, flaring nostrils and thick, soft lips. Her eyes saved her face from ordinariness. They were like a startled deer's, almond-shaped and dark brown, with blue-tinged whites. Her eyelashes curled extravagantly on to her high, round cheeks. Around her long, thin neck was a wide band of metal, attached to which was a ring.

Cherry-Ripe stretched her long arms over her head. 'That was Captain Ric, of the King's Guard. I am his favourite whore, he told me.' Cherry-Ripe was a nut-coloured girl of about eighteen. She was not very bright but she had a pleasing body; slender, but full of curves and hollows. Her small, round, apple breasts curved upward and bounced pleasingly on her narrow ribcage. Her bottom was round and rubbery and very popular with the soldiers and other regular customers, who liked to part her buttocks with greedy fingers and glimpse the dark, puckered hole that nestled in the depths of her cleft.

Lana was of mixed blood, and her red hair and pale skin were proof of the coupling of her brown mother and white pirate father. Her lips were negroid and soft, voluptuous promise bloomed in her proud face. Her mien was haughty and her expertise and inclination was to dominate. She had a supply of birches, whips, chains and straps in the chamber that she used. Samson had attached metal rings to the sturdy bamboo uprights in one of the copulation rooms.

The girls continued their toilet, depilating and smoothing scented oils into their skin. It was just another day on Isle de Paradis.

But this particular morning there was a new excitement at the Forbidden Apple. A group of workmen had arrived to help Samson and Bartolem build an extra room on the hut. Business was good. Jezebel was expanding.

Chapter Three

Prince Hari, Princess Angeline and Adam

*B*londe clouds of curls bounced about her lightly tanned cheeks. Dark blue eyes peered out from her long black lashes. Her brows lowered in a typical frown as she searched the surrounding rocks and bushes. She looked up into a palm tree. Her pouting mouth exploded into a burst of laughter.

'I can see you, Adam, you foolish boy! Come down from that coconut tree or I'll send my monkey up after you and he will pull your tail.' She giggled at her naughty thought.

'Come and get me, then! You can pull my tail any time you like!'

'No, you know that my father-in-law doesn't really approve of me climbing like a boy.'

Adam shimmied down the diamond-patterned trunk. His loincloth, catching on the rough bark, unravelled, and Princess Angeline, who still thought of herself as newly wed, giggled into her hand and turned away modestly, so she could not see the naked loins of her husband's manservant.

13

'Come on, Angeline, let's race to the promontory.'
Adam set off, and she ran after him instinctively, the sea
breeze catching her golden crown of curls and spreading
it behind her like a silken curtain. She raced as if her life
depended on it, keeping pace with the strong and
muscular Adam. The slender Prince Hari dawdled
behind them, fruit juice dribbling down his chin.

Next day, Angeline was dressed by her handmaiden in
a pretty flowered sarong, her breasts uncovered but for
a garland of scarlet flowers. She had tiny breasts, still
adolescent, but her waist was narrow and her hips were
becoming softer and more round and she stuck out her
bottom proudly.

Hari followed her like a pet dog, three steps behind.

'Don't follow me, Hari, I don't want you to. I want to
be alone,' Angeline told him.

He looked at her in dismay. She shook her hand at
him dismissively and he stood and watched as she
walked away, her hips swaying provocatively.

'Hi, Angeline!' A dark-skinned comely girl, with dark
short curls and plump, round, exposed bosoms
appeared. 'Come and walk with me on Rocky Beach.'

Angeline smiled agreement and the friends ran
together, barefoot.

'I know where the guards do their fighting practice,'
said the dusky, knowing Sylva. She looked much older
than Angeline, though she was, in fact, six months
younger. 'We can flirt with them,' Sylva promised.

Angeline looked excited at the idea. 'I'm not supposed
to talk with the lower orders.'

'You mean me?' Sylva chortled. 'Who else is there to
talk to? There is no-one in Paradis except the royal
family and the lower orders. You would be bored stiff
just talking with your stuffy relations. I prefer the lower
orders. Look! The guards!'

The two young females, like budding roses with their

14

flowery sarongs and their soft flesh, hid behind a rock and watched as the company of six guards lifted long wooden pikes and hurled them at targets twenty feet away. The guards were youths of about nineteen years old; fine specimens of burgeoning manhood. They wore the uniform leather tunics, consisting of leather straps crossing their naked chests and wide leather thongs hanging from a wide waistbelt. Their feet were encased in leather sandals strapped and tied around their muscular calves. The girls watched, enthralled, as the leather kilts rose and fell, revealing the young men's naked loins and buttocks.

'Surely they wear something underneath?' Angeline sucked her thumb in disbelief at what she saw. The young men's dangling genitals were uncovered, and with every run and lunge the girls were given a wonderful lesson in human biology.

'Wow! Look at that whopper!' Sylva giggled.

'Mmm! I don't believe it!' Angeline's eyes were round and her mouth fell open.

'And I don't believe this!' The heavy hand of Ric fell on the shoulders of the girls. They started in embarrassment.

'What are you doing? Admiring my soldiers, are you? Your king shall know of this.'

'Oh, Ric, please don't tell King Aristide,' begged Sylva. She had never yet been chastised by the king, and she dreaded it.

'Would you rather I punished you, then?' said the guard.

Sylva looked at the strong limbs and swarthy face of Captain Ric and liked what she saw. Her legs grew weak and her sex felt moist. A blush rose to her cheeks.

'You wouldn't dare,' said Angeline.

'Oh please, Ric, punish us,' said the forward Sylva, rolling her eyes at him coquettishly.

'I will spank you both in full view of my men. That

15

will pay you for your stolen glances at them.' He dragged the two girls on to the sand and the men stopped their target practice and stood to attention.

'Hold this one.' He ordered two men to hold Angeline while he uncovered the buttocks of the younger girl. She wore a narrow leather thong between her full, brown buttocks, and when she was bent over his knee her sex pouch was revealed to the surrounding men. The thong went under her legs and held the sex lips apart. Angeline could not tear her eyes away from the voluptuous sight of her friend's genitals. The guard spanked Sylva hard, his broad hand covering her buttocks fully and making them rosy with the blows. She yelled, her head held low to the sand, her breasts pressed against his legs. She screamed in rage at being humiliated in front of the men, but at the same time, she felt the fire in her swollen sex. Her buttocks were hot under his powerful hands. She moved her body slightly so her sex was lifted towards his blows and he complied, slapping her genitals lightly – a sensual torture, which she endured, moaning quietly.

It was soon Angeline's turn to be chastised for her naughty voyeurism. She struggled in vain and two young men, whose swollen pricks she could feel pressing against her, dragged her to the rock where their commander sat. They placed her over his broad lap, and his cock raised itself through his leather kilt and pressed into her belly. The young men stood close, eyes wide, as they watched the voluptuous punishment. Sylva, wild-eyed and tearful, sat on the sand, her clothes in disarray and her hair dishevelled, and watched her royal friend being humiliated. The rough soldier was enjoying his role as teacher of good manners. Angeline's sarong had been torn aside and her round bottom exposed to all, and she writhed under his blows. She wore nothing at all under her sarong, as was usual on this tropical island. Her sex was inflamed as the soldier let his hand wander under her bottom. She instinctively struggled against his caress, but he insisted his rough fingers into her soft flesh. She cried out in a sudden thrill of intense sensation and lay still. The youths were all in a state of high excitement at what they had witnessed and were caressing themselves furtively.

'All right, off you go, and don't let me catch you peeping again, or I'll tell the king.'

The girls ran off home and Ric said to his squad, 'I expect you might need to visit Jezebel's establishment, later, eh!' He laughed, and they laughed too. The intensity of the moment gone.

Hari was lying on the sand reading *Moby Dick* or *The Whale*, by Herman Melville. He devoured books as if his very life depended upon it. He was a gentle lad, not at all like his father, the ageing King Aristide, who had been a great warrior. Hari was a sensual boy, who spent his days with his darling little wife, Angeline. He read and painted and made music with his friends, who were mostly the sons of natives in the village. He wore casual, floral-patterned loincloths and brightly coloured feathers in his long, straight hair, which was tied back in a ponytail.

His father disapproved of him. 'Why don't you stop that awful caterwauling, Hari?' he always said to him. 'It won't get you anywhere. No-one wants to hear that music. Become a soldier like Ric. It would do you good to get some discipline, my boy.'

Today, King Aristide was not in the best of moods. His wife, the delectable Clementine, who had been his daughter-in-law's old schoolfriend, was not talking to him. He was in disgrace, but he could not remember what he was supposed to have done. Something she disapproved of. Oh yes, he had not given her a good seeing to last night. He was tired and he had a headache, he had told her, but she did not believe him. Clementine had grown rounder since their marriage. Her flesh was a

17

subtle blend of rose and cream. Her white throat was a column of marble-made flesh. Her dimpled buttocks trembled under his palms. Her belly shook and her large breasts rose and fell in emotion. He recalled their conversation.

'Aristide, my darling, do I not please you still?'

'Of course you do, my little honey pot,' he murmured into her ear.

'Do you not want to bury your face in my breasts?' She pushed his head, still blessed with thick black hair, into her generous cleavage. He snuffled and coughed.

'Not now, my sweetness,' he said, 'I don't feel like it.'

'Oh, you are awful! How are we to have children if you do not make love to me?'

'One son is more than enough,' he murmured and then snored lightly, pretending to sleep.

Clementine was only 22 years old and she wanted children. But Hari, King Aristide's son by his first wife (now deceased), would become king one day.

Adam, Hari's manservant of only two months, had a secret desire. He wanted to be a painter – an artist. He had another secret passion: he had found one of the queen's discarded old corsets that she could no longer lace up. It had been thrown away in the rubbish heap outside the palace compound, and when he found it, he asked Hari if he might keep it.

'What are you going to do with it?' asked the bemused Hari, as they sat in his bedchamber one afternoon.

'I shall find the perfect girl and get her to model it for me. Then she will become my muse and make me famous.'

'You are pretty enough to wear it yourself,' said Hari, grabbing the pink satin corset and wrapping it around the slender waist of his manservant. 'There, you are a picture.' Hari pinched the boy's nipples and turned him around. 'Let me fetch Angeline. She likes games like this.' He shook a bell pull and a maidservant appeared. 'Tell my wife I want her here, please,' said the polite prince. The maidservant lowered her gaze from the erotic sight of Adam in the corset, and ran to fetch her mistress.

Angeline stared with pleasure at the unexpected scene. Her husband had his loincloth unwrapped completely. His cock, erect and glossy, pointed straight out in front of him. He sat and looked at his manservant, Adam, who now not only wore the corset but a pair of Angeline's split-crotched drawers.

'Oh, he is almost as pretty as you, Hari,' said Angeline.

The married couple tied the corset more about Adam's hips and waist and did the ribbons up behind. His narrow hips flared under the satin, and the boned corset held his waist in a vice-like grip. His flat nipples peeped over the corset and Adam's cock flickered and rose up to lie against it. Hari grabbed Adam's swollen member. 'Oh yes,' he murmured, and rubbed the purple rod up and down between his fingers. Adam rolled his eyes up into his head and lay back in surrender. The two young royals caressed themselves in the excitement of the homosexual game. They garlanded the manservant with flowers and his pubic hair was embroidered with flower buds. Hari leant over his friend and kissed his lips.

Adam groaned. 'Kiss my prick!'

The dark head of Hari covered his straining groin. Angeline was holding Hari's long brown cock in one hand. The three young people, drunk on their own beauty, gave in to the desire that tugged at each one of them. Their mutual admiration exploded in an orgy of masturbation. Afterwards, Adam begged them to undo the queen's corset and free him from the erotic bondage of silk and velvet and ribbons. He bundled up the clothes and took off on his own to think and recover.

19

Chapter Four
Tom Meets Jezebel

*S*amson and Bartolem spent the day preparing the bamboo poles that were to form the fabric of the new room of Forbidden Apple and overseeing the weaving of the makuti walls and roof.

Jezebel could not help but admire the boys who were on the work team of weavers and builders. The bar girls were of course flirting with them outrageously, flaunting their charms. The youths were a mixed bunch of island-ers, but among them was a red-haired lad with blond skin. He looked familiar.

'What is your name, boy?' Jezebel swayed her volup-tuous hips and pushed out her upholstered breasts, which were only half hidden, towards the youth.

I am Tom Johnson of England, Madame Jezebel,' said the blushing youth.

Jezebel remembered the red-haired Tom, who had been a ship's engineer's lad in his younger days.

'Well, Tom,' Jezebel whispered in his ear. 'You are a fine, strong lad. How would you like to do some extra work for me later?'

Tom stood to his full height of five feet ten inches and pumped out his hairless chest so his pectoral muscles stood out proudly. 'All right, I don't mind,' he said, blushing, as the notorious madame of Isle de Paradis stared openly at his crotch and his sturdy thighs.

'Come to my chamber when you have finished here.' She threw the command over her shoulder and gave him a tantalising glimpse of her shivering buttocks, half exposed under the flowered sarong, tied high on her left hip.

She didn't have long to wait. Tom soon entered her own private hut, built separately from the bar and brothel.

Jezebel was practically naked, yet seemed to be dressed; her erogenous zones visible through the carefully arranged satin garment. Her fat thighs were camouflaged under swathes of cloth, but her triangle of dark, curly pubic hair was proudly displayed, as were her nipples and large, brown areolae. The overall impression was of voluptuousness and sexuality. Her lips were painted scarlet and she wore a scarlet flower in her wiry, thick Mediterranean hair.

The boy sat at her feet, and his face was soon hidden in her plump thighs. She moaned in delight as he parted her pubic hair with his tongue.

'Yes, there, there! Push your tongue right inside.'

Tom was in a dream of sensuality. He could hardly believe this invitation to make love to the island's whorehouse keeper. Sure, he would rather it was one of her bar girls he was making love to, but who cared? Any woman was worth fucking, he knew. He was ripe for experience of any sort. The fleshy woman whose thighs he parted smelled of oranges and lemons, olive oil and garlic. Her scent was pungent and salty like sea creatures, oysters and mussels. He drank the flavours deeply and breathed in her musky smells. He stared at the plump sex lips hidden in the forest of black hair. They were scarlet as her lips – painted with sweet-tasting pigmented oils. He licked the sex lips tentatively and she pushed hard on his golden head.

'Yes, that's right, good, good.'

He penetrated the red slit with his probing tongue and licked inside her. He felt the walls of flesh cling and pulsate to his delicate tongue. She writhed on his face, forcing him to press his teeth on her clitoris. His smooth chin and long nose rubbed her pleasingly on her belly and buttocks. She came noisily as he lapped and sucked.

'Well done, my lad, you are a good pupil. Do you want to put your young prick inside me now?'

'Yes please, madame,' he stuttered, his erection straining against his loincloth.

Jezebel lay down on the wide, low bed and opened her legs wide. He leapt on her with enthusiasm and unwrapped his loincloth to expose his pale loins and mauve cock. She grabbed it in delight. 'You are a good size for a lad,' she practically slobbered. Her eyes were dilated and her sensuous lips were swollen with lust.

The boy rubbed himself over her big belly and pressed her breasts with hungry hands. He licked and nuzzled the mountain of comely flesh like a starving man. She stopped his grazing. 'Just put it in me and get on with it,' she ordered.

He happily complied and felt the silky slithering of his young cock slide up into her fleshy purse. He groaned in pleasure and strained against her. She suddenly held his cock at the base and he felt the threatened orgasm fade. She held him there firmly, at the same time allowing his gentle thrusts into her. Then she let him go and his cock once more filled with blood and began to throb. Her fingers held his small buttocks and thrust him into her. She was a cushion of soft, warm flesh and he buried himself in her. His cries were loud as he exploded into her. Her moans grew like a sudden hurricane and then, as suddenly, she fell quiet.

After a brief doze they began again. His prick was immediately thick and swollen and purple with blood, she was gratified to see. This was the thing about

22

youths – always ready for love. She had forgotten; her consorts were in their thirties and past their best. She, on the other hand, was at the peak of her sexuality and needed far more sexual attention than they could give her. It was time she had a new lover. She would have to try a few more, of course, before she could make up her mind, but this one might well do. His colouring was interesting too. She liked the yellow freckles on his chest and face. The hairless young body was without fault; he had a flat stomach, tight buttocks and firm, bulging pectorals. She ran her experienced eyes over the sturdy body. He was strong and muscular and well made. She liked the gold-red hair, darkened now to a chestnut brown by perspiration, which curled on to his young neck. He would be useful to have around too, with his carpentry talent.

This time she licked his shaft and pressed her tongue on the thickening rod. She held him by the balls, stroking them and caressing the base of his cock. He sighed and moaned and threatened to come straight away but she stopped him with the squeezing caress and quietened him with soft cooing. She took his straining weapon and stroked herself with the swollen, purple tip, its little open eye weeping a pearl of moisture. She lay him down, knelt over him and pushed his cock between her fat thighs. He blushed red on his chest, neck and face. His breathing was fast and hard as she pushed down on his cock so it filled her to the mouth of her womb. She thrust again and again on to him, her thighs clutching his cock. He came almost out of her, the purple, shiny crown of his cock poised on the brink of her plump sex, then plunged into her again, his throbbing cock disappearing completely. His balls caressed her buttocks and perineum in a way she loved. She grabbed the base of his cock and rubbed hard while he plunged in and out of her. The orgasm was mutual and loud with juicy slapping of flesh.

'Well, did you enjoy that little game, Tom, my fine boy?'

'Thank you, ma'am!' He could hardly speak.

Forget the girls, he thought. It's the mature woman for me, every time. He thought of what he would tell his mates. Would they believe him? He sighed in pleasure and was ready to doze again when he was rudely awakened by a slap on his bottom.

'Back to work, you lazy boy. There's a room to build this afternoon.' Jezebel was already dressed and clearly wanted him gone. 'Your boss will be looking for you. Siesta is over.'

Tom leapt out of bed with the enthusiasm and *joie de vivre* of youth, washed himself quickly at the basin of water, and smiled cheekily at the whore.

'Thanks for the lesson, madame. May I come for more?'

'I'll let you know,' she replied flicking her plump, red-nailed fingers.

Chapter Five
Adam and the Mermaid

*A*dam had his paints and brushes packed in a ruck-sack. His easel was folded away and tied to his back. He had Queen Clementine's corset and Angeline's split-crotch drawers wrapped carefully in a silk bag tied with ribbons and he was off to find someone to model for him. He had made arrangements to meet with some friends and go to find some likely girls. The boys were ready for anything. They had their slings and quivers of arrows, their little horn-handled daggers, and they wore their most fetching sarongs. All this was to make themselves more attractive to any girls they might need to impress.

They walked slowly past Jezebel's establishment, daring to glance in the dark doorway in the hope of glimpsing a bar girl. Jezebel herself was leaning on the door post, and she whistled at the boys as they shuffled by, embarrassed.

'Come on in, baby!' she called. 'I am looking for a young lad with a fresh face and smooth skin just like you.' Adam and his two friends giggled and looked at each other in mock horror. They broke into a run and disappeared over the brow of a hill, leaving a laughing Jezebel fanning herself and swatting flies.

Arturo, Jimi and their palace playmate idly chased the huge coloured butterflies and tried to catch them. They climbed up into a tall tree and swung on the liana roots. They were like boys anywhere in the world. Their thoughts were mostly about sex. They plotted how they would attract the prettiest girls on the island.

'I think Princess Angeline is the most beautiful girl in the world,' said Arturo.

'No, she isn't. Sylva is better; she has bigger titties,' said Jimi, cupping his hands to show how big they were. The others giggled and punched each other playfully and fell down in the sand and wrestled.

'Come on, fellas, let's find some girls! I need a model, for goodness sake! How am I ever to be the greatest living artist if I don't have a muse?'

'What's a muse?' asked Arturo.

'A model. An exquisite creature who will inspire me to make beautiful pictures,' said Adam. The other two continued to sprawl and fight each other, and Adam became annoyed with their adolescent insensitivity and ran off, wanting to be on his own.

'I shall count to one hundred, and then I shall ask the next female I set eyes on to be my model,' he rashly promised himself.

He walked along the forest path, which skirted a perfect palm-fringed crescent beach, and counted slowly. 'One, two, three, four . . .'

He walked through a coconut plantation on the edge of a beach, having passed a notice pinned to a palm: DO NOT PICK THE COCONUTS. PRIVATE PROPERTY.

He stepped down on to the white beach where pink shells lay piled in heaps like baby's ears. He gathered a few in his hands and threw them in a spray into the turquoise water. He was hot and sticky from running. He dropped his rucksack on the sand and stripped himself of his sarong. He plunged into the warm water, walking up to his thighs.

26

From the green, spreading branches of a tamarind tree, almond-shaped eyes watched the lovely youth. They saw his firm, tanned buttocks rest on the water. He turned and the almond eyes saw his balls bounce on the supporting wavelets. The eyes became round as they saw his young cock stretch and grow up towards his belly. He clutched his erection firmly and rubbed it. The unseen voyeur grew hot and bothered as the youth rubbed himself and his cock grew in his hands.

'Ninety-four, ninety-five, ninety-six . . .'

Adam's cock was close to explosion when the girl who had been hiding in the tree fell out.

'One hundred!' Adam had his eyes closed as a spray of white foam arced into the sea from his overexcited cock. 'Ohhhhh . . .!' He fell into the water and began to swim away from the shore to cool off.

The girl, wrapped only in a very short pink silk sarong tied around her waist, with flower garlands wrapped around her long black hair and tucked behind her little ears, sat and laughed merrily at what she had witnessed.

She ran towards the water and plunged in, swimming strongly towards Adam. As she drew close to him she dived under the youth and grabbed his legs. He was pulled down under the water, and he saw the mermaid – for that is what he thought she must be – smiling at him from between her swaying locks of dark hair.

'Ahhh!' He inhaled water inadvertently and spluttered and coughed his way to the surface. She grabbed him under the arms and swam in to shore with him.

'I am so sorry! I didn't mean to alarm you,' she laughed.

'You idiot!' He spat out the salt water and wiped his nose with his fingers. 'You could have killed me.'

'I said I'm sorry!' The half naked, slender creature, her sea-blue eyes blazing, turned from him and ran off into the trees.

Adam sat on the sand, cross with himself and her. He

suddenly remembered his promise to himself. The artist's muse! This must be her! He called after her but she had gone. Who was she? He did not recognise her, and he thought he knew everyone on Isle de Paradis.

He collected his rucksack and easel and walked off through the coconut plantation, hoping to come across the beautiful, mysterious creature.

'Hi! Tom! How are you?' Adam raised his arm in greeting to the lad who had appeared.

'Fine, Adam.' The youth carried a saw and a bag of tools.

'Where are you going?' said Adam.

'I have work to do at the Forbidden Apple.'

'Have you really? Gosh! Have you been inside?'

'Of course!' Tom stood a half a head taller than Adam and was much stronger in form. He had always worked hard and his muscles were well defined on his sturdy frame. His arms bulged and his chest curved with strong pectorals.

'What's it like?'

'Makuti, you know, the usual construction,' said Tom.

'No, fool, what is it like? Are there naked girls? What do they do? Have you seen the bar girls at work?'

'Better than that!' bragged the newly deflowered youth.

'What do you mean?'

'Jezebel . . . I have slept with Jezebel.'

'You haven't!'

'I certainly have.'

'Did you pay for it? Isn't she revoltingly old and fat?' Adam's mouth turned down at the corners and his face showed the distaste he felt at the idea of the grossly sluttish madame with no clothes on.

'She was very nice,' Tom said, smiling.

'Nice! How can you say that?'

'She smells wonderful and is very generous with her . . . charms.'

'Charms! Yuk!'

'Don't be so unkind, Adam. She is a fine woman; a beautiful woman. Her breasts are magnificent and her pubic hair has to be seen to be believed. And her buttocks are heavenly – such large, soft globes of flesh. And she holds me inside her with strong muscles that do amazing things. Honestly, Adam, she is terrific!'

Adam stood and gazed at the carpenter. He looked suddenly older and wiser; not such a boy. Adam was jealous.

'Take me to her now,' he said.

'I can't do that,' said Tom.

'Why not?' insisted Adam.

'You are not invited,' said Tom, unsure of how to manage this unexpected intrusion into his new intimacy with the voluptuous madame.

'Oh, come on, Tom, I am your friend. Anyway, I command you as your prince's bodyguard.' He slapped the youth's buttocks playfully and they both laughed at the ridiculousness of the situation.

'Oh, all right, I expect she will welcome you with open arms, a pretty boy like you,' said the resigned carpenter.

Jezebel had showered under the waterfall for the third time that sultry day. Her girls were having a siesta. Samson and Bartolem were sleeping too.

She expected her new boy to arrive and she was ready for him. She was dressed in an intricate arrangement of chamois leather straps which wrapped her hips, thighs breasts and buttocks but left her nipples and sex bare. The straps were tied at the waist where she could tighten or loosen them as she chose. She was perfumed and powdered and her sex lips and nipples were rouged.

She was surprised to see Adam enter the chamber with Tom.

'Well, well, the prince's manservant! I am charmed to have you visit my humble establishment. The girls are resting now, but you may come back later if you wish.'

29

'Oh no, Jezebel, it's you I want.'

'Ho, ho, ho! Me you want, eh!' Her bosoms shook with delight. 'Well, what do you say to that, Tom? Shall you share me with your palace friend?'

'I don't mind.' The boy seemed suddenly shy.

'Come on in then, boys. Make yourselves comfortable.' She moved over on her wide bed and patted the surface invitingly.

Adam had left his belongings at the doorway. He undid his sarong, threw it flamboyantly on to a couch and threw himself on to the bed. Tom did the same and soon Jezebel was inundated with youthful erections, enthusiastic mouths, long, lithe limbs and prodding fingers. The boys wrestled to get their cocks into her; they were like animals in their lustful haste.

'Wait, wait, not so fast,' laughed Jezebel.

She held both boys' cocks and milked them slowly, allowing them to kiss and suck her breasts and sex. When they were nearly ready to burst, she knelt on all fours over Tom and placed his cock into her front passage.

'Get over me. Put it in my arsehole,' she ordered Adam.

Adam nearly fell off the bed in his haste to do as she said before he exploded. He guided his slender penis between her large, quivering buttocks and pushed into the brown rose. It opened magically and his cock's head thrust through the narrow aperture and disappeared into the generous depths. He groaned. Under him Jezebel writhed on Tom's throbbing prick. Her breasts fell into his open mouth and he sucked automatically. His cock was swallowed up in her moist tunnel and Jezebel knew he would be able to feel the pressure of Adam's rod pressing from the back passage. She thrust harder on to the boy's thick prick and savoured the enjoyment the two boys were giving her.

'Yes!' she cried. 'Yes, oh yes!'

They all collapsed on to the bed, sighing contentedly.

After a short sleep, the boys began to feel desire creep through their bodies again. They were lying on top of each other, their breath sour and sweet with Jezebel's flavours.

'Let me see you play with each other,' Jezebel commanded.

Adam took Tom's thickening cock between his fine, long fingers and began to rub rhythmically. Tom groaned and lay back with his head on Jezebel's lap. He idly played with her breasts with one hand, easing his fingers under the tight straps.

'Tom! Take his prick in your other hand and milk him,' said Jezebel, watching the youth's cocks grow and thicken. She was an expert on men's private parts. She had seen many hundreds in her time. These young cocks were not special or unusual; just the ordinary run of boy's cocks. But Adam's balls were magnificent, she saw. They hung like ripe peaches beneath his penis and nudged it upward. His rod was slender and long and he had no pubic hair. Most of the native population went in for depilation on Isle de Paradis. It was the tradition. If they had pubic hair it was removed daily. Pumice, which littered the beaches in some parts of the island, was used to keep the shaved skin smooth. Jezebel, however, had always been proud of her exceptional hirsuteness. She combed and shampooed her sex hair and sometimes cut it into interesting styles. The black hair curled into ringlets which grew up on to her belly, down her thighs and around and behind her sex to her bottom cleft. The youths of Paradis had never seen anything like it. They were intoxicated by the pungent melange of scents which came from her nether regions and armpits, which were similarly graced with thick curly hair. Her upper lip had the faintest hint of a fine moustache. Her strong teeth glittered as she strained against the boy's cocks, now pressing and squeezing to defer their ejaculations.

'All right. Now, Tom, sit on my face and let me take you in my mouth. And Adam can put his pretty prick into my honey pot.' She arranged her limbs to accommodate the energetic young men. Tom lowered himself gingerly on to her mouth. He was immediately rock hard as she sucked him to the hilt of his thick cock.

Adam slid his legs alongside her plump thighs and pressed himself into her fleshy sex, parting the hair aside with trembling fingers. He sunk into her soft flesh, while his friend's cock went in and out of Jezebel's red mouth. The boys came again, violently.

Chapter Six

Angeline Finds Solitary Consolation

'Angeline, my little frangipani blossom, is what I hear true?'

'What is that, Father-in-law?'

'You have been seen with one of Jezebel's bar girls – Sylva?'

'Yes, King Aristide, I know her well.'

'I thought the high priestess told you that you were not to have anything to do with her?'

'Oh, Father-in-law! Viva is so old-fashioned! Why shouldn't I talk with Sylva?'

'You know very well, my dear. Don't be naive. Sylva and the other bar girls are a bad influence.'

'But father . . . !'

'No buts, Angeline, I agree with High Priestess Viva. You must not have anything further to do with Sylva. Be polite to her and pass the time of day, by all means, but do not consort with her.'

Angeline tossed her blonde curls and gave her father-in-law a look of anger and frustration before she ran off sobbing.

King Aristide returned to the high priestess to report on what he had said to Angeline.

'Well, Viva, I did it, and very awful it made me feel,' he told her. Viva, his first wife's sister, had spent many years after her untimely death as consort to the king, but had failed to give him more children.

'Good! Thank you, Aristide. I know you like Jezebel, but we really must do something to tame Angeline. She is still such a child in many ways and very impressionable.'

'Yes, and since her parents died in the shipwreck, we are in *loco parentis*, I suppose,' he said.

'How are the young couple getting along together?' said Viva.

'Well, I'm not so sure,' said the king. 'I discern a little dissatisfaction in her attitude these days.'

'Is the trip to Monkey Island all fixed yet?' asked the high priestess.

'Not yet. I am working on it.' The king clapped his hands and a maidservant brought in a tray of sweets and fruit.

Angeline ran into the forest and hid in the hollowed-out bole of an oatu tree. This was where she went when she was unhappy. It had been her own private hiding place since she found herself on Isle de Paradis, having been shipwrecked three years ago. She still hid treasures there sometimes. At the moment there was a book which she had not read for a long time; she had found the forgotten ancient volume in a trunk in the palace. Also in the trunk were strange, carved horns and wooden banana-shaped objects covered in monkey skin, but the book captured her eyes as soon as she saw it. It was highly illustrated with erotic drawings. There were anatomical drawings of male and female genitalia, and strange creatures who had both sexes. There were pictures of breasts of all shapes and sizes. The most interesting pictures were of men and women doing strange things to each other. Angeline was fascinated. She settled herself into the tree trunk, placing a cushion under her bottom and one behind her head. She stared in amazement at the erotic pictures and felt herself grow sticky between her legs. Her thighs felt as soft as silk and her little breasts were swelling, she was sure.

Perhaps my breasts are growing at last, she thought. If only I had breasts like Sylva! Oh, Sylva! Bother the king and Viva. I will see her if I want to. The princess turned a page and was transfixed by what she saw. Two men were simultaneously impaling a woman with their members. One man, dressed in frockcoat and breeches, the breeches pulled down to his knees, had his erection in his hand and was pushing it into the woman's hairy slit, coloured red in the picture. The other brutish-looking thug was unclothed and his balls and cock were shown in all their swollen glory, about to be thrust between her large, upturned buttocks. The woman was smiling lasciviously.

Princess Angeline grew hot and bothered. Her hand drifted down between her breasts and undid the loosely tied sarong. She stared down at herself and saw that her breasts were rather pretty. Her little brown nipples stared back at her. She touched them and they stiffened. She pressed a hand on her belly and the feeling she had in her pussy was not unpleasant. She went lower, sliding a finger down between her legs. Her pussy was charming, she thought. The rise of her belly; the fall of the curve down to the slit. The lips were plump and well formed. She slid a finger into the hairless slit. She moved it inside, just a very little, and felt the sudden moisture, as if a spring was inside her sex. Her fingers felt the fleshy tunnel, discovering the folds of soft flesh. She took out the finger and put it to her nose. It smelt charmingly of the seashore, sea creatures and salt. There was a musky, warm smell too, like the toffee cook made her when she was a child. She licked her finger and replaced it more confidently in her private parts. She dropped the interesting volume, open at a page showing a voluptuous woman parting her sex lips and shoving what looked like a huge cucumber into the hole. Angeline pushed two fingers inside and felt a tiny bud grow under her touch. She wrapped her fingertips around the bud and stroked it. It felt wonderful. Her thighs were hot and she wanted to move them fiercely. She panted and sobbed quietly to herself. Her breasts heaved and blushed, and her mouth grew dry. Her lips were swollen – not just her mouth lips, which were always slightly swollen, as if she had bitten them, but her sex lips. She strained against her fingers, pushing them in and out. She found the sensation particularly satisfying when she almost withdrew her fingers and they pressed on the mouth of her sex. She squeezed the lips together and rubbed over the area of her vagina with the palm of her hand. This was nice too! She stroked her bottom and the space between her arsehole and her vagina. That was lovely! She suddenly lost control of something and felt as if she would wet herself. Her insides started to throb and pulsate and she thrust her fingers right inside. She needed something for her inner muscles to hang on to. Instinctively, she rubbed herself on the outer surface of her sex.

'Oh! Oh! Oh!' Princess Angeline sighed in contentment.

She had been unhappy for some time. Her two very best friends – Kelila and Isadora – had left Isle de Paradis twelve months before to set up a dance academy on Kelila's home island, which had a reputation for dance and music. They had tried to make a go of it together on Isle de Paradis but there wasn't enough interest. Angeline missed them so much. She was discontented with her young husband, too. She needed some excitement.

On her way back home, Angeline remembered the

strange objects she had seen in the trunk where she had found the erotic anatomy book. She determined to make use of the dildos at the first opportunity. Perhaps Sylva would like to try them too?

At the Forbidden Apple that night, the usual crowd were gathered: Ric and several other soldiers, Samson and Bartolem, one or two fishermen, who had sold a big catch of tuna and felt the need to throw their money around and Jezebel, the whore-mistress supreme. In times gone by she had enjoyed the powerful position of a slave-mistress, but that life was gone now and she led a respectable life these days. She sighed as she thought of her mis-spent youth. However, she was still healthy and vigorous and her sex urge was as good as ever, if not better. She ate with pleasure, enjoying the curried fish that her house-husband-cum-consort, Bartolem, had prepared. Samson sat on one side of her while Ric and his young soldiers were otherwise occupied with her girls. The fishermen had drunk too much banana wine and were singing loudly outside, giggling like girls. They had brought a tuna fish with them as a gift to the house and they too had enjoyed a fine meal.

Next door, in one of the copulation chambers, the scene was one of the greatest lasciviousness. Ric watched as his boy soldiers rooted and screwed the bored girls. The guards' first fucks were unsatisfactory for the girls, as they knew they would be. These lads needed to be shown what to do. They were hopeless lovers.

After their first climaxes, they lay back, drinking more wine. Ric took the floor and gave them a fine performance.

'Look, watch me carefully,' he said. 'This is what you must do, you stupid fools.'

He sat on the low couch and patted his lap. Cherry-Ripe giggled and sidled up to him. She wore nothing but a G-string of chamois and a flower behind one ear. Her olive skin shone with perspiration and her eyes glowed in the gloom. There was quiet as the girl sat on the soldier's lap. He placed her hand on his crotch and she took the soft penis between her fingers, her knees parted. He played with her breasts, moving them up and down and bouncing them in his big hands. He pulled back her head so her long neck curved outward. He kissed the edge of her lips and her tongue flicked out. His cock grew in her sly fingers and the young soldiers grew hot and erect again, witnessing their captain's tumescence. He had his fingers inside her G-string now, and was churning them inside her red sex lips. She squirmed and rocked on his cock. She let it out of her fingers and it slipped up between her legs and poked out in front, looking obscenely as if it were growing from between her soft thighs. She touched its swollen head, which was dark purple and looked ready to explode, with moistened fingers. But Ric was adept at holding his sexual excitement for a long time. Young men might well have the advantage when it came to getting another erection soon after an orgasm, but the older man could make his erection last. Ric was confident he could keep his organ swollen and useful for many minutes more. The young girl rose and fell on his cock, her thighs rubbing it as it rubbed her sex and inner thighs. He held her breasts in his large, callused hands and hid them all except for the taut, puckered nipples.

'Enough!' he said. 'Turn over on my lap, upside down.'

Cherry-Ripe did as she was told, knowing that this was what Ric liked best.

Lana had gone out. She had been summoned by madame to deal with the fishermen, who had realised that they were getting too drunk to perform and needed a little extra something. Petite Gigi was lounging with the two lads, her breasts and upper body in the lap of one, her legs entangled with the other. They unconsciously began to play with her, practising the art of love

38

on this passive young body. As her lips kissed one boy, her sex was penetrated by the fingers of the other. Her breasts were fondled by four hands, her sex lips parted and her privates explored. She closed her eyes and enjoyed the unexpected pleasure she was experiencing.

Cherry-Ripe had her head low and her hands on the ground in front of her. Her dimpled bottom was proudly high and Ric's hand came down hard. Smack! Smack! She cried out in pretend pain. Smack! Smack!

The soldier boys looked over at the pantomime and their cocks grew. Cherry-Ripe's bottom was facing them. Its pinkness and ripeness held their gaze as they probed and stroked, fondled and grabbed at the female flesh in their grasp. They saw again, in their imagination, the princess's bare bottom being spanked and the desirable Sylva's naughty nether parts bared. They fought like puppies to put their desperate pricks into Petite Gigi's sexual orifice. She reorganised herself so that she could accommodate both boys at once, sucking the one and fucking the other. They came in two minutes flat and left her high, dry and disgruntled.

Ric had finished pleasing the upturned Cherry-Ripe and clapped his hands to Petite Gigi. His men watched as he, still rampant, sucked the juicy sex lips of the frustrated girl until she came loudly.

'I sure needed that, thank you, monsieur!' she said smiling.

He turned her over and penetrated her from behind, hunched over her and twice her size. She knelt, her buttocks high and her sex pouch raised to his thrusts. He pushed his big cock right into her and moved furiously like a big dog. She quivered and held herself steady to meet the thrusts. He came at last with shouts of jubilation and she sank to the ground with Ric sprawled over her.

* * *

Gertrude, the English wife of Captain Ric of the King's Guard, sat on the veranda of her home on her own, miserable and frustrated. Little did she think, when she had fallen for the ruggedly good-looking soldier four years before, that she would be sexually frustrated. Being married to a soldier of Isle de Paradis was not what she had hoped for. Ric, the attractive ruffian, was popular with many other women and certainly had never pretended to be faithful to Gertrude – but he did expect her to remain faithful to him.

She sighed loudly and listened to the song of the cicadas, splitting the air with their constant scratching screech. She longed for love, excitement and novelty. Her life was lonely. She had arrived here with her charge, Clementine, on a visit to Angeline and Hari after their marriage, and the king had married Clementine, and she, Gertrude, had fallen for the captain of the King's Guard. Ah, how dreams fade, she thought sadly. She had tried to keep Ric's interest but he preferred the company of his young soldiers and other women – especially the bar girls of the Forbidden Apple. Yet Gertrude's nature was passionate and she needed sexual satisfaction.

'Oh, for a love affair, or a wild romance!' she said to the blue-spotted, yellow lizard who crawled up the wall next to her to lick off the flies. A praying mantis, green as English apples in September, turned its triangular head and gazed at her.

Chapter Seven

Adam Searches for the 'Mermaid'

King Aristide had always indulged in sex play with his charming daughter-in-law, Angeline, ever since he had had the privilege – *doit de seigneur* – of deflowering her on her wedding night in the 'End of Childhood' ceremony. He had shared his pretty 'daughter' with his only son, Hari, even though he had married her friend, Clementine, after a whirlwind courtship. The king, Clementine and Angeline had spent many a night together. Now he was less vigorous than he had been as a young man, and he was having difficulty with his erection. He started to make excuses to his wife when she demanded her conjugal rights, and he had not called Angeline to their bed for months.

Clementine was less than satisfied with the status quo. She decided to do something about it, before her husband thought of finding other pleasures.

She took a walk around the island one day on her own. The islanders were used to their royalty taking the air. It was not unusual to see Hari and Aristide playing football with the natives on the playing field. Isle de

Paradis was a safe kingdom, and there was never any fear of robbery or attack from the mostly happy island-ers. Clementine laboured up the hill and through a little forest, perspiring heavily.

I must do something about losing a little weight, she thought for the seventh time that week. But Aristide does like something to grab hold of, or so he tells me. When did he last tell me that? Let me think.

She remembered passionate couplings with her hus-band in the early days of their marriage, as well as erotic spankings at his hands. She and Angeline would take turns to be spanked, upended over his lap, his hands brushing their sex mounds as he smacked the offered bottoms. She grew hot just thinking about it.

Clementine suddenly came across a scene of innocent love-making in a bosky forest clearing. She stood behind a tree and watched a young native girl sitting on top of a native boy, rising and falling on his erection with obvious pleasure. They did not notice their queen as she stayed behind the thick trunk of a tree. The lad was a fisherman, she thought, but she did not recognise the girl. Clementine quietened her breathing as she wit-nessed the private act in the almost-public place. The girl had her flowery sarong hitched up to her waist and her thighs glistened. Her head was flung back in joy as she pushed herself down hard on the young cock. His hands were holding her little breasts, covering them completely. She cried out and he grimaced as he ejacu-lated, then they both laughed happily and held each other. Clementine felt sad and contented at the same time. Youth is wasted on the young, she thought sagely.

She walked on, having successfully hidden herself from the young lovers. The air was hot and sultry up in the hills. There was no breeze. A toucan clattered its strange cry in the tree tops. A family of Vervet monkeys stared at her from the branches and chattered noisily. She came across another amorous pair and recognised the young man as Hari's manservant. She liked Adam. He was a healthy, cheerful lad with good manners. Hari had told her about Adam's obsession with her corset and she smiled as she thought of it. She hoped he had found a girl to model for him. Perhaps he could assist her with her problem. Yes, Adam would know a pretty girl who could help put the joy back into her married life. Clementine set off again, her sarong gathered up in one hand to keep it out of the dirt, with hope in her heart.

Adam had met the native girl he was with in the forest. She was not pretty, and quite plump, but desperate for sex. She hung on his arm and whispered in his ear.

'Oh, all right then,' he agreed, and lay down with her on the mossy earth. He put his hand up her sarong and felt the bare, soft flesh open at his touch. He closed his eyes and thought of the mermaid. She soon cried out loud and kissed him. Then it was his turn. She sucked his cock and he pretended the mermaid was between his legs. It was all over in less than two minutes. They shook the leaves from their hair and said goodbye.

Adam walked on. 'Oh where are you?/ with your sea blue eyes/ your glistening thighs/ dripping wet/ I'll find you yet . . . No. I don't like the last line; it's terrible.'

Adam spoke the verse out loud, alarming the monitor lizards who leapt from his path.

He reached the village and asked his friends if they knew his mystery mermaid.

'What does she look like again?' asked Jimi.

'She was wet all over . . . her hair was slicked back . . . it's difficult to say. But she was beautiful and had blue eyes and dark hair. And she was curved in all the right places.'

'It sounds like Joshua's little sister. She's growing up fast. But she's a real wild thing. Lives in the forest most of the time, and only goes home for food. She's friends with the animals, or so Joshua says.'

Adam had not seen Joshua for months – not since he had started to work for his father. Now he went straight to his house. Joshua's father was in the coconut plantation overseeing his men, and his mother was in the little dirt yard, hanging out washing.

'Good afternoon, ma'am,' said Adam, aware that the best way to a girl's heart was through her mother's approval. 'Is Joshua around?'

'Adam, how are you, boy? How is the prince?'

'Very well, thank you, ma'am.' He waited patiently for her to answer his question.

'Joshua is love-sick. I don't know who the lucky girl is, but he is off every afternoon to follow her, I think.' Poppy-Flower laughed loudly, her plump arms shaking in tune with her bosoms.

'And where is your daughter?' said Adam bravely. 'I have something to ask her.'

'Trixie-Jane? Who knows? She's never here when she is needed.' The woman grumbled quietly to herself and fixed a tall pole to the line of clothes in order to catch any breeze.

Adam went on through the village. The little huts were almost hidden in the ever-encroaching forest. Most of the front yards had lemon trees, banana trees and bright coloured flowers lightening the gloom of dark glossy leaves.

Now he had a name for his muse he only had to catch her. The velvet corset was in his rucksack on his back, as were his paints. He went down towards the coconut plantation and the beach where he had seen the girl, then sat at the top of the beach in the shade of a casuarina, being careful not to sit on the spiky fallen fruit. The heat got to him. He took out a notebook and pencil and lay back with his head on the canvas bag. He didn't know whether to write a poem about her or draw her from memory. He doodled idly, drawing a curvaceous figure with the corset laced tight about her waist

44

and hips. He drew two round breasts peeping out the top with cherry-like nipples. He drew the dark triangle of thigh and pubis, then stopped and thoughtfully drew out his cock, which throbbed slightly and ached. He stared at the primitive likeness he had drawn and felt his cock harden in his fingers. He pressed his fingers around the shaft and drew them to the base firmly. Then he pulled the loose skin up and over the swollen head. He took out the corset and unravelled the ribbons. There was no-one to see him, he thought. He wrapped the soft stuff around his waist and tied the ribbons around his cock. He pulled on them and stared at the drawing of Trixie-Jane. His cock rose and fell as he tugged the ribbons. He pulled tighter, enclosing his rod in the silk. He admired his own silky flesh pressed under the corset's bones. He took his cock firmly in one hand and pumped at it.

Suddenly there was a cry, and Trixie-Jane fell out of the tree on to him. He yelled in fear and fury. His cock shrivelled to a dark plum. Panicking, he grabbed his sarong, leaving the rucksack, corset and drawing pad on the sand. He ran off, holding the sarong to his crotch. He did not stop until he was 50 metres away. She had not followed him.

Trixie-Jane was sitting on the sand, laughing. She saw the drawing, but did not recognise her own likeness. She picked up the corset and tried it on. It fitted her beautifully, as if it had been made for her, and she danced around on the empty beach, admiring herself. She moved seductively, the garment giving her grace and femininity she did not know she had. Her apple breasts jiggled above the boned silk velvet. Her strong thighs and buttocks curved beneath. She felt a strange moistness between her thighs. She rubbed them together and felt the moisture quicken and her sex lips quivering and pouting. She licked her lips and lay down thoughtfully on the sand where Adam had lain. He had looked so

45

pretty wearing the woman's clothes, she thought. She drew a sketch of the boy with the corset ribbons tied around his erection. She took the ribbons and placed them between her legs, drawing them into her slit and pulling them back and forth in her slick wetness. She pressed her belly and squeezed her breasts, admiring their bounce. She pushed the ribbon right through her legs and drew it up behind. She sawed it between her legs, sighing as the silk rasped her sex. Her insides fluttered and her thighs shuddered and heat invaded her from head to feet. She cried out as the 'little death' took her into brief unconsciousness.

At that moment, Adam was furious with himself. He thought of all the things he could have done or said. He could have grabbed her and made love to her. He could have shown her the drawing and asked her to model for him. He almost sobbed in frustration. He hurried back to the beach and the casuarina tree, but there was no sign of the girl or the rucksack. And now he had lost the queen's corset and Princess Angeline's drawers, as well as his sketchbook and paints. How was he going to get them back without humiliation? He walked slowly back towards the palace compound, bumping into the queen on his way.

'Your Highness,' he said, blushing guiltily.

'Oh good, I have been looking for you, darling boy. Adam, you look flushed.' She took his face in her hands. 'Are you sickening for something?'

'Oh, ma'am, I need your help.' The boy threw himself into the queen's generous arms, burying his head in her large breasts.

'What is it, my boy? Oh dear, tell me, Adam.' She seemed delighted that this young man showed such affection towards her.

'It's your corset, ma'am. I have lost it.' He told her how he had run off when the girl fell out of the tree, omitting to mention what he had been doing at the time.

'Well, Adam, that's no problem. If it was who you think it was, I am sure she will have taken it home with her to her mother. You must go and thank her nicely for rescuing it. It could have been ripped apart by monkeys by now.'

'Yes, ma'am,' he said.

'Is she pretty, this girl?' asked the queen.

'Yes, very,' he said quietly.

'Perhaps I will come with you and meet her. I haven't seen the family for a long time. It's about time I paid Poppy-Flower a visit.'

Adam didn't know whether to laugh or cry. The queen go with him to meet his love, his muse! But at least he would not have to go alone, embarrassed and stuttering, to reclaim the erotic garment. He could laugh it off. The queen could help ask permission for Trixie-Jane to model for him. They could not refuse their queen.

Chapter Eight

The Muse Comes to Court

The queen and Adam were soon back at the coconut plantation owner's house. Poppy-Flower was nursing a baby, and her daughter, Trixie-Jane, was not to be seen.

'Hello, my dear, how are you?' said the queen, fanning herself with a woven palm leaf fan that Adam had made for her as they walked along. She held a parasol over her fair skin to protect it from the sun.

'Come in and sit down,' said Poppy-Flower, beckoning the queen and Adam to come in the gate and take seats on the veranda. 'How lovely to see you, Queen Clementine. You are looking hot and bothered, my dear. Hold baby a minute and I'll get you some lime juice cordial.' She handed the plump, gurgling baby to her friend and waddled off into the gloomy interior of the hut.

'Oh, isn't he sweet!' twittered Clementine, kissing the little creature's milky face. 'I do wish I had babies.' She laughed as the baby grabbed at her jewelled ears.

Adam took the baby's little hand in his big one and marvelled at its perfection. The baby had black hair in tiny curls and the same startling blue eyes as his big sister.

Poppy-Flower returned laden with glasses of pale yellow, faintly jellied liquid, decorated with hibiscus flowers.

'Poppy-Flower, is your daughter home?' asked Clementine.

'No, she is never here. I was telling Adam – she is not a homebody. She spends her days doing I don't know what. She climbs like a monkey and swims like a fish. She is no good at looking after the baby, I know that.' Poppy-Flower took the baby again and nursed him.

'Has she been home and left my rucksack here?' asked Adam.

'No, my boy, I told you, she has not been seen since breakfast – Oh! There she is! Trixie-Jane, my poppet, everyone has been looking for you.'

The small figure of Adam's muse slowly walked through the little wooden gate and closed it behind her, giving her audience a chance to admire her curvaceous behind and straight brown back. She wore her pink flowered sarong and it was tied tight around her hips to show off her maturing curves.

Adam could imagine her dressed in the corset and drawers and he felt himself grow hot and erect under his sarong.

'Come here, my dear. How you have grown! You are a little beauty – your mother's looks and your father's eyes!' said the queen.

'Um, hello, I'm Adam!' said Adam, putting out a tentative hand to her. 'I believe that is my rucksack that you have there.'

'Yes, I found it on the beach,' she said, grinning cheekily as she handed it to him.

He opened it a little and saw the corset and drawers were there. He coughed to the queen in an attempt to remind her why they had come, or why he had come.

'Oh yes! Trixie-Jane, we wondered whether you would like to come to the palace and pose for a portrait, my

49

dear? Adam needs a model in a hurry and thinks you would be perfect – and so do I, my child. I think you would be just what we are looking for.'

Adam looked at Queen Clementine. What did she mean? What *they* were looking for? Trixie-Jane shook her hair from her face and smiled openly.

'All right, ma'am, I'll come tomorrow, early. After I've fed my animals.'

'Wonderful! Now, Poppy-Flower, may I have a private word with you, my dear?'

The two young people sat together while the women went inside. Trixie-Jane swung the baby around in her arms, showing Adam her lithe form from all angles as she did so.

Adam smiled weakly and did not know what to say. He was overwhelmed at the possibilities the future now held for him. The queen came out of the hut, smiling with satisfaction. Poppy-Flower tucked something into her sarong.

'Come along, dear boy,' Clementine said, and Adam finished his drink and took the queen's arm. They walked home together, both excited at what they were planning.

Next morning, Trixie-Jane was up at dawn. She ran down to the little beach and begged a few fish from the fishermen resting on the beach after their night's work.

She dived into the clear blue water from a promontory and swam strongly out to sea. As she rounded a headland she saw them – the dolphins. A school of eight leapt and dived and played in the deep water. The sun sparkled on their black, rough skin as they rose in pairs and leapt into the air. Trixie-Jane swam among them and they swerved near her and nuzzled her with their snouts. She gave them the gift of fishes, which they accepted. They all swam together back to the promontory and she pulled herself out of the water and shook herself like a dog.

Later, showered and changed into a becoming pale green sarong covered in blue flowers, one blue flower behind her ear, her black silky tresses drawn back over that ear and hanging thickly over the opposite shoulder, she presented herself at the palace of King Aristide and Queen Clementine.

Guards in leather kilts stood at the gate. They saluted her as she passed through, and stared at the lovely girl as she swayed her hips provocatively at them. She laughed at their obvious consternation. The leather thongs of their kilts rose and quivered. The guards held tight to their spikes and stared ahead again.

'There you are, my dear. How pretty you look! Now, Adam wants to see you first and later I'll bring the king to visit you. Off you go, Trixie-Jane.' Queen Clementine ushered her towards the private chamber of her son's manservant.

Trixie-Jane knocked tentatively on the heavy door and Adam opened it immediately, as if he had been waiting – which he had. He had hardly slept for thinking of her. His muse! He had smoothed out the corset and pressed the ribbons. He had borrowed one of Hari's couches and had it brought to his chamber. His easel was set up with paints, palette and brushes ready.

There was a makuti screen in the corner and he told her to go behind it and change into the garment she would find there.

He busied himself with mixing paints. She giggled behind the screen.

'Adam, you'll have to help me, I can't do up the ribbons tightly enough.'

Trixie-Jane emerged from behind the screen. Adam gasped involuntarily. She was a vision. Her lithe, curvaceous body had been poured into the restraining corset. She turned her back to him and offered him her

51

buttocks, or that was the way he saw it. In fact, she wanted him to tie the ribbons. Her bare bottom shone glossily, honey smooth, and her muscular thighs jutted from the velvet. He tied the bows with shaking fingers. His knuckles grazed her flesh briefly. He shuddered. She turned her face to him, an open flower, and he gazed into her laughing, blue eyes.

'You are supposed to wear the drawers too,' he said.

'Oh, really, I didn't know what they were. I've never worn drawers.' She turned towards him and he saw her pink, hairless pubis; the curved mound; the slit.

He gasped and turned away. 'Well, put them on for me, please, Trixie-Jane,' he said.

She went behind the screen once more and came out wearing the white lawn drawers that Angeline had made for herself many years ago, before she was shipwrecked on Isle de Paradis. Adam knew the story well.

'There, how do I look?' said the beautiful girl.

'You look – you look – very nice,' Adam stuttered, and wanted to hit himself for such stupidity and lack of finesse. But he was having trouble hiding his burgeoning erection under his tightly wrapped sarong. He turned sharply away and knocked over his palette and pot of brushes. She knelt to help him pick them up and he felt her warm breath on his neck. He was very aware of the scent of her skin, like salt and sea and fresh air, with the hint of something else; some promise of mystery, a spice as yet unknown to him.

'To work now,' he said, and placed her on the leather couch, lying on her side, one hand dangling on the floor, the other on the back of the couch. Her drawers – or rather, Angeline's drawers – lay open at the crotch, and there was just a glimpse of flesh. Her breasts were held in by the tight-boned garment and although they were smaller than the original model's had been, the curves of them showed above the corset where they were pressed together.

Adam could still feel the touch of the velvet and the silk of her thigh against his hands as he had tightened the ribbons. He was feeling very warm and tried to loosen his sarong. He too had no undergarment on, and his cock rose impertinently against the cloth. He rubbed himself just a little, unconsciously. She saw the movement and smiled. He blushed.

'Close your eyes,' he ordered her. 'That way, you will not tire so easily.'

She did as she was bid. He tried to concentrate on the painting, sketching in the pose quickly and covering the canvas with line and block of colour. Her face was hidden by her heavy hair, so he went to her and pushed it behind her ear. She opened those startlingly blue eyes and glared at him.

'It is all right, I'm just adjusting the pose,' he said.

'Am I all right like this?' she said.

'Oh yes, oh yes!'

He pretended to concentrate on the painting. Her bosoms rose and fell, straining to free themselves from the tightness of their velvet prison. Her nut-brown limbs hung in suggestive abandonment. He saw the split-crotch fine lawn drawers gape. He could put a finger inside and feel her soft flesh. He could rip the corset from her. He could press himself against her body and come all over the queen's corset.

He painted for an hour and then stopped.

'You may rest now, Trixie-Jane. I'll call for some refreshment.'

She rose from the discomfort of the long pose and stretched herself. At that moment, there was a knock at the door and in walked the queen with King Aristide.

Trixie-Jane stood, not knowing what to do. She curtsied, briefly, in the incongruous costume.

'Well, I say, Clem, you are right, she does look just like you did in that garment – what is it called?'

'A corset, my dear.'

53

'Yes, of course, a corset! Ha Ha! Corset is!' He laughed again and his queen and Adam smiled at his little joke. Trixie-Jane had her mouth open and her hands over her crotch. It was all very well to pose practically naked in front of Adam – who, after all, was only a boy, and a manservant at that – but the king!

'There, there, my dear, don't be embarrassed,' said the queen. 'You look charming, doesn't she, Aristide?'

'Certainly she does, my dear.' The king stood up straighter, pulled back his still-powerful shoulders, and held in his stomach.

'You are delightful, my dear,' he said to Trixie-Jane, and she smiled nervously.

She had heard, as everyone on Isle de Paradis had, that the king was a rampant master, or had been in the past. She had also heard that he had a penchant for a little sado masochism, in the form of spanking and caning. Her own mother had spoken of it many times. Poppy-Flower had once been handmaiden to the late queen, and had enjoyed many intimacies with her, including the pleasuring of the king.

'After your modelling session you must come to our chamber, my dear. Don't forget,' said the queen, nodding cheerfully at Adam and drawing the king away by his hand. He looked over his shoulder at the young model and smiled broadly.

'We will be waiting for you, my dear,' he said. 'How long will you be, boy?' He frowned at Adam.

'Not long, sire.'

Adam worked for another half an hour, not talking and trying not to get an erection. He was pleased with the painting so far. He had caught the general shape and fall of the limbs, he thought.

'Will you come back tomorrow?' he begged her.

'Yes, of course, but only if you come with me first thing in the morning for a swim.'

'I – er – I would like that. Thank you.'

'You'll have to untie me now.' She turned her back to him again, and he had the distinct impression that he could have her if he wanted. But he was too shy, and she was too precious. He undid the ribbons, loosening them with his fingers. He felt the warm flesh beyond the velvet. She clutched the undone corset and disappeared behind the screen.

A few minutes later she knocked at the door of the king's chamber. A servant opened the door and ushered her in.

'Oh, you are not wearing the corset!' The queen looked disappointed. 'Go back and get it, dear.'

Trixie-Jane returned to Adam's room and was met with the interesting sight of the young man wrapped in the garment again.

'Oh dear, I'm sorry, Adam, but the queen wants her corset,' she said quietly.

Adam, who had not yet started to masturbate seriously, ran behind the screen when the girl entered his room. He threw the corset over the top of the screen and said, 'Here, take it, take it!' He sounded angry.

Trixie-Jane, sure of her charms as she had never been before in her seventeen years, giggled cheekily and went back to the king and queen, wondering what they were going to do with her.

Chapter Nine

Regeneration of the Royal Love Life

The king's chamber was decorated with pink and white shell-encrusted coral walls. The enormous bed was low and square. Elephant tusks were its four corner posts, from which hung wreaths of white muslin covering the whole. The floors had been updated in recent years. Hardwood boards gleamed beneath fur rugs. An Egyptian cotton sheet was stretched over the ten foot square bed. Various swan's down pillows covered in embroidered cotton pillowcases were scattered on the bed.

Attached to the coral walls were several metal rings. These did not impinge on the susceptible Trixie-Jane's consciousness immediately, but they did later.

'Sit down, darling girl, here by me.' The king, a handsome man in his late fifties, was dressed in a voluminous white silk loincloth. His chest was still well muscled and his stomach flat. He swam and fished almost every day and fought mock battles with his guard. His English wife had taught him to fence and he and she did this once a week without fail. He enjoyed the sight of her in the tight gilet, with her plump bottom and white thighs quivering under the leather jacket.

Trixie-Jane was suddenly very shy. She had the corset clutched to her and sat by the king as he bade her. The queen was dressed in a loose kimono, flatteringly folded to enhance her plump curves. She was only in her early twenties. She had been just a girl when she married King Aristide; only a year out of school.

She had learnt to enjoy female flesh and what it had to offer her many years before and she had mourned the loss of her friend, Angeline, in their bed in recent months.

It was Clementine who first touched Trixie-Jane.

'Let me dress you in the corset, my dear. Do you realise it was mine?'

'Yes, ma'am, I did know. Adam told me. He likes it very much, doesn't he?'

'Yes, dear, and so do we, don't we, Aristide?'

Her husband was lost for words as he watched his wife slowly undress the girl. The sarong dropped to her ankles and she stood, curved in youthful perfection.

Clementine hurriedly wrapped the corset around the girl's narrow waist and turned her around to pull the ribbons tight. She pushed her foot against the girl's bottom and pressed hard, pulling the ribbons at the same time.

'Oh, that is very tight, ma'am,' gasped Trixie-Jane.

'Yes, it is supposed to be, ninny,' she laughed.

'Oh, that is even tighter. I can hardly breathe.'

'But you look gorgeous, my dear. Look at yourself.'

There was a wide mirror from floor to ceiling next to the bed. Trixie-Jane stood and admired herself, turning sideways to see her jutting backside and proud breasts. Clementine lifted the little breasts from their silken prison, resting them on top of the garment like proffered fruit. She stroked the pink nipples and pinched them lightly. The girl stood quietly, her thighs growing warm.

The king had a hand inside his loincloth and a dreamy look in his eyes. The queen carried on with her tender embraces. She leant over the girl and sucked her little breasts gently. The girl was between them now, sitting on the low bed.

'Do you like that, my dear?' asked the queen.

'Oh yes, ma'am, it is very pleasant.'

Trixie-Jane had shared intimacies with her brother's friends in the past. They had shown her their ripe roots and she had shown them her pussy and let them play with her breasts. She was aroused by the situation she now found herself in. The king was handsome and the queen was a lovely woman. Trixie-Jane was a virgin, but there was no dishonour in losing her virginity. On the Isle de Paradis it was usual for girls of fifteen or so to be deflowered by an older male relative, and Trixie-Jane was unusual in that she had not yet been deflowered. Her father was not from this island and that made a difference. He had not always wholeheartedly approved of some of the island's traditions, though he now thought himself an adopted son of Isle de Paradis. He had been shocked when his wife, who had been the first queen's handmaiden, was included in royal sexual games, but he had had to put up with it.

After the queen and Adam had left, the previous evening, Poppy-Flower had talked for a long time to her daughter. She had told her that this was her big chance to make something of herself. If the king and queen were pleased with her, and if she did as they asked, new worlds would open to her. Poppy-Flower had enjoyed her years working in the royal household, with all that entailed. She was proud that the queen had chosen her daughter to help resuscitate the royal sexuality. She kissed her daughter and patted her on the head.

'You will be so happy, dear child,' she said. 'This is a great honour for us.'

When her husband returned from his work, she told

him the exciting news. He was only too aware of the duties his daughter would have in the royal household. He shouted and railed against it, but his wife convinced him that Trixie-Jane would be perfectly happy with her new life, and they were to be grateful that she had been chosen.

Trixie-Jane knew she was lovely. She was aware that her beauty was her greatest possession. She liked it when Adam stared at her pussy. She enjoyed the sight of his erection pushing the cloth of his sarong. She had yearnings and sexual longings. She wanted things to happen to her – and now they were.

'You are a naughty girl, I'm sure, aren't you?' Aristide whispered, stroking her breasts.

'I am?' she said.

'Yes, you are a naughty, naughty girl, showing your titties and your pussy like that. You must be spanked. Taught a lesson. Don't you think, Clem?'

'Oh yes, my dear, she must be spanked.'

They placed the half naked girl over the king's lap, her bottom raised high, her arms to the ground. The king's loincloth was unwound now, the length of cloth arranged on the floor in coils. Only a belt of cloth remained around his hips and loins and his prick stood proud: a royal erection. The velvet corset and the girl's naked belly rubbed his cock as she slid from knee to knee on his lap. She wriggled playfully, aware of the wetness between her legs and the thick member pressing her belly. His hand came down hard on her bare buttocks with a powerful slap.

'Ouch!' she yelled. 'That hurt!'

'Of course it did, dear, it was supposed to, to teach you a lesson. You are naughty, naughty, naughty!' He smacked her again and again and her flesh grew hot from the erotic blows. The queen was also undressed now, and touching herself between the legs, clearly finding the sight of her husband, obviously so aroused, with the upended reddening buttocks writhing on his lap, more than she could bear. Her thighs softened and throbbed as her fingers palpated her fleshy sex.

After this initial climax, she suggested to her husband that they all get on to the bed. He complied happily, carrying the excited Trixie-Jane, his hands clasping her under her arms and around her legs below her bottom. Her bare flesh glowed where he had spanked her. Her nipples were little pink peaks, surrounded by swelling areolae. She was a delightful sight, and when Trixie-Jane saw her own reflection in the wall mirror she liked what she saw. King Aristide was a fine figure of a man, a warrior still, and justly admired by his subjects. His rampant cock was huge. She had never seen such a monster. It made her wetter still to think of it inside her. Would he deflower her? She grew hot and cold at the thought of that immense root filling her pussy.

The king placed her on the bed, her skin dark against the gleaming white sheet. She half lay, leaning back on her elbows, and watched curiously as the queen leant over her and began to caress her. The king stood behind the queen, slightly to one side, so he could witness his wife's love-making. He had his big hands around the root of his cock and was slowly moving them up and down the length of it. Clementine kissed Trixie-Jane on the lips, first softly, her hands brushing her breasts, then firmly, taking her lips into her lovely mouth and churning her tongue round inside Trixie-Jane's.

Trixie-Jane was in a state of semi-consciousness; a swooning daze. Her legs fell open and the queen's hands were delving into the soft flesh. Trixie-Jane raised her hips instinctively to encourage the caress. The queen took the girl's hand and placed it on her breast. Trixie-Jane was amazed at the softness of the large cushions of flesh. She fondled and squeezed, encouraged by the queen's murmurs of approval and encouragement.

Meanwhile, Aristide looked after his own needs. He

was standing close to his wife's back, his cock rooting between her plump thighs. He held on to her hips and shoved into her. Clementine touched the girl lightly but firmly, cupping her crotch and rubbing with the palm of her hand. She kissed her, still, and Trixie-Jane returned the embrace willingly. There was a sudden quickening of breath and pulse and the girl cried out. A second later came more cries from the royal couple. They fell together in a heap on the bed, and laughed and smiled and kissed each other happily.

'Oh, that was just like old times, darling, wasn't it?' said the queen later, as she and the king renewed their intimacy in private.

Chapter Ten
Madame Lana

*T*he Forbidden Apple was full, as was usual at sunset. Men sat on the sand outside, drinking banana beer and eating sweet potato chips. The fishermen were in good spirits as they had recently made a fine killing. Not a catch of tuna, but a fine bit of wrecking had made them rich. A ship had foundered on an offshore rocky islet, with loss of life of all crew and passengers, but they had managed to salvage much from the damaged vessel, including a fine gramophone in working order. The large trumpet blared out music now, and one of the fishermen had invested himself with the duty of winding up the machine as the music slowed. They had given Jezebel the gramophone in return for the promise of delights yet to be given. They had insisted on a night's pleasure with Lana, the most interesting and expensive of the establishment's employees. However, they were in danger of being unconscious when their debt was paid.

Cherry-Ripe and Petite Gigi were dressed in fine clothes from the wreck – American dresses of fashion, in silk chiffon. They wore the garments with panache, naked beneath the transparent folds and frills. They sat on the fishermen's laps and tickled their ears and kissed their beery mouths. Jezebel also wore some of the treasures taken from the wreck, and was dressed in magnificent red satin. Her big breasts, like olive silk cushions, were encased in boned satin. Her nipples jutted from the centres of each carefully stitched cup. Her hirsute triangle was shaved into a heart shape and glistened black through the split-crotched drawers. She swaggered up and down in front of her customers and girls, whirling a whip.

Lana came out of the copulation hut and calmly took the whip from her mistress's hands.

'Come on, you ugly lot of lazy idiots!' she railed at the fishermen, and cracked the whip. They looked up from their half-coconuts of beer or wine and gazed dreamily at the vision before them.

Lana was encased in a black leather costume which consisted of straps and belts and buckles, erotically entwined about her lithe, tall figure and exposing portions of her olive-skinned anatomy. Her bosoms were high and jutting; her hips flared from a narrow waist. She had a haughty expression on her face. Her chestnut hair was tied back in a severe knot at the nape of her long neck.

'I want you now, all of you. Come on!' She cracked the whip again, more convincingly this time, and the three men staggered to their feet, pushing Cherry-Ripe and Petite Gigi from their laps, whose disarrayed chiffon skirts were above their heads.

Lana loomed imperiously over the cowering men. Jezebel laughed good-naturedly.

'That's right, my sweet, you tell them. Ah, I taught you well!'

The three fishermen, trying to compose themselves and looking forward to their punishment at the hands of the luscious Lana, stepped into the gloomy new 'dungeon', which was simply another makuti-roofed chamber, done up to look like a chamber of horrors, with dark curtains at the window and chains and iron rings in the floor and in suitable positions on the wall. There were wooden rafters, too, from which hung chains and ropes. The three men let themselves be tied up by the other two girls, who giggled in delight as they strapped the men's wrists and ankles so they were spreadeagled. At a sign from Lana, the men were stripped of their loincloths – all they wore.

One, a fine lad of nineteen or so, was strongly built and less drunk than his friends. His cock was already tumescent. It bounced on his flat, brown belly, as if searching for a soft, warm nest. He moaned slightly and licked his lips. He had a pleasant expression, with wide-set almond eyes and a broad nose. The other two were poor specimens; one scrawny and middle-aged, the other a smug man of 30 or so. He thought he was the cat's whiskers, and when he looked down at his cock he seemed surprised to see it had not yet risen. Scrawny's penis was thickening slowly. Lana cracked her whip threateningly close to his thighs and his cock rose in anticipation. Lana stared at the older man's genitals and laughed.

'What do you call that? It is a poor excuse for a cock.' She flicked at it with the handle end of the whip and raised it, only to see it flop again on to his shaking thigh.

She stood behind the men, who were arranged in a row for her, then flicked her hand fast so that they each received a sharp cut on the buttocks. She did this several times, shouting abuse at them at the same time. Each man was clearly having trouble not crying out. The erotic pain hurt as well as gave pleasure. Scrawny came quickly, his arc of come spraying the dirt floor, which was covered in sand. The smug man needed more to make him come, and begged Lana to hit him again. She untied him and insisted he lick her feet, which he did willingly, his hands tied behind his back still. Then she leant over and pushed the whip handle between his fleshy buttocks, pressing the leather into his crack. He winced and knelt, licking her ankles and legs. She sawed the whip between his buttocks and he opened his legs wider. He reached her thighs with his tongue and licked the golden fleece of her crotch. She did not move, except for her whip hand. As he licked, she caressed his arsehole with the leather and his prick waved sadly, trying to feel for something warm to fill. She quickly tied it up with the knotted leather tail of the whip so it was bound to his belly. He seemed happier like that. He licked more vigorously and Lana stood, her legs open for him and her hands on her hips. She swore at him if he paused his tonguing for a second, and she came, wetting his mouth with her juices. As he felt the stickiness fill his mouth his cock erupted, spouting gobs of white jelly on to his own belly and chest.

Lana saved the best until last. The strong lad was standing, still tied by his hands to the rafters. His legs were slightly apart, fixed to the floor. Lana leant against his belly, rubbing her leather-clad breasts and thighs over him. She licked his cock briefly to see it twitch. She had another weapon now – a thin cane. She brought it down hard on his thigh.

'You are a bad boy, aren't you?'

'Yes, Lana, a bad boy,' he agreed.

'No! How dare you call me Lana!' She brought the cane down hard on his buttocks this time and he flinched and caught his breath. 'Madame, you must address me as Madame Lana.' She gave him six of the best and his buttocks grew red and swollen. His prick was in an even more interesting state, trembling and waving about. It was of extraordinary girth and Lana was tempted to try it for size – but Madame Jezebel did not like her girls to give in too easily to their lusts. Instead of putting it between her legs, where she wanted it, she licked it again, starting at the tip and sliding her tongue to the base. She cupped his fine, plump balls and milked the root behind them. She leant against him, pressing herself on his cock but not letting it go inside her. Her sex lips were wet and swollen from previous administrations and the merest touch of his cock was enough to send her over the edge of ecstasy. Then the boy burst suddenly, his foam covering them both. The other girls and fishermen, who had witnessed the last act, were quiet, subdued and all suffered a similar *tristesse*.

At the palace, the king and queen were happy. They had sent the girl home for now, but she would return on the morrow to model for Adam before continuing the therapeutic practices with them.

'We must appoint her handmaiden to me, of course, then she can live in the palace quarters. It will be better for all concerned,' said the queen decidedly.

'You are so clever, my pumpkin,' said the contented king. He stroked the queen's peach-like bottom with one hand and placed the other round the front of her, insinuating his fingers between her thighs. She sighed loudly and allowed his fingers entry into her honey-filled sex. She enjoyed foreplay as much as the sex act itself. Her intimacies with the pretty girl had left her wet with longing and in a state of heightened eroticism. She was dressed in her very favourite nightdress of dark pink silk. Her bosoms rose like moons over the hem of the bodice, and the king's tongue found her stiff nipples. He patted her sex pouch fondly, then harder, causing her to open her legs more for a closer contact. His other hand was still fondling her nether parts, stroking the buttocks and pushing a little finger into her bottom cleft. She felt the finger find its mark, and settled her bottom more comfortably on her husband's hands. He had her in an intimate embrace, attacked from both sides. She held his surprisingly hard cock in her delicate hands and caressed him. He suddenly moved on top of her, lifting her legs up on to his strong shoulders. Her hips tilted and her pubis swelled towards his cock. He pushed it into her sex mouth and it enveloped the fleshy rod and swallowed it whole. He gazed at his wife's well-loved abundant flesh and saw her bosoms topple out of the silk garment. Her white thighs shone like moonlight, and he thrust into her firmly several times before spurting his love into her belly.

Adam, poor lad, was alone in his bedchamber. Did he love Trixie-Jane? He thought of Jezebel and her womanly charms. He thought of Princess Angeline and her smooth face and kissable lips. He thought of Queen Clementine's large breasts. He rubbed his cock through the split-crotch drawers he had managed to retain when Trixie-Jane had claimed the corset for the king and queen. His young cock was sore from masturbation, but he could not stop. He thought of the sight of Trixie-Jane's pink pussy through the open crotch and came for the fourth time that long night.

Next day Trixie-Jane was there, on time, on the beach. Her hair was wet where she had already bathed.
'Look, I have a present for my fishy friends.' She waved the fish at Adam. 'Come on, I'll race you to the headland.' She ran off into the water, Adam close behind her.
They swam powerfully together, though she was the better swimmer and Adam had to try hard to keep up with her. They reached the headland and turned the corner and there were the dolphins. Adam had seen them many times, but not this close. The fishy beings were bigger than the puny humans but looked upon them kindly, especially Trixie-Jane, as she always had fish for them. They took the little snack and clicked their thanks. Trixie-Jane and Adam swam with them under water, marvelling at their speed and beauty. Adam suddenly got cramp – he was not used to staying in the

water as long as this – and he cried out in pain. He couldn't keep his head above water, and he sank, coughing and spluttering. He lost consciousness, but not before realising that the dolphins were helping to save his life. He was kept afloat by the strong muscular dolphins, two of them under him and either side of him, nudging him along gently. As they reached shallower water Trixie-Jane took over the burden and half carried, half dragged him ashore.

He lay on his side, water pouring out of his mouth, coughing and vomiting. Just then Princess Angeline appeared for a morning swim.

'What has happened? Is he all right?' she asked.

'I think so, Princess Angeline,' replied Trixie-Jane.

'Do I know you?' said Angeline, clearly curious as to who her friend was consorting with so early in the morning.

'Yes, I'm Joshua's sister.'

'Goodness, how you've grown!' said the princess. 'Of course it is. Trixie-Jane.'

The manservant had recovered and was embarrassed at his ignominious position. He rose, staggered and sat down again.

'Well, well, Adam. I see you have found another playmate,' said the princess, grinning. 'I'll see you later,' she called out as she headed for the sea. Her sarong fluttered to the sand, revealing her naked limbs and a flash of her buttocks before she disappeared into the blue-green water.

Chapter Eleven
Angeline Sets Sail

Gertrude was bored with life on Isle de Paradis. She had come here several years ago as chaperone to Clementine and she had stayed to marry the handsome warrior, Ric – she never could resist an attractive man in uniform. It had been her downfall in the past. However, they had not been enjoying conjugal relations recently and she was unhappy with her inactive life. She had been teaching native children to speak English, but now it was the school holidays.

'Your Majesty, I would be happy to do as you ask. I would be sincerely happy,' she told the king one morning.

'Oh, good. I thought you would like the idea,' said King Aristide. 'I want Adam to go too. He can guard you both against any unexpected dangers. It is only for three months.'

Three months! Heaven! thought Gertrude. Perhaps absence will make the heart grow fonder.

Later, Adam was called to the king's quarters. Adam was unprepared for the joy that overwhelmed him as he heard the news, and blushed red as he bowed and thanked the king for the honour he bestowed on him. He could not think of what to say except, 'Thank you, sire. I will guard your beloved daughter-in-law with my life.'

Afterwards, though, when he had had time to think, he realised that he would not be seeing Trixie-Jane for several months. His happiness at being chosen to look after the princess, whom he adored, was suddenly deflated. He had not even got beyond kissing his muse yet, and the painting was not nearly finished.

Angeline was also overjoyed, but knew she would pine for her husband while she was away.

'I will miss you, Hari,' she said tearfully, that night in bed.

'You know you will enjoy yourself with Kelila and Isadora. They have always been kind to you, darling,' said Hari. 'It will be a holiday for you from me. And you could do with some dancing lessons, my love.'

Angeline smiled contentedly and wrapped her legs around his slender back. She secretly thought that Hari would miss her terribly when she was gone and be extra loving to her on her return.

Angeline, Gertrude and Adam stood on the royal yacht and waved to their friends, relations and interested natives who had gathered to see them set sail for Monkey Island.

Adam wore the guard's uniform of leather strips which hung from a wide waistbelt. His broad chest was criss-crossed with wide straps and he wore a bandanna of red cotton, which made him look heroic, he thought. Gertrude was magnificent in a travelling outfit of cream linen, made from a bale of cloth saved from the wreck. She even wore a straw hat. Her skin was as white and smooth as it had been when she first set foot on Isle de Paradis four years before. She looked such an English lady. Ric was on the pier with the king and queen, as was Prince Hari, who was both sad and relieved that his wife was off for three months. Ric looked forward to blessed freedom from marital strife. He knew his visits to the Forbidden Apple had not gone unnoticed by Gertrude, but now he would be able to spend more time with the forbidden fruit.

The yacht steamed off into the calm blue sea. There was a small crew of three men. The captain was a tall, good-looking native of one of the off islands, wearing a white uniform of light cotton with tight-fitting trews which showed off a taut pair of buttocks, and a fitted jacket with gold buttons and gold epaulettes. His peaked cap was worn at a jaunty angle, casting a blue shadow on his proud, angular, clean-shaven face. His hair was worn shorter than most of the islanders.

Gertrude has noted his broad shoulders and fine figure on boarding the yacht. She now made sure that he noticed her. She kept her hat low over her face and also carried a parasol to protect her from the strong sunlight. She took off her jacket and displayed her buxom charms. Her cleavage was magnificent and her white breasts rose like twin moons above the plunge-necked linen dress. She saw the captain glance at her bosom. Once he had seen, she knew he would not be able to turn away, and she was right. He was straight away bewitched by Gertrude's fair skin and thick brown hair, that had recently been cut in a short and flattering wedge that met her round cheeks with a sharp edge. Her eyes were lowered demurely and her lustrous eyelashes brushed those same fair cheeks.

He coughed. 'Madame, can I interest you in seeing the wheelhouse?'

'Oh, that would be delightful, thank you, Captain . . .?'

'Captain Barnabus, ma'am, at your service.'

The cook had prepared parrotfish for their lunch. Gertrude, Angeline and Adam sat in the small cabin, which was open at the sides but covered in a canvas screen above, and drank wine while enjoying the food.

'Being on the water always makes me hungry,' said Gertrude.

Adam could not speak, he was so happy and he beamed stupidly at everything. He grinned at Angeline every time she looked at him. He was very irritating, but he looked most fetching in the leather uniform and she blushed as she remembered the last time she had seen the uniform. She also remembered the sight of the guard's naked loins. Did Adam wear anything under his kilt? She knew she should not look, but she could not help but give him side glances as he moved about the boat. Angeline had also dressed for the occasion. She wore a blue and white striped dress with a sailor collar. It was made of soft stuff which clung to her curves and fell into her clefts. She looked charming in it; slender as a reed.

Suddenly, Adam got up and tripped over a large brass cleat screwed to the mahogany deck. Angeline turned and saw right up his kilt as he fell. No, he was not wearing any underwear. His bulging balls nudged his impressive organ forward and up. He saw her look and she blushed.

The voyage was smooth. The weather was kind. They saw dolphins and flying fish ride the wake, while frigate birds swooped for scraps.

The third day drifted by and brought a moonlit night, with the blue light spread over the sea like a glimmering highway. After Angeline had retired for the night, Gertrude sat at the stern with her arms on the rail.

'Good evening, madame.' It was the captain. His white uniform looked blue in the moonlight, and he looked exceedingly handsome. Gertrude was hot with thoughts of love, and his slightest touch on her chiffon-covered arm was like an electric shock. She gasped, and let out a short laugh.

'Good evening, Captain. Do sit down and enjoy the peace.'

He sat next to her, close enough to smell her flowery scent.

'Do you see the phosphorescence on the water?' he asked, pointing to the wake.

He brushed her hand with his. She recognised the signal and did not draw back from the promise of lust that was in his dark eyes.

'Would you like to come to my cabin for a nightcap?' he asked suddenly.

'That would be delightful, thank you.' Gertrude rose and followed him to his mahogany-lined, small cabin, which had in it a large single bunkbed, with sides of wood to stop the sleeper falling out in high seas. She looked around her quickly, noting the porcelain basin and water taps, the bidet and the side table which folded away. The captain lit a glass-shaded oil lamp and lowered the flame.

'What a charming cabin, Captain.'

He stopped her chatter with his mouth over hers. She gasped at the passion in his embrace. Her arms were pinned to her sides and he tore her flimsy garment from her shoulders, and pulled it down over her breasts, which fell out like ripe melons into his eager hands. He kissed them fiercely and she nearly swooned. Her garment dropped to her ankles, leaving her wearing only a thin silk slip. His hands were all over her. He grabbed her crotch and rubbed hard at the bulging mound. She allowed his hands freedom over her freshly prepared body. She depilated daily, as was the island custom, so her skin was smooth all over. He felt her plump sex lips through the thin silk. Her breasts tumbled out of the bodice of the slip. Then he was on his knees, still in his uniform trousers and shirt, but he had taken off his jacket. She felt his tongue move up her silk-stockinged leg. He came to the white flesh straining at the thigh and

73

he kissed it, wrapping the elastic of her suspender in his fingers. Her thighs melted and she sank on to the edge of the bunk. He had his hands inside her plump pussy and she was very wet. She pressed a hand on his head encouragingly. He sucked at her bare mound, making slurping noises as he did so. His hair was sleek and silky like a dog's.

The captain fumbled with his flies and released his eager organ. He rose to clasp her around the waist and push her backward on to the bunk. She allowed him to kiss her hard and she sank back, her hips thrust forward to meet his embrace. His cock was held in his hand, aimed at her softest, most vulnerable part, and she opened her thighs to allow him access. He pressed the thick cock into her and she cried out as the warm weapon found its target. It slid into her, hard and silky, and she clasped it between her thighs. His ardour was keen and she worried that he would come too quickly and not give her the satisfaction she craved, so she calmed him with a hand around the base of his thick stem, squeezing firmly. He understood and eased his straining thrusts, meanwhile touching her lightly with his masterful hands. He rubbed her bare mound, slipping fingers into the welcoming slit and sliding them into her, next to his cock. The extra pressure on her delicate flesh was like fire. She rose to his touch, impatient for his caresses. He bit her nipple lightly and sucked at it strongly. Her head was thrown back and her white neck was covered in kisses. He was overwhelmed by her fairness; her delicacy; her Englishness. Her white thighs were stretched wide and he thrust into her, his cock slithering in and out to caress her outer lips. His heavy balls pressed firmly on her perineum. She lifted her legs to clasp him around the waist, her feet entwined on his back. Cock and scrotum pressed in just the right places and she yelled out in delirium and enjoyed the slow ecstasy of orgasm, giving the captain his cue to let go and spurt into her.

'Well, Captain, that was delightful. Perhaps we may partake of another nightcap tomorrow?'

'At your service, ma'am.'

Next day dawned, pink with the promise of a fine day. Angeline woke, put on a negligee over her thin night-gown, and went to her chaperone's cabin.

'Gertrude, are you awake?' She knocked and entered through the low door.

Gertrude was washing at the little sink, leaning forward to bathe her breasts. Angeline stared at the pleasant picture. Her chaperone was naked, and a very charming shape. Her plump buttocks were large and round and very white. Gertrude pulled a towel from the rail and covered herself with it. She turned and smiled at the girl.

'Good morning, dear Princess, what can I do for you?'

'Well, Gertrude, you see, I am used to help with my toilet, and I cannot seem to manage to depilate on my own. I wonder, could you help, please?'

'Of course, dear. There is not much room, is there?' Gertrude giggled girlishly. 'Shall we do it here or in your cabin?'

'Oh, in mine, it's bigger,' said Angeline.

Gertrude threw a bright pink silk kimono-style wrap around her naked body and followed the princess to her cabin, across the passage from hers.

The princess disrobed and sat on her bidet, facing the chaperone. She had no modesty about her private parts, having been used to a handmaiden bathing her.

'You are very charming, my dear,' said Gertrude admiringly. She prepared the soapy foam and brushed it on to the princess's pubic mound and between her legs with a monkey-hair brush. She was aware of the pink folds of her princess's sex shining through the white foam. It seemed to open at the delicate touch of the fine brush. Gertrude's eyes gleamed. Her sleeves were in the way and she drew them back over her elbows. But they slipped down over her wrists again and were a hindrance to the operation.

'Oh, do take it off, Gertrude. You'll only get hot and bothered if you keep it on.'

'Thank you, Princess, you're right. It is very warm in here, is it not? Is your porthole window open?' She rose and opened the porthole, which looked out on to the foredeck, then she slipped off her kimono to reveal her stiffened nipples and her rounded belly.

'That's better, Gertrude. You look cooler now,' said the princess, admiring the mature chaperone's generous curves. 'Oh, I wish I had a more womanly form,' she grumbled. 'I am shaped like a boy.'

'Nonsense, darling, you are lovely; charming. A pretty shape.' Gertrude was hot and bothered by the proximity of naked female flesh. Her touch on the princess's skin was inflaming her desires. She used the razor gently but firmly, sliding the blade across and under the thighs to remove the light fuzz of fair hair. She splashed cool, soothing water over the shaved area and patted it dry with a soft towel. Her breasts touched Angeline's thighs as she knelt to do this intimate service for the princess. Angeline bent forward and kissed Gertrude lightly on the cheek.

'Thank you, Gertrude, that was well done. You are more gentle than my handmaiden.'

'A pleasure, Princess. Shall I perform this service for you daily?'

'Yes please.' The princess rose and admired herself in the mirror, pirouetting and twirling. 'Do you think I will make a good dancer?' She craved approval from everybody.

'Certainly, darling, I'm sure you will.' The chaperone allowed herself another 'accidental' touch of the princess's lithe young body as she passed her to pick up her kimono and put it on.

Neither of the females saw the peeping tom at the porthole. The sailor had noticed the fluttering curtain, almost closed but allowing him to glimpse the princess and her chaperone cavorting naked in the cabin. He moved away sharply before Gertrude left the cabin, but not before he had heard them agree to repeat the performance. He noted the time and made his plans.

Chapter Twelve
Hari Takes Up the Art of Portrait Painting

Hari had decided to take up painting too. Since his wife's departure, a week ago, he had been bored. He had hung around the palace, putting himself in the way of Trixie-Jane.

'I am sure Adam would not mind if I used his paints to give it a try,' he had said to Queen Clementine. 'Do you think he would?'

'No, Hari. It's a good idea.' She had patted his hand. 'Use his model, too,' she then suggested.

His painting was improving in leaps and bounds. His model had come daily for a week and the painting was nearly finished, but he had not touched her, becoming more shy with her as time passed. He was aware that his father and stepmother had hired her as handmaiden and he knew well enough what her duties would be. He was therefore afraid of incurring his father's wrath if he made love to their servant. But it was difficult, because she gave him every encouragement, flaunting her open crotch at him so he could see her swollen lips peeping out. Her nipples were always swollen too, as if from constant kissing, and her firm buttocks were pinkly marked from his father's hand. She cunningly leant over him as she admired the painting, allowing his eyes to alight on her little breasts, letting him smell her musky perfume.

He spent nights pulling at his tortured cock, imagining her mouth around it. He tried hard to reach his cock with his own mouth, nearly causing himself a spinal injury.

In the end he went to his father and asked for an allowance so he could spend it at the Forbidden Apple.

'Of course, my boy, you must have what you like in the way of an allowance. But don't you think you should be considering the future? I think you should be seconded to Ric's battalion for a while – make a man of you, my boy. You start in three days!' He strode off, jaunty in a new silk loincloth, his chest and back oiled to a glossy mahogany. Hari groaned, miserable in the belief that this was the end of his artistic ambitions.

The queen and her rejuvenated husband now enjoyed the spanking and fondling of the delectable handmaiden dailing, so Trixie-Jane moved into the palace compound, with her mother's blessing. Poppy-Flower was pleased with the jewels and gold she brought home to them.

'Are you still a virgin, my child?' she asked her tentatively, on one of her visits home.

'Oh, yes, Mother. They only use me to titillate themselves. It is very amusing really.'

She too enjoyed the caressing and fondling the royal couple gave her, and the spanking aroused her lust and made her wish for more firm handling. She desired penetration by the king's impressive organ, but so far had had to make do with his hand or the queen's fingers. She also wanted the king's son, Hari.

Later that day, Hari told her his bad news.

'But does that mean I won't model for you again?' Trixie-Jane asked him.

'Yes,' he said dramatically, failing to tell her it was only a temporary secondment.

He put down his paintbrush and went over to the couch, throwing himself on her and kissing her. She placed her arms around him and drew him close. Her tongue found his and they imparted to each other their mutual desire. Her legs fell open and he placed his fingers into the gap of her drawers – his stepmother's drawers. She gasped at his cool touch, more delicate than the queen's fingers on her. He was slender as a girl and his weight was light on her. She opened his loincloth, to reveal his swollen cock; paler than his brown belly and more slender than his father's massive member. She took it into her fingers and felt its length and breadth. He swooned in her arms, kissing her neck and shoulders and the tops of her swelling breasts. She turned away from him and asked him to undo the corset.

'I want you to wear it,' she whispered, and he eagerly agreed.

Soon he lay there in the tight velvet and satin, his cock sticking up rudely beneath it. She admired his slender form, which strained against her. She was naked and sitting astride him so he could see all of her sex gaping at him. Her hands caressed him, using the lessons she had learnt from his father. She wanted the slender stem inside her. She placed a flower behind his ear and stroked his long hair. She painted his kiss-swollen lips a bright red, like hers. She kissed him. She painted his slender cock too and kissed that. It swayed and throbbed at the delicate touch of her mouth and tongue. She sat over him and impaled herself on his proud organ.

'Oh! That's wonderful!' she sighed, and pressed down hard on him. He groaned loudly and came inside her immediately.

'Oh, you brute!' she said, and the disappointed girl

leapt off the selfish prince. 'I don't care if you do go to be a soldier, so there!'

On the royal yacht, Gertrude had again shaved her charge's pussy. They were watched as usual by the young sailor, who stood outside the cabin, perched on two metal protuberances either side of the porthole to give him the necessary height to see through. The older woman was crouched by the bidet between the open legs of the princess. Her face had disappeared between the long legs of the prone girl. The princess sighed loudly. 'Oh, Gertrude, that is a delightful feeling. Lovely! Do it some more.' Gertrude was wielding the monkey-hair brush, not covered in soap this time but dry, and she was using it to caress the girl's newly shaved sex.

'It is good practice, darling, to conceal your pleasure and prolong it as long as possible,' said Gertrude, her lips and eyes shining. She caressed the youthful thighs, pulling open the princess's outer lips to reveal the more closed inner lips, which swelled like an oyster's flesh. 'You like that, don't you?' Her voice caressed the feverish Angeline.

'Oh yes, Gertrude, I do indeed. Can't you push it up into me a little?'

The blunt, furry bristles swept across her pubis back and forth and penetrated her just a little. The princess was flushed all over. Her little bosoms rose and fell, her nipples hard as buttons. Gertrude bent over to kiss them. The girl's head hung back and Gertrude pushed the shaving brush a little further up inside the open sex. The bud was swollen; pink and ripe. Gertrude felt inside her own thighs and rubbed hard. The princess sighed and moaned loudly. Her belly thrust forward on to the erotic weapon.

The peeping tom fell from his precarious perch in a crash as he also came into his white duck trews.

'Oh, what was that?' The two females gathered their wits and clothes and looked outside the cabin door.

There they found the captain with the naughty sailor. The captain held one ear of the boy, and the boy's face was red with terror and pain.

'He was trying to see through your porthole, Princess,' said the captain angrily. 'What shall you have me do to him?'

'You will thrash him, of course, and we shall be witness to his humiliation,' decided the princess.

'As you wish, Princess,' said the captain, smiling.

The princess and her chaperone dressed quickly and prepared themselves for the entertainment. The sailor, who was a lad of twenty, shy and solemn, and had never before this voyage seen a woman naked, was bent over a capstan, his bare buttocks exposed to the captain and cook, and to Adam and the two female passengers. His trews were pulled to his ankles and his legs looked frail. He was sobbing in anticipation of the cat-o'-nine-tails.

The captain was holding the leather weapon, testing it on the deck. The loud crack made the peeping tom wince.

'Captain, may I make a suggestion?' said Gertrude.

'Of course, dear lady,' said the captain.

'May I thrash the lad, please? I think the punishment would be more memorable if I did it.'

'Very well, dear lady.' He handed the many-thonged whip to the smiling Englishwoman, who felt it lovingly. She threw it behind her and tried her strength with it on the wooden deck, as he had.

The lad, whose bottom quivered in fear and trepidation, felt his cock grow under him. Gertrude's hand touched him briefly on one bottom cheek then he felt the sudden sting of the whip. He yelled. She struck again and he yelled, but felt his cock thicken and swell to its full tumescence. It was thankfully hidden from the gaze of the women. His bottom was hurting terribly as she

82

struck mercilessly six times. He came all over the metal capstan as the sixth blow flicked across his back and thighs.

'There, young man, perhaps that will teach you not to peep at ladies at their toilet,' said his captain.

The captain himself later enjoyed the whip at the hands of Gertrude, who beat him about the thighs and buttocks and balls. He had implored her to tie him down and chastise him erotically, and she had not known that she would enjoy being so rough with him. She rubbed herself over his big cock and swung his rod up and down over her sex lips. She made him suck her breasts, then she sat on his face and churned on his mouth. She came like this while his cock pulsated in her hands.

She wished the voyage would not end.

Erotic handling by her sensual chaperone had made Angeline blossom like a flower. She felt that her breasts were growing bigger. She made herself up with black kohl eye make-up, lengthening and enlarging her almond eyes. Her lips were made to look even plumper with red glossy paint. Gertrude had shown her how to paint her sex lips also, to enhance their bright colour. She became more aware of her emotional hold over Adam, and started to use her charms on him mercilessly. He, poor boy, could not resist.

'Adam! Come and lace me up, would you? Gertrude does not seem to be about and I need to dress.' She turned her back on the lad, smirking in satisfaction as his large hands tugged at the ribbons on the back of her gown. 'How is a soldier's life then?' she asked coquettishly.

'Boring, mostly – I mean, I didn't mean . . .'

She laughed at him. 'Come on and sit with me at the stern for a while, if you've nothing else to do.' She led him by the hand and he stumbled after her. Her charms were well displayed in the low-cut gown; her shoulders bare, her breasts swelling under the blue stuff. His leather kilt slapped against his thighs and buttocks. She sat on the stern thwart and bade him sit next to her. He sat sideways on to her, gazing into her slanting, painted eyes. She fluttered her eyelashes at him.

'Do you like my gown?' she asked.

'Oh yes, Princess.'

'You may kiss me if you like.' She puckered her painted lips and closed her eyes, raising her face to his.

He leant over her, almost fainting in the excess of emotion he felt at this historic moment –

'Darling, there you are!' It was Gertrude, flushed and half dressed. 'Adam! I am afraid the captain has been taken ill, I believe. Would you come and see, please?'

The frustrated young people followed the chaperone to her cabin, where they found the prone, naked captain slumped on his knees. His bottom was striped with red marks and his face had a bluish tinge. He had red marks around his wrists and neck but Gertrude had hidden the straps and whip that had done the damage. As they walked into the cabin, Gertrude tried to keep the princess from seeing, but knew that she could not hide her predilections for ever, and anyway, it had been the captain's suggestion. Adam slapped his face and placed him on his side. He came to quickly and choked a bit, then recovered himself.

'I'm fine,' he whispered, blushing when he saw the princess.

'Give the man air,' said Adam. 'Princess, please leave us at once.'

'Oh, all right then,' said the princess, not wanting to miss any excitement. 'What happened to him?'

'Ssh! I'll tell you later, dear,' said her chaperone, and closed the cabin door on her.

Chapter Thirteen
Monkey Island

Kelila and Isadora were waiting at the pier for the royal yacht to dock. They had seen it since it was a dot on the horizon and they were anxious for the princess to arrive. The white yacht slid into the harbour and smoothly edged up to dock. The young sailor who had peeped at Gertrude and Angeline leapt from the deck on to the pier and wrapped the aft and fore ropes around cleats. Angeline was surprised to see a large crowd gathered to see her alight. She had not realised her royal importance before this – or she had not cared. Now she rose to the occasion. She was dressed in her best travelling costume – the sailor dress – again, and she felt her breasts swell against the thin bodice. Her legs looked tanned and shapely as she stepped down on to the wooden pier. The captain handed her down, and waited to help the sweet-scented Gertrude down also. She smiled coldly at him, only allowing a slight up-curve of her lips as she bade him goodbye until he should return to fetch them again in three months' time. Adam looked every inch a soldier. His leather-thonged kilt slapped his thighs in the rising breeze and his firm flesh glimmered beneath the leather.

'Welcome, sweetie, welcome!' Isadora flung her arms around the young princess, who she hadn't seen for twelve months. 'My, you've blossomed!' she enthused, kissing both her cheeks. Kelila did the same and they kissed Gertrude too. They knew her well, and remembered many happy times together on Isle de Paradis.

Adam was greeted enthusiastically, and sent off to his own private room in a hut close to the dancing academy. Gertrude and Angeline were to sleep in their hostesses' home. Once there, they washed and dressed in clean clothes and joined Isadora and Kelila on the airy veranda with the view of the sandy beach.

'And how is Ric?' said Kelila to Gertrude.

'Oh, you know, he's a soldier. And soldiers will be soldiers!' laughed his wife, more confident now she had proved to herself that her own charms had not lost their power.

'Oh, right!' Kelila and Isadora understood immediately that the couple were not faithful to each other.

'I am really fearfully sleepy,' said Angeline, yawning loudly. 'Will you excuse me?'

'Of course, honey. Goodnight!'

She leant over them all and kissed their cheeks, then went to her room. Kelila had carefully unpacked her trunk and she saw that the dildos had been left in their silk wrapping. Angeline had brought them with her in a sudden moment of madness, thinking that maybe she could give them to Kelila and Isadora as a gift, but in all truthfulness, she had brought them for her own entertainment. She had not had time to make use of them with her friend, Sylva, on Isle de Paradis, but they intrigued her. She had also brought the erotic volume with her on this trip.

She yawned again as she pulled the thin sheet up over her naked body. It was so exciting to be here! She couldn't believe she had been so reluctant to leave home.

She missed her handsome husband, but it would do

them both good to be away from each other for a little while. They were together too much. She wanted to learn how to dance too. Kelila and Isadora's dancing had been much admired on Isle de Paradis, but Angeline had not taken advantage of their expertise when she had had the opportunity. This term of dance tuition was just what she needed. Adam was attentive, flatteringly so, and Gertrude's tender administrations were not unappreciated either. She sighed and reached for a dildo.

Meanwhile, her husband, Prince Hari, was learning how to be a soldier. Ric, his lifetime friend and now his captain, took him by the arm and lifted him from his bunk, where he had slumped after a day's running and training. 'Come on, Prince, the day is not finished yet,' he joshed.

They arrived at the Forbidden Fruit and Hari pushed aside the beaded curtain and went inside. The powerful scent of sex hit his nostrils. He peered through the gloom and saw Lana wielding a long black whip. He whistled at her costume – she was dressed from head to foot in black animal skins, but with holes left to show her intimate zones. Her sex triangle shone and glistened with oil, as did her magnificent breasts. Her erect nipples were painted bright red and her long scarlet fingernails were sharpened to a point. She stared at him, then she lifted the hem of his kilt with her whip handle. His erection was swelling up towards his belly. She smiled wickedly and then rearranged her features until they were stern and forbidding. Hari shivered in anticipation. The curtain divided and Sylva and Petite Gigi swept in, giggling.

'Tie him up,' ordered Lana.

He allowed the scantily dressed girls to attach his wrists and ankles to the wall rings, opening his legs and lifting his arms to their touch. They tickled him under his kilt, touching his taut thighs and stroking his balls.

His erection stiffened imperceptibly, and he strained against them.

'Enough!' said Madame Lana.

The girls withdrew from the chamber and left him in the clutches of the dominatrix. She knew who he was, of course. He was almost as handsome as his father, she thought, yet his slenderness was too pretty for her. She preferred big men. She was much more attracted to Samson, who was huge and powerful, or Bartolem, whose shoulders and arms were like tree trunks. Their muscles were honed and oiled, and they were easy with their strength. This was only a boy, really, but his cock was long and thickening nicely as she licked his buttocks with the whip end. She wore a black mask over her face, giving her a demonic air, and she stroked his loins with a leather-gloved hand. His balls tightened as she weighed them thoughtfully. She called in Samson and the giant swept through the doorway, his shadow huge on the wall.

'Samson, insert your finger up the prince's pretty arsehole, will you?' she commanded, softly but firmly.

'With pleasure, Madame Lana.'

Prince Hari winced as the big man's smallest finger pressed into his anus.

'Shall I oil him first?' said Samson.

'Of course, fool.' She cracked her whip furiously.

The prince felt the fingers smooth the oil over his buttocks and into his arsehole, which gradually opened up at the subtle touch. He relaxed and felt his anus widen, and then the black consort had his thumb pressed into Hari's puckered hole. Hari groaned. The dominatrix cracked her whip on his thighs and belly, and watched his cock jump.

'Hold his cock, now, Samson. Milk him.'

Hari hung from the metal wall rings, unable to help himself or protect himself from the erotic torture. The dominatrix was out of reach; her whip was the only contact he had with her. It stroked his buttocks. He felt its velvet touch on his flesh. His skin was on fire. But the huge hand of Samson enclosed his cock and milked it. He threw back his head and groaned as the white fluid pumped from his sex. The dominatrix struck him once more then turned away, leaving Samson to undo his bonds.

Angeline woke to a perfect day. The sky was blue as the bluebell woods of her beloved home, the New Forest, which she had left years ago. There were few white clouds racing across the horizon and the air was cooler than on Isle de Paradis. She felt refreshed after her sleep. Kelila had come into her chamber earlier but had not disturbed her. She had just picked up the dildo from the floor and taken it away to clean it.

Gertrude was late for breakfast too, but today was a rest day for the dancing academy. Isadora and Kelila were determined to show their guests the delights of Monkey Island before the princess started work on her lessons.

They all sat together at a table groaning with fresh-plucked fruit. They drank starfruit juice and ate fresh baked bread spread with honey.

'Where is Adam staying?' asked the princess.

'He is close by, but his meals will not be taken with us, Angeline, unless you say so, sweetie,' said Isadora.

Angeline wore a little tunic of white silk, with a short hem which showed her round bottom when she walked. Here, as on Isle de Paradis, the custom was to wear as little as possible. Underwear was not worn usually. Most people wore sarongs, tied around their hips or waist. The princess and Gertrude's Western-style clothes were a novelty to the Monkey Islanders, as they soon discovered when they toured the island after breakfast, but they were all friendly, and waved and cheered as the princess walked by. She waved back, happy to be with her old friends again after so long. Adam joined them for the walkabout in his role of bodyguard and couldn't keep his eyes off Isadora. Her legs were long and her green eyes glittered. She wore a theatrical costume and looked like a man, her white jodhpurs fitting her like a glove. Her high, round buttocks were like twin moons, straining to escape the cloth, and her pointed breasts showed erect nipples through the thin stuff of her full-sleeved shirt, which was tucked into the waist of the jodhpurs. She wore black, knee-length boots with a small heel. She carried a riding crop and held a long leash.

'Where's your horse?' he joked, smirking.

'I'll show you later, if you like.' Her smile was a threat.

Kelila walked three steps behind, her head bowed. Her garment was a short sarong that covered only one breast. The nipple ring on her exposed breast had a fine silver chain running through it that was attached to the lead that her lover held. Kelila trotted behind, occasionally lagging a little so that Isadora could tug the leash. When this happened, Kelila's brown nipple stretched and grew longer and she licked her lips at the excitement it clearly gave her.

Gertrude looked every part the lady. She was corseted and curvy in her bright pink costume, and her dark head was shaded with a pink parasol. She was used to the outrageous costumes of these dancers – she remembered them well. She wondered how she would occupy herself while staying on Monkey Island. Her ardour had been awakened on the voyage by the handsome captain, but would she find a substitute?

The tour of the island took several days, and they stayed at various places along the way. The huts were larger and more elaborately designed than on Paradis. The natives were artistic: there were potters, fabric designers, silversmiths and tanners. Jewellers showed their wares to the royal guest and she bought several pieces, liking all she saw.

Geographically, Monkey Island was similar to Isle de Paradis, but there were more mountains and a large, deep lake in the middle called the Lake of Lost Love, where pink pearls were the prize of daring divers. These boys and young men dived naked into the dark green water, holding their breath for minutes while they searched the lake bed for the treasure-filled oysters. It was exciting to see them slit open the ugly, grey-brown shells and reveal the gleaming pearls. Mostly, of course, the shells contained nothing but the edible bivalve. Gertrude and Angeline watched the slim brown bodies dive like daggers into the water. They sat under wide parasols, placed there specially for the royal guest and her retinue. One of the divers was especially good-looking, with long, black, curly hair and an angular face with wide-spaced brown eyes. His mouth was wide and generous and he smiled through an explosion of water droplets as he emerged from the water. He pulled himself out of the lake and took an oyster-filled bag off his shoulder. His powerful, naked body was close to her as he crouched on the bank, and she was aware of the heaving of his chest and the muscles of his shoulders. His long cock hung between his strong thighs and nearly touched the ground. She watched as he took his knife and inserted it into the divide between two shells. The pearl inside was huge. A delicate pinky white, with depths of blue and mauve, it shone like a miniature planet in his palm. He gave it to her, and she held it in the palm of her pink hand. It was the biggest pearl she had ever seen.

'How much is it?' she asked.

Kelila translated, and Angeline paid his price. He stood, a slender, muscled, proud man. Angeline felt his erotic power and her thighs felt weak. She thanked him and the royal party left.

She turned and saw him still standing there, watching

91

her, and holding his cock in both hands and rubbing hard. She giggled in embarrassment and excitement.

When she got back to Isadora and Kelila's hut, Angeline asked to see Adam.

'Yes, Princess, can I help you?'

'Yes, Adam. Tell me; do you think I am pretty?'

'No, Princess, you are beautiful!' He bowed down and kissed her hand.

She sighed happily. 'That's all, Adam. You may go now.'

Chapter Fourteen
Dancing Lessons Begin

Gertrude had also been aroused by the sight of the naked divers, though she preferred her men to wear uniform. There were not many men wearing anything but loincloths or sarongs on Monkey Island, but she lived in hope. Angeline was to start her dancing lessons, and after helping the princess with her toilet and dress, which took two hours of the morning, she was free to wander.

Angeline had been bathed and depilated, as usual, and had her hair dressed. Gertrude was learning fast to be as good a handmaiden as Isadora and Kelila had been to the princess in the early days. Angeline was dressed in her favourite tutu of white frothy net, with her sex left bare except for a narrow thong of silk. It was fairly loose, to allow the violent movements she knew she would have to perform. Her breasts were just hidden under the tight bodice. She wore ballet shoes and white stockings to just above her knees.

Gertrude kissed her charge farewell and watched the young princess run off to the academy, which was just across the dirt path from Isadora and Kelila's hut.

The chaperone was dressed in a light blue gown held

tight at the waist, with a full, long skirt. Her bosom heaved under the constricting corset. She carried a white parasol of cotton and lace above her dark knot of hair and set off to see some more of the island.

'Ma'am, may I come with you?' It was Adam, bored with his own company and in need of a talk. His guard duties had lessened and he had little to do.

'Of course, dear boy, join me by all means. Here, hold my parasol, will you? My arm tires so.' She had not really appreciated before how handsome the lad was in his uniform. The leather thongs flapped loudly on his thighs as he trotted at her side, and she remembered that soldiers traditionally wore no underwear. Her own husband had taken great delight in exposing his heavy balls to her as he climbed the ladder to their hut. His thick erection would poke through the leather straps and make her almost faint with joy and anticipation.

Yes, the lad had great potential. Her eyes met his, and she was glad her breasts were still plump and firm. Her nipples rose in interest and his gaze fell to her half-exposed bosom as if he was hypnotised. He was a head taller than she was, and his strong male scent enveloped her as his arm was held high to protect her from the strong sunlight. The parasol lent an intimacy to their walk, and she held a white feather fan to her face to hide her smile. They walked through the village of makuti homes and small shops, which sold rice and maize flour and candle wax and other basic necessities. They dipped into the dark shade of the forest and Adam folded the parasol, while at the same time Gertrude stumbled over a tree root.

'Oh! My ankle!' she exclaimed, and sat down on the root which had tripped her.

'Let me see!' Adam took her small, neat foot in one hand and removed the satin shoe.

'Ouch! Be careful!' she cried.

He gently lifted her foot. 'Does that hurt?' he asked.

'No, I don't think I've broken anything,' she murmured, and stroked his silky black hair. 'Lift it higher
and just check, please, Adam.'

He lifted her foot and held her plump calf in the other
hand. His hand slid up under her long silky skirts, and
he pressed and turned the ankle gently.

'Oh, oh, yes, go higher, please. Lift my leg up.' He
lifted her foot until he could see to the top of her skirt.
The skirt slid up to her thigh, revealing that she was
naked underneath. Her plump pussy glistened between
her round thighs. Adam gazed, mesmerised by the fleshy
mound and the red slit. His hand moved inexorably
towards her sex, and she swooned back and lay there,
her head on the mossy bank. Then his lips were sliding
up her leg, kissing her ankle and calf and knee. He
kissed behind her knee, lifting her leg so it rested on his
shoulder. She lifted her other leg and put it on his other
shoulder. He licked and kissed slowly up both her bare
legs. Her thighs strained open to his touch. His mouth
was on her sex. His tongue sipped and lapped at her
flowing juices and she moaned appreciatively. Her buttocks quivered under his palms. He held her thighs and
bottom and slipped fingers into her wide open sex. She
pushed herself up into his embrace. His mouth covered
her sex and she writhed on his tongue and titillating
teeth. His cock was tumescent. She reached down and
held it between her firm fingers and massaged it with
precision. His balls tightened and throbbed. They eased
themselves into a suitable position and his cock slid into
her. She held it at the base and kept his eruption at bay;
she wanted more fondling first. Her orgasm was near,
but she needed to wait for it; to hold off the moment as
long as possible. She allowed his cock its instinctive
thrusts and her feet clasped behind his head. His balls
knocked against her buttocks and gave her the exact
right pressure she required. Her hips raised to him and
he thrust hard into her. One of his leather kilt thongs fell

on to her inflamed sex and his cock trapped it on the next inward thrust. Her heavy hair fell out of its constraint of hairpins and fell to her shoulders. Her face flushed pink. Her bosoms heaved. Her juices ran freely, and she cried out as she orgasmed. His climax was triggered by her ecstatic cries.

Kelila was dressed in a chamois-skin outfit and she looked like a warrior queen. Her hair was tied back in tiny plaits, intertwined with red coral beads, and her limbs, like brilliant copper, were golden arrows shooting from her hips and pubis. Her breasts were hidden by a leather corset which drew in the small waist even tighter and made her flaring hips look rounder. She wore a thong of chamois between her legs and narrow belts of the stuff were wrapped around her legs. Her sex lips were painted red and were visible either side of the chamois G-string. Her proud, full buttocks were oiled.

Isadora was dressed in animal skin breeches and a loose-sleeved shirt, and she wore thigh-length black skin boots.

'Well, look at you, you little darling!' Isadora clasped the princess around her slender waist. 'You still look good enough to eat! Let's get started.' She clapped her hands and Kelila whisked the princess up into her strong arms and twirled her around.

A boy drummer had appeared and started to hammer loudly on a huge drum, throwing his slight body at it in a frenzy of rhythm. Another lad played a smaller drum, which sat on the floor between his knees. He used both hands to tap and pound, and between them the sound was terrific. Isadora stood to one side and watched Kelila take the princess through her paces.

'Watch my steps and follow the beat, Princess,' Kelila said. 'Dance as you feel; feel it inside your stomach.' She moved slowly, sinuously, writhing her lithe form like a snake. Angeline listened to her heart and closed her eyes before moving in time with the native dancer. She opened her eyes to see what Kelila did with her body, and then tried to follow her steps as best she could.

'One two, one two – that's right, Angeline, you are doing well,' called Isadora.

Kelila held the princess around her waist and lifted her high. Angeline lifted her arms high and pointed her toes, flashing her moist, pink sex from beneath the loose ribbon of silk. Kelila feasted her eyes on the sight.

'All right, Kelila, let her down, dear, thank you!' Isadora said sternly, although she was smiling at the same time.

Later, over a light lunch of fruit and goat's cheese with warm, homemade bread, Isadora explained to Angeline their plans to expand the dance academy and introduce modern American dance routines. Her ambition was to open a dance theatre and attract important guests to first-night performances. Isadora had been an exotic dancer in San Francisco before the fateful voyage which had landed her and Angeline on Isle de Paradis. The rest was history. Isadora had fallen for Kelila, and Angeline had married the king's son.

Isadora was a drama queen, a tragedian, a romantic, an actress. She sang (not well) and danced (divinely). Her red hair, only slightly helped with henna paste, and her white skin, long slender limbs and straight carriage raised her from the ordinary and made her unforgettable. Her love for Kelila was real, as was her abiding affection for Angeline.

Kelila was edgy. She knew she had punishment to look forward to. She should not have so openly admired the princess's body. She knew she would have to wait until the work day was over before she received her just desserts.

* * *

Gertrude had showered and changed and was languishing in the shade of her hostess's veranda. She smiled to herself as she felt the heat of her sex still. She had not felt so alive for a long time. She felt young again. There was an understanding between the bodyguard and the princess's chaperone. She looked forward to many similar walks while the princess practised her dancing.

Adam was feeling smug and satisfied. He had not really expected such immediate satisfaction as Gertrude had bestowed. He had only wanted to be near a womanly scent; think of her constricting garments; imagine her breasts. His success was a wonder to him. Were all older women this grateful? he thought. Were they all so lascivious? He hoped so. He still yearned after the princess, of course. She was so sweet, so pretty; perfect, in fact. But he was gratified that his attentions had been so appreciated by the handsome Gertrude. He was suddenly aware that he had fucked his captain's wife. It would mean death, probably, if he was found out. Somehow, it only made it more exciting. He went through the seduction in his mind. Had he seduced her, or had he been seduced by her? Who cared? He was satisfied – for now, at least. He wondered if she would lend him her corset.

Angeline slept well that night. Her narrow bed was cosy and she enjoyed the privacy of her small room She could hear the gentle snore of Gertrude in the next chamber and felt physically exhausted after her day's work. It was a good feeling. She fell asleep and dreamed that she was being whipped by her dancing teacher.

Meanwhile, Kelila was being whipped by her mistress, lover and dancing partner. Isadora was dressed in black satin jodhpurs, thigh boots and nothing else. Kelila was chained over a low stool, her buttocks naked and high and her head low.

Thwack! Thwack! The riding crop hit its target –

Kelila's open thighs. Her sex was pouting, plump and moist. She could not raise her head as the metal band around her neck was attached to the floor. She flinched imperceptibly.

'You know why you are being punished?'

'Yes, mistress.'

'Why?'

'Because I desired the princess.'

The crop sang and her buttocks stung.

'Yes!' Isadora struck with all her strength and her lover's buttocks reddened under the fearsome blows.

'She is delightfully young and pretty, isn't she?' she murmured encouragingly.

'Yes!' The answer was interrupted by the sting on Kelila's tender flesh.

'But we must teach her to dance, must we not?'

'Yes, mistress, we must teach her to dance.'

Afterwards, Kelila fell into her lover's arms and they embraced.

'Do you remember the fun we all used to have together?' said Isadora.

'Yes. Even Hari joined in. Do you remember playing Blind Man's Buff?'

Isadora giggled. 'Yes!'

'We always blindfolded Hari and he used to grab us both and feel our big titties and think he had found Angeline. He would kiss me on the lips and call me his little wife.' Kelila burst out laughing. 'What a simpleton he was!'

'Yes, and he pulled my labia rings and kissed me and called me his little wife, too,' said Isadora. 'He wasn't such a fool!'

'We must make Angeline's stay a happy one,' said Isadora decidedly. 'After all, we have been paid very well by Hari to teach her dancing.'

'Yes, darling, I am very happy about the money,' said

Kelila. 'Perhaps we can start thinking of building the theatre?'

'Oh, shush about the theatre and bite my nipples,' Isadora ordered.

'Your every wish is my command,' said Kelila, giggling, and did as she was told.

Chapter Fifteen
Men Behaving Badly

C aptain Ric and Prince Hari were men on the loose.
Ric encouraged his latest recruit to go with the other
soldiers to the Forbidden Apple most evenings. Hari
could not make up his mind who he liked best. He
decided to try all the girls.

Petite Gigi had long, wavy, black hair like most of the
native girls of Isle de Paradis. He particularly liked her
high, little breasts. They disappeared behind his hands
as he squeezed and caressed. She was lithe as a monkey
and acrobatic in her love-making. He felt her slip out of
his grasp as he went to grab her buttocks. She wanted to
get it over and be paid. She sat on his cock and he came
almost immediately.

He admired Sylva's cheeky smile but she talked too
much and reminded him of Angeline by asking him if
he had heard from her yet. It put him off his stroke, and
he failed to retain his erection. He fell asleep over his
drink and had to be carried back to barracks by Ric.

The girls of Forbidden Apple did not truly appreciate
the prince's royal charms. He was too young and inex-
perienced to give them the pleasure they craved, as were
the other young soldiers. Ric was more to their taste. He

knew what he was doing. His cock was no bigger than many they had held between their legs, but he knew what to do with it. He also talked to them sweetly and kissed them where it felt good. Ric often gave demonstrations of love-making to his soldiers. They had to watch his technique and take mental notes so they might improve. But mostly they lay in a drunken stupor, enjoying the voyeuristic experience, but did nothing to satisfy the girls.

Jezebel, however, was very satisfied. Her sex life was full. The boy, Tom, had finished building the annexe to the brothel, but his duties to the brothel keeper continued. Bartolem and Samson were sometimes invited to join them too, and she enjoyed again the foursome sessions she had been used to in times gone by. Samson was grateful to the boy for letting him have a rest from Jezebel's awesome demands, and Bartolem had more time to cook and market for food. He had started a vegetable garden behind the new room and he could often be found there, happily digging or hoeing weeds.

Jezebel had Tom hooked. He went to the brothel after work.

She waited on her bed, naked but for a red satin corset which pushed up her big breasts until they were two swollen cushions of flesh. Her chubby legs were encased in black silk stockings and left her olive thighs swelling above. Tight ribbons held her stockings to her corset. He was like a tom cat, helpless to ignore the female on heat. That is what Jezebel called him – Tom Cat. He purred. She stroked him and he rolled over and showed her his belly. His red cock stuck up rudely and she took it into her scarlet mouth and sucked hard and long on it, lengthening it and swelling it to a thick rod of solid flesh. Her breasts hung down, caressing his flesh. She stuck her bottom in his freckled face and he licked her. When his cock was big enough for her she impaled herself on it. He watched her big thighs divide and saw the red slash of sex open to accept his offering. He shoved into her to the hilt and she wriggled her buttocks to feel the rod hit her womb.

'Put a finger up my arse,' she begged on one of these occasions.

He licked his longest finger on his right hand and pressed into her.

'More, more! Bartolem, where are you?'

The consort was busy making a compost heap.

'Samson!'

He did not appear.

'Samson!'

They were in Jezebel's bedroom and the noise of music in the next room drowned her call.

'I'll have to make do with just you, boy, so you had better be good.'

Tom found a dildo hanging on the bedstead. It was long and slender, made of wood and covered in white monkey skin. Moistening her arsehole once more, he pushed the hairy rod into her back passage. His own thicker rod filled her front channel and she was soon groaning with intense satisfaction. He drew the dildo in and out slowly, thrusting in time with it. Her generous flesh began to quiver uncontrollably. She held on tight to the lad's buttocks, encouraging him to go faster, then slower. She held his cock at the base to hold back his climax. He panted loudly in her ear. She imagined the two rods rubbing her, at the back and in front, and she let go of his cock and came loudly. Tom emptied his seed into the woman's clutching sex.

Ric and Hari were beaten by Lana. They had paid to be beaten together. Cherry-Ripe and Sylva helped tie them together, face to face and naked. Their arms were tied high above their heads and they were blindfolded. Sylva caressed each man's arsehole and reached beneath their buttocks to stroke the heavy balls. Ric's cock was much bigger than Hari's. They rubbed together, swollen in anticipation of their erotic torture. Lana was magnificent in a full, swirling, black satin cloak and high boots. Her breasts were divided by leather straps and her sex was similarly displayed. The cloak hid her body except when she pushed it back to better deliver the blows she inflicted with the long whip. Her narrow, haughty face showed no sign of emotion. Her duty was simply to punish, not to condemn. The men, face to face, breathed heavily as she moved in a circle and struck them both in turn. The striped flesh reddened, while the cocks grew bigger and rubbed the other's belly. They leant together to feel the pressure more, writhing away from the whip towards each other. Sylva and Cherry-Ripe watched as the dominatrix whipped harder, moving together instinctively and caressing each other. They clearly found the sight of the naked, blindfolded men – one so sturdy and rugged and the other so young and pretty – erotically entwined, very moving. They kissed each other and fell in a heap on the floor, touching each other's sex and breasts. Lana frowned at them, then continued her punishment.

Ric called out, 'For goodness sake, hold my cock, someone.'

Lana moved closer to the men, wrapped them together in the whip and placed her gloved hands between them. Ric and Hari groaned and sprayed their white foam over each other's bellies.

Queen Clementine missed Adam's company and Hari's handsome face, but her conjugal relations with the king were improving daily, thanks to the delightful presence of Trixie-Jane.

Trixie-Jane, however, was becoming more and more frustrated. Her presence in the royal bed was titillating for the king and queen but she was left unsatisfied. Her excitement gathered but could not explode. They fucked each other, as was only right, but she was desperate for her own satisfaction. Prince Hari had been a terrible disappointment to Trixie-Jane and the little romance with his bodyguard and manservant, Adam, had come to nothing. She wondered what Adam was doing. Had he kissed the princess? she wondered. He was so shy, it probably hadn't even occurred to him. But Trixie-Jane had noticed that Angeline had been jealous of Adam's attentions to her.

One day, when the queen was out having lunch with Trixie-Jane's mother, Trixie-Jane took matters into her own hands. She went for a walk on her own in the forest. She had a deliberate plan.

The king was busy sorting out brightly coloured feathers. He had recently learnt how to tie fishing flies and he was now an enthusiastic fisherman. He sat alone in his private shack in the forest. Suddenly he heard a little cry. He looked outside and saw Trixie-Jane, seemingly hurt. She was on all fours in the dirt, her skirt over her head.

'What is it, my dear? Are you hurt?'

'No, sire, I don't think so.' Trixie-Jane went to stand but cried out again and slipped back to the ground. Her little bottom jutted up prettily and her sex pouch pouted at him temptingly.

'Er, let me help you, my dear,' he said, and went to her. He crouched down and lifted her into his arms. She was as light as his feathers. He clasped her under her warm bottom and carried her inside his hut. Her young arms were around his weathered neck, and she clung to him and nuzzled his grizzled chin.

'Oh, thank you, sire. I will be better if I rest awhile.'

'Of course, my sweet, lie down here.' He cleared a space on his old leather couch with one hand and placed her on it. She sprawled out, her legs open and her knees up.

'I think it is my knee that is hurt.'

He knelt by her and his member stiffened. Her hot breath was on him.

'Oh, sire, please comfort me,' she begged.

'Of course, darling child, of course.' He slid on to the couch over her, his cock straining under its loincloth. She reached for it, twisting the cloth away and holding it firmly.

'Oh, sire, your prick is so big and royally thick. Would you not like to stick it in me?'

'Er, yes, er, yes! Indeed I would.'

'Please do it to me, sire. I am your obedient servant.' She opened her legs wide and pulled him on top of her. His cock found its target and her sex enclosed him. Her little bud swelled and throbbed at the pressure of his big cock. He held her little breasts and kissed her tenderly. Her nipples were taut and stiff. He put his hand under her and held her sex in his big palm. He rubbed it firmly and pushed in and out of her gently. She pressed towards him, eager for more. He thrust more ardently, his cock surprisingly hard. Trixie-Jane knew the geography of his body, of course, having caressed his balls, belly and cock many times in the queen's presence. She rubbed her little body over his broad chest. She kissed the smiling face. He slapped her sex mound gently and she felt his fingers slip into her folds. His cock moved sensuously and slowly, its veined surface caressing her inner folds and her erect bud. She felt her whole body contract and throb. She felt as if she would wet herself. She tried to withhold the climax but his thrusts became ardent and needy. She read the signals and let herself relax. His strong body held her tight in his firm embrace. She melted into him, her thighs stiffening and her breath quickening. He moaned softly as his sperm spilt in spurts into the girl. She cried out joyfully.

Meanwhile, Queen Clementine was paying Poppy-Flower for her daughter's services. 'She is a delightful companion. Always so obliging, you know?'

'I'm glad to hear it, ma'am,' said Poppy-Flower, smiling.

'Yes, she is a little darling. We are both so fond of her. I don't know what we would do without her now, we have grown so dependent on her.' The queen ate the avocado pear with lashings of prawns and coconut milk, and smiled contentedly.

Joshua entered the hut and smiled at the queen, who was licking her fat fingers.

'Oh, Joshua, my boy, come and sit down. How lovely to see you!' The queen sipped at her drink of highly alcoholic manioc wine and patted the chair next to her. 'Come and sit next to me. Have you eaten?'

Poppy-Flower quietly placed a plate of food in front of her son and withdrew.

Later, she returned to find the queen gazing lovingly into the youth's dark brown eyes. His bare chest was glistening with well-earned sweat and there were finger-marks striping it. The queen's hair had fallen on to her plump shoulders and she brushed it behind her ears with a casual flick.

'Oh, Poppy-Flower, I was just saying to Joshua that he ought to come and visit us at the palace sometime soon. How about tomorrow? Would your father give you time off from the plantation? Aristide would be so pleased to see you, dear boy. About one o'clock?'

'At your service, ma'am.' The half-naked youth smiled and kissed the queen's plump pink hand.

Next day, at one o'clock, the palace guard let the youth enter the compound. He knocked at the queen's apartment door. She opened it.

'Joshua, dearest boy! How well you look!'

He was dressed in an ankle-length, kingfisher-blue sarong slung low on his hips. He wore a bandanna of the same blue. His chest was naked and his broad shoulders

107

glistened. She was mesmerised by the muscles quivering on his arms. 'Come in!'

She held open the door and he walked in; a fly into her web.

'Aristide is off, fishing still, I'm afraid. He hasn't been in since breakfast. He'll turn up later. He will be devastated if he misses you.' She turned away from him and swayed her hips provocatively. He followed, a puppy scenting a bone. She wore a loose garment made of thin layers of cream silk, which clung to her ample bosoms and hips and skimmed her plump waist flatteringly. Trixie-Jane had earlier washed the queen's hair and dressed it with diamonds, before depilating her sex mound and legs, oiling her abundant flesh and painting her sex lips and nipples before setting off for her own exercise and entertainment for the day. She had told the queen she would be swimming with her friends, the dolphins. The queen had given her some tuna and lobster left over from the previous night's supper to feed them with.

Clementine was certain her husband would not be back before dark, and she had given her handmaiden the day off.

'Follow me, Joshua, dear boy. We will entertain each other until he returns.'

Chapter Sixteen

Feathers

Queen Clementine led Joshua to her private chamber. A large, low bed sat in the centre of the cool, shady, coral-walled room. Seashells and mother of pearl encrusted the walls, shining like precious stones in the chinks of light coming through the wood-shuttered windows. The bed was covered in Egyptian cotton sheets and pillows of various shapes and sizes. There was a low leather stool with a strange protuberance in the middle, shaped like a rhinoceros horn. A muslin curtain hung from the wooden beams to cover the bed completely. There was a gentle sea breeze wafting through the room from one side to the other, as there were floor-to-ceiling windows on three sides.

The queen began to discard her gown. She slipped the shoulder straps down and wriggled her shoulders until they were bare. Her bosoms rose magnificently from the creamy folds of silk and tipped over the top like white coconuts. Joshua leant towards her, pressing her to him. She sighed, feeling his eager cock through his sarong. He kissed her red-painted lips and her hands found the bulge of his erection and pressed it encouragingly. He squirmed against her hand.

'Let me undress you, my boy,' she whispered, and he stood while she unwrapped his brightly coloured sarong. She looked like she was opening a precious gift. She took her time unravelling the cloth and exclaimed over the smoothness of his hips and loins. She touched his firm, taut buttocks and his brown thighs. He purred, while his cock quivered and rose. He was naked now and his penis was throbbing painfully.

'Ah!' she said, and touched the plum-like balls. She took pity on his condition and held the rod firmly. She could see he was rather too aroused, so she squeezed firmly at the root of his erection and calmed him. She kept her middle body covered up, only exposing her bosoms and thighs to his eager gaze. She was lacking in self-confidence, lately, owing to her increased girth, but Joshua seemed extremely happy with the charms she saw fit to show him. Clementine was in a haze of arousal and her thighs parted to his rough fingers. Her bosoms heaved and her large brown nipples stiffened. He licked and sucked her breasts hungrily, kneading the soft cushions of flesh. The lovers sprawled on the bed under the white lacy curtain. He was on top of her, his thighs grinding into her, his cock digging into her belly. She threw back her arms and abandoned herself to his ardent demands. He held his cock and pushed it into her. She hungered for more of him. She lifted her hips up towards him and he pushed hard into her. He held her plump buttocks in both hands and gripped while he thrust.

'Oh yes! Yes!' she cried.

Her white breasts swung to the rhythm of his penetrations. His fingers pressed into her sex beneath her buttocks and she felt herself stiffen. Her orgasm shook her whole body like a minor earthquake. He cried out and pressed as deep as he could into her generous flesh. His cock was held on all sides by her soft silkiness. He felt the throbbing of her muscles; the after-shocks that gradually died down.

'Did the earth move for you too, Joshua?' she murmured, laughing softly.

Later, after they had eaten giant prawns, tearing off the bright pink shells with their fingers and licking the juices from each other's chins, they made love again.

'Oh, you are so potent, my boy. The king, bless him, is a wonderful lover, but his potency has faded, of course, as is only natural in a man of his age. How old are you, Joshua?'

'Twenty, Your Highness.'

'What sort of love shall we make now, do you think?'

'I am your humble subject, ma'am.' Joshua lay on his back, and the queen's face was hovering over his crotch, her flickering tongue darting out to kiss his cock.

She took his arms above his head and attached them to the leather straps that were tied to the bamboo bedhead. Then she blindfolded him with a silk scarf and put a gag of silk over his mouth and tied that too, before opening his legs and strapping them apart. He was totally helpless. She stripped her gown from her plump hips and stepped out of it. Joshua's cock was flaccid, his anxiety over being tied up clearly affecting his erection. She sucked his cock gently, taking the whole soft rod into her mouth. Her fingers slid under his balls and caressed them. He groaned under the gag as his cock grew in her mouth. She did not release it, but sucked harder until it filled her wide mouth. Its salty flavour filled her throat. She undid his gag and almost sat on his face, her plump bottom hovering over his mouth. Then she leant forward and licked his cock and he sucked automatically on her shaved, plump pussy. His tongue and lips and teeth embraced her sex, and she licked and sucked and nibbled his fat stem. She rotated her hips and experienced his mouth over her perineum and anus. She moved to lie on top of him, her back to his chest, her legs tight closed, his cock pushing into her bottom cleft. She balanced with cushions under her elbows so she was

111

directly on top of him. His arms were still tied above his head, but she realised she needed his hands so she changed position to untie them. She resumed her erotic posture over him, his penis now piercing the gap between her fat thighs. It rubbed on her tightly closed pussy, the swollen lips so tender and sensitive that they felt every slight pressure. He pulled in and out of her thighs and she placed his hands on his cock and encouraged him to caress both her and himself simultaneously. He did this enthusiastically and soon her climax came. Her thighs were still held tight together, her buttock muscles clenched. Then she allowed the silken rod to penetrate her, and she rose and fell on it and came again, with fluttering thighs, as he let go his seed into her depths.

She left him there, after cleaning him herself. He slept, his shrivelled cock, paler now, lying on his thigh. She showered and went back to him, ready for more. This was a marvellous way to spend an afternoon, she mused. This time she sucked him to a climax and he sucked her, lying side by side.

His blindfold had slipped and she was aware now that he saw her abundant flesh, but she realised with relief that he liked what he saw. His excitement was obvious. His young prick throbbed with desire and his hands touched her in all her intimately secret places. Her arsehole was penetrated by his fingers; her mouth was filled with his tongue.

She spanked him lightly, then more firmly as he sucked her breasts. His cock grew and she held it tightly with one hand, spanking him harder now with the other.

His teeth bit gently on the stiff stalks, and she felt dizzy with lust. His cock was enveloped by her fingers, rubbed firmly from the base to the tip, the loose skin taken over the swollen helmet and back again. His hands cupped her bare sex and he rubbed hard and smacked the swollen purse. She opened to him, her flower open-

112

ing to the heat of his caress. Her clitoris sung with the intensity of his pressure on her. She squeezed and rubbed and spanked firmly, and his spunk spurted through her fingers.

'Ah!' She sighed for the fourth time in as many minutes.

King Aristide staggered into the palace compound. His legs were shaky.

'My goodness, I haven't felt so randy since Angeline and Hari got married and I had to deflower her,' he said to himself. 'I had quite forgotten what it was to be so hard.' His hand went to his stiff penis, straining under the silk loincloth. His manservant tried to stop him going into the queen's chamber by suggesting that the king might like a cool drink first, but the king was eager to try out his erection on his wife. He pushed open the door of the chamber, calling, 'Darling frangipani blossom! I am back! I want to fuck you!'

He strode into the chamber and found his wife, naked, gagged and blindfolded, her arms and legs apart and tied to the bed, and the rampant Joshua between her legs, humping away like a rabbit. They had not heard his entrance, so lost were they in the throes of passion and lust.

When Joshua suddenly became aware of the king standing by the bed, however, his erection wilted. He slid out of the queen's sucking sex and knelt at the king's feet, his head bowed.

'Oh, don't be so silly, boy. Get on with it! Or rather, let me help you. You have made a good start, I see!' And Aristide leapt on to his wife with great gusto, his erection proud and thick and – more importantly – stiff. He dropped the heavy prick on to his wife's pubis and she moaned appreciatively.

The boy and her husband took turns to fuck her, and she lay there, passive, tied up, gagged and blindfolded. The two cocks pounded at her and penetrated her. Four

113

hands fluttered over her, and two tongues wrapped around her clitoris. She was overwhelmed; fucked into a heavenly state of semi-consciousness. They removed the gag and penetrated her mouth. Her anus and sex were simultaneously entered, and her breasts were sucked and caressed. Her lips were kissed and she heard the grunts and moans and cries of enjoyment as they used her orifices for their lustful gratification. She hid under the pretence of senselessness but her joy was great. They had both achieved their own satisfaction, but hers had been greater. She swooned with happiness.

King Aristide withdrew and left Joshua to untie his wife and take off her blindfold.

'My! Joshua, you were wonderful, darling! How did you do that?' she joked.

'It was nothing, ma'am. I am always at Your Highness's service.' He kissed her hands and left.

Soon after the boy had left, his sister arrived to attend to the queen's toilet. Clementine's skin glowed as if it had had a strong touch of sun. Her eyes glistened excitedly. She squirmed as Trixie-Jane washed her, her skin was so sensitive.

'Have you had a good day, ma'am?'

'Yes, indeed I have, my little magnolia flower,' she sighed. 'And you?'

'Yes thank you, ma'am. A lovely holiday!'

'Tell me about it!'

'Well, I fed the dolphins and climbed with my monkey friends and then I helped the king tie his flies.'

'Did you, dear? How nice for him!' The queen opened her legs wider and allowed her handmaiden to swoosh water between her labia and stroke her pubis.

'Did he catch any fish?' she asked.

'I have no idea, ma'am. I only helped with the flies, not the fishing.'

'I hope he caught something for supper,' said the

queen, moving her hips gently to better feel the girl's fingers on her sex lips.

Trixie-Jane was moved by the sight of Queen Clementine's swollen privates. The outer labia were open wide, and the smaller lips also gaped. The bud was prominent, a little erection, pink and pert. The handmaiden stroked it thoughtfully. Her own sex was moist. She rubbed her legs together. The queen was leaning back on her wrists, her legs wide open. The handmaiden wiped gently between the folds of flesh with the silk cloth. She pressed under the thighs and dabbed at the tender skin. The queen turned over on to her stomach and the handmaiden washed her bottom and thighs. She poured warm clean water over the queen's buttocks and watched it flow down between the white fleshy mounds. She rubbed the queen's anus dry with a soft white towel made of Egyptian cotton and dabbed at her thighs.

The queen lifted her hips and said, 'I am not dry underneath.'

'I beg your pardon, ma'am,' Trixie-Jane said apologetically. She stroked the perfectly dry area carefully.

'I want you to soothe my privates with the special ointment, please,' said the queen.

'Yes, ma'am.' The handmaiden was gone for several minutes while she prepared the mixture. It consisted of coconut oil scented with essential oils of jasmine and apple-mint. Trixie-Jane had changed out of her sarong and wore only a silk thong between her legs and wrapped on her hips. She placed the bowl of perfumed oils on a low chest next to the bed and fetched a selection of feathers from a calabash. The queen, naked, stretched luxuriously across the wide bed. Her skin shone. Her thick, wavy hair spread like a shawl around her white shoulders.

Trixie-Jane dipped her fingers in the bowl and soaked them with oil. She bent over her queen and began to massage the inflamed shell-like sex parts gently. Her palms moved softly, smoothing the oil carefully into the folds of tender flesh. Her fingers were butterflies alighting on Clementine's flower.

The queen sank into a dreamless slumber, her eyes closed, and the girl continued her delicate massage. When she awoke, Trixie-Jane was tickling her parts with a long feather. The feather fluttered like hummingbird wings, faster and faster on her clitoris. Clementine's little climaxes fluttered, one followed by another, then another. She opened her legs wider and bent her knees so her feet touched her buttocks. She was wide open to the erotic caresses. Each feather gave a separate sensation. The peacock feathers had tiny, fine thread-like filaments at the tip which tickled her. The tail feathers of the hoopoe bird were stiff and penetrated her vagina. She wanted the bunched parrot feathers swept across her perineum and anus.

Trixie-Jane was clearly enjoying the operation as much as the queen. Her sly fingers crept into the queen's private parts as she massaged more oil between her plump thighs. The queen sighed and moaned appreciatively and when Trixie-Jane lay down next to her she reached over to the girl and kissed her. She touched her handmaiden's small, round apple breasts and pressed against them with her own ripe melons. Their caresses became more frenzied and they cleaved close, their legs entwined and their fingers pressing into each other's intimate orifices. They rubbed and squeezed and fondled and gave each other the echoing pleasure they received. Their loud sighs woke the queen's songbirds in the aviary outside her chamber, who sang a sweet, melodious, sad hymn to love.

Chapter Seventeen
Diving for Pearls

*I*t was ten days after the arrival on Monkey Island of the princess, her chaperone and her guard. The morning was clear and fresh, with a light, warm breeze blowing, and Angeline was being prepared for her day's dancing practice by Gertrude. She enjoyed these intimate sessions with her chaperone more and more, so much so that she was in danger of being late for her lessons. She had personal tuition on most days and shared her teachers with several other would-be dancers on two days of the week.

'Oh, Gertrude! You must stop my massage now, darling, as I will be so late again and I don't want to incur the wrath of Isadora.'

'She wouldn't dare whip you, Princess!'

'No, but she would spank me.' The princess smiled as she remembered Isadora's threat to punish her when she arrived late the day before.

'There, you are finished. And you look gorgeous!' Gertrude had laced up Angeline's pink satin corset and tied her ankle boot laces. Her blonde hair was knotted high on her head and her very short pink, chiffon skirt floated over her pert bottom. She wore loose knickers of pale pink, the colour of her skin.

'Goodbye, Gertrude, see you later.'

Gertrude was eager to go and find Adam. She dressed in her most fetching blue corset and white silk stockings held up by suspenders, and arranged her hair high on her head. Then she slipped a loose blue gown over her head, sliding it over her large breasts and plump hips until the hem caressed her ankles. She completed the outfit with suede booties, then picked up her blue parasol and fan and went outside into the balmy air. Large yellow butterflies fluttered past her.

Gertrude had arranged to meet Adam in the forest, in a clearing where they had found a grassy knoll, but after waiting there for five minutes he had not arrived. Cross, and rather warm, she walked on and eventually found herself at the banks of the Lake of Lost Love. Several divers were in small dug-out canoes, naked and wet. She sat on the lakeside under a large woven canopy of coconut palm leaves. She took out her fan and cooled her face with it.

The handsome pearl diver who they had particularly noticed the first time they had been there dived into the deep, dark water. He was gone a long time and Gertrude worried that he might have been caught by weeds or met with some other accident. But he suddenly emerged, like a dolphin surging out of the water. His long black hair was plastered to his head and water slipped from his brown loins. He climbed into his boat and paddled it to the bank near her. Gertrude didn't know where to look. His cock was erect and pointing at her.

'Oh! Goodness me!'

He showed her his catch – a fine pearl of medium size and pale pink hue. It was a regular sphere. She put out a hand automatically but he withdrew the pearl from her reach and smiled, pointing at his cock. He made it clear that she could have the pearl if she gave him something in return. She strove to understand.

'What do you want for the jewel?'

He flapped his tongue at her lewdly and waggled his cock.

'I can't possible do that,' she said, shocked. But she peered about her anyway. The other divers had disappeared into the lake and there was no-one else in sight.

The pearl diver pointed to his mouth and made sucking noises, then masturbated gently. He took her hand and led her to his canoe, where he helped her into the rocking craft and she lay down. She took his long, thick, black cock into her red mouth. It became even stiffer and began to throb. She was in a swoon of disbelief. Was she really doing this? She rubbed his plum-like balls and sucked harder. The native was handsome and lean with years of swimming, and his muscled thighs grasped her head. Then he was doing some more diving. His tongue had found her pink pearl and was edging it out of its shell. She almost fainted as his tongue twirled around her oyster and tasted her salty flavours.

'Oh,' she murmured, the diver having almost swallowed her precious stone.

She drank his white foam almost automatically as she throbbed with passion in her 'little death'.

When she returned to the village, her face was once more that of a well-born English lady and her smile was composed. She had forgotten that Adam had not kept his appointment with her.

Angeline was exhausted after her lessons, and was in the bath, resting her tired limbs. Gertrude knocked and entered the bath chamber, then sat on the edge of the wooden bathtub.

'You look happy, Gertrude, my dearest,' said Angeline, rousing herself. 'What have you been doing?'

'Negotiating the price of a pearl, my darling,' she

replied, smiling wickedly. 'I might go back for more at that price,' she added.

'Scrub my back, please, Gertrude, will you?'

The chaperone removed her gown, which had got slightly muddy from the bilge of the canoe, undid her corset and breathed a big sigh of relief as it fell from her ample bosoms. She stepped out of her stockings, which were also a little grubby from her 'shipboard romance', and climbed into the large bath. Angeline shifted slightly so Gertrude could get behind her, her legs either side of the princess's hips. Angeline pulled a bell-pull next to the bath and Kelila came in with a large jug of warm water, which she proceeded to pour over the tired couple.

'Oh, that's lovely. Is there more?' said the princess.

'More coming, Princess. Shall I soap you both?'

'That would be lovely, wouldn't it, Gertrude?'

'Oh, yes, thank you, Kelila. Delightful, delightful.' Gertrude sank back into the water and watched avidly as the princess's erstwhile handmaiden scrubbed and pummelled the lovely young flesh. A large loofah appeared, and then a giant sponge. The princess was soaped in all her little crevices until she purred with pleasure.

'Now it's your turn, Gertrude,' said the rejuvenated Angeline. 'Let me help, please, Kelila.' She took the sponge from Kelila and began to squeeze soapy water over her chaperone's breasts.

'Your breasts are like lovely bubbles,' she said, smiling.

'You will burst them if you squeeze too hard,' Gertrude giggled. Kelila leant over and squeezed one breast as the princess pressed the other. Kelila stepped into the bath and the water level rose dangerously high. All three delectable bodies were soaped and scrubbed and caressed with soapy fingers, and when they were so clean they squeaked, they climbed out of the bath and fell on to the princess's bed. Here they were found some time later, still erotically entwined, by Isadora, who was also tired and rather annoyed.

'Kelila! You are here! Where is our supper?' She flicked a small riding crop at her lover's naked bottom and Kelila leapt out of bed as if she had been stung by a bee.

'Oh, Isadora.' Kelila bent to kiss her mistress's bare feet. 'Forgive me, mistress!' She backed out of the room on her knees, and Isadora stood with her arms on her hips, still looking very put out.

'Issy, don't be so cross, darling,' said Angeline, in a consolatory tone.

'Come and let me unwind you after your hard day's work.'

Isadora wore a scarlet kimono and nothing underneath. She sighed and laughed and threw off the garment.

'You're right, Princess, but I am hungry. Aren't you two hungry?' She looked at the sleeping Gertrude and smiled. 'She's had a busy day, by the look of her.'

Gertrude's inner thighs were bruised with purple suck marks, and her bosoms, too, showed signs of violent love-making.

Angeline looked hard at the marks and wondered at them. Gertrude did not stir as Isadora kissed the princess and caressed her.

'You were very good today, honey, you worked well. Kelila and you look good together.'

'Thank you, Isadora, I know you are only being kind. I'll never make a dancer – I mean a real dancer, like you or Kelila.'

'Sure you will, honey, it just takes time. We'll knock you into shape, don't worry!'

Angeline relaxed under the tender administrations of the dominatrix. She missed her husband, Hari, suddenly, and wished he was here to enjoy the fun. Then she forgot him as Isadora pressed her close and kissed her full on the lips.

Later, Angeline asked Isadora a question that she had been meaning to ask for some time.

'Why is the Lake of Lost Love called by that name?'

'I don't know, honey. I'll have to ask Kelila. She knows everything about Monkey Island.'

Kelila had prepared a wonderful supper of cold avocado soup followed by spicy prawns cooked in coconut milk. There were half a dozen different vegetables and as many herbs flavouring the sauce. The four beautiful women sat on cushions around a low bamboo table. They ate with their fingers from banana leaf plates. The soup was served in gourds and eaten with spoons made of large bivalve shells. The pearly interior of the shells reminded Angeline of the pearl diver and she asked Kelila to explain the reason for the lake's romantic and rather melancholy name.

'Well, it was said that long ago a visiting princess fell in love with one of the pearl divers and visited him there every day for a month. They were lovers, and when the king found out he forbade his daughter to go there. But the princess could not live without her lover and he could not live without her, and so they dived together from a high cliff with heavy stones tied to their legs and together they drowned.' Kelila gave a rueful smile and carried on eating.

'Oh, how sad!' said Angeline. 'Is it a true story?'

'Oh yes, I believe it is. Even now, star-crossed lovers go to the lake and commit suicide together.'

'How terrible!' said Angeline, who had never been unhappily in love though she wished Hari would be more attentive sometimes, and less demanding at other times.

'Where is Adam, by the way?' asked Gertrude, who had been concentrating on eating so far and so had not contributed much to the dinner conversation. 'I haven't seen him all day.'

No-one knew where Adam was, and they suddenly realised that this was unusual.

Although his guard duties were not onerous on Monkey Island, he usually made contact with the princess at least three times a day. And, of course, Gertrude had recently been used to more intimate contact with him on a daily basis.

'Well, he must be exploring, I suppose,' said Isadora, who didn't have much time for young men, or any man, and did not see the need for them except for procreation purposes. 'He'll turn up. Don't worry.'

'Oh, I'm not worried,' insisted Gertrude.

'Well, I am,' said Angeline. 'Hari would be furious if he knew that Adam was failing in his duty to me.' She was, in fact, sorry that Adam had not been showing her much attention lately. He seemed to have forgotten how lovely she was.

'Have some more dhal, darling,' said Kelila, passing the bright yellow spicy mixture. 'Have some rice with it,' she urged.

'You are a wonderful cook, Kelila. Isn't she, Isadora?' said the princess, licking her fingers.

The four friends had a relaxing evening together, and afterwards Isadora sent out a servant to look for the bodyguard. She was secretly worried about his disappearance, though she would not let the princess see how concerned she really was.

There had been a recent spate of kidnappings of young men from Monkey Island. No-one knew who was responsible, but half a dozen youths had gone missing over the last few months. These events had not touched Isadora and Kelila before now, but Adam's absence suddenly brought the problem home to the royal party's hosts.

Next day, there was still no sign of Adam. Gertrude was cross with him, but she at least had the consolation of the pearl diver. Her first thought, after bathing, depilating and dressing Angeline, was to dress herself in suitable attire for the uncomfortable but exciting love-making venue of the narrow canoe. She showered and then depilated herself, a difficult operation on her own. After smoothing scented oils into her limbs, she brushed her hair a hundred times and tied it high on her head with ribbons. Then she chose a loose gown of sea-green cotton, folded into many small pleats. It hung flatteringly over her full breasts, showing them in all their glory. The skirt was full and she wore nothing underneath. She painted her mouth and the lips between her legs a bright scarlet colour. She admired herself in the mirror before setting off for the Lake of Lost Love.

Chapter Eighteen
The Powerful One

A dam had been where he said he would be, in the forest clearing, waiting for Gertrude. He had got there early, so eager was he to be joined intimately again with the older woman, but this time he was going to ask her to model for him. He had his paints with him and a small canvas. He also had one of her corsets that she had left behind on one of their trysts. He stroked the white satin, marvelling at its softness.

He wore his usual uniform – the kilt made of individual leather strips. He was impatient for her to arrive, and his cock was already stirring under his kilt at the very thought of Gertrude's heaving bosoms and her plump belly quivering in passion. He thought of her white thighs; the softness of her touch, her tongue. He needed to urinate, but his erection was a hindrance. He stood up and walked around, trying not to think of the sexual contact he would soon enjoy. His erection died sufficiently and he went into deeper forest and found a broad-trunked tree. He took his cock into his hand and began to pass water. As he did so, he was suddenly aware of a movement above and behind him. He looked up and saw a hooded, masked figure leaping down on him. That was all he saw for some time.

When he came to, he was blindfolded and his head hurt. He was tied by the feet and wrists to a pole, and was being carried like an animal caught for food. He was aware of several harsh voices and the crunch of leaves underfoot. He sank back into unconsciousness.

When he awoke again he was in a cave. His blindfold had been removed but it was dark, and only a chink of daylight far away lit the gloom. He was still bound, hands and feet, but he could shift to get more comfortable. He waited for his eyes to become accustomed to the darkness. He was alone, he thought, but he was wrong. There was a guard at the entrance of the cave, with a fearsome dog on a leash. The man slept but the dog did not. It growled as it became aware of movement inside the cave. The guard woke and led the dog into the dark depths. He looked down at the frightened youth and the dog sniffed Adam's legs. He flinched and edged away from the growling beast.

'Don't move or he'll kill you,' warned the man.

Adam could not see his face but he thought he was masked. He remembered the masked, hooded figure in the forest.

'What do you want of me?' he demanded bravely.

'Ha! It's not what I want of you! It's what she wants of you.'

'She? Who is she?' asked Adam, extremely confused.

'You'll see, soon enough.' The guard left Adam and took the dog back to the cave entrance.

Some hours later, voices grew louder and several men appeared. They blindfolded Adam again after giving him water to drink, then carried him again on the pole so he felt totally helpless and humiliated. He hung and swung as they carried him fast through the thick forest to a small beach. There he was transferred to a long canoe where he was thrown, unceremoniously, into the bilge. He slept again, only aware of dizziness and nausea.

'Clean him up and take him to The Powerful One,' a voice commanded. Adam was still faint and weak and he drifted in and out of consciousness. He was aware of his body being bathed gently by many hands. He was dressed in a loincloth of silk. His hair was brushed. He felt like a sleepy, helpless child.

Someone slapped his cheek and threw cold water into his face. He roused himself and his vision cleared. He was held on both sides by strong men and his wrists were tied behind him. He became aware of a figure sitting on a throne in front of him.

'He is a good-looking youth, for once. Well done, Thor!' The woman who uttered these words was dressed in a gown which seemed to be made of silver and pearls. It shimmered over her slender body. Her breasts were bare, her nipples pierced and hung with large pearls. She wore a mask of silver which covered the top half of her face; only her green eyes and her wide nostrils were visible. Adam stared drowsily, not knowing if he was dreaming.

'Strip him and show me what he is made of,' she ordered.

'Yes, O Powerful One.' The guard untied the loincloth, unravelling it and revealing the flaccid penis.

'Yes, he is a good specimen, you did well. Give him a helping hand, will you, Thor. I want to see how big it can get before I use him.'

The guard casually held Adam's prick and rubbed at it expertly. Adam was still in a half-dream, but his cock enjoyed the massage it was receiving from the powerful, hooded man. It rose and swelled.

'Yes, it looks good. Put him to me.'

The masked man oiled Adam's prick and anus, then half carried Adam to a low seat with a straight back and no arms. The wooden seat had a small penis-like protuberance made of carved wood sticking out of the centre. Adam was pushed down on to the seat and positioned so the carved penis pressed up into his anus. He was suddenly wide awake. The masked woman stood and walked over to where he sat. She swayed her full hips and her pearl-hung nipples quivered on her pomegranate breasts. She lifted her heavy silver skirt and he saw black shiny skin. Her sex lips were red – a red slashlike fire on black embers. She lowered herself slowly on to his fine erection. Adam groaned as she sat on him. His large cock had gone right to the hilt. Her breasts were in his face, the nipples close to his mouth, and he instinctively went to suck them.

'No, do not dare!' she whispered. 'Do nothing. I am in charge here.' She rubbed herself over his thighs and held his balls in her ringed fingers. He was going to explode. Suddenly he felt something going over the head of his cock. She had slipped a gold ring over his erection and pushed it down to the base. He could not come now, he was stuck with the enormous erection and unable to orgasm.

The woman satisfied herself several times on his huge, swollen rod. He was in an agony of frustration. He felt the sperm gather, the throbbing begin, but he could find no relief, and she made it worse by demanding more of him. The small prick inside his anus tortured him erotically. She writhed and churned her insatiable, voluptuous body on him. She turned her back to his chest and sat on him again. Her hands went to her sex and her fingers sank into the juicy depths. His cock was being unbearably used and abused by this woman, and he cried out in an agony of frustration. She cried out as her fingers smacked her sex lips and gave her just the exact sensation she craved. He felt as if he were just a sex toy; a dildo. She rose at last, her passions satisfied for the time being. Two hooded and masked men wiped her sex parts clean with wet cloths and dried her with towels. She stood and allowed them to do this service before she slapped their faces with the flat of her hand.

'Enough, fools. Leave me,' she spat.

'Shall we take him away?' said one, bowing low to her.

'Of course. What more is he good for, fool?'

The guards lifted Adam roughly, causing his anus to contract suddenly as it lost hold of the carved protuberance, and he cried out.

'Bring him back later,' The Powerful One ordered. 'Do not remove the ring.'

Adam was dragged from her presence and taken to a dark room. He was washed and oiled again and placed on a bed, where he lay in great discomfort, untied now but still unable to lose his erection. When he was alone he tried to remove the restraining ring, but to no avail. He rubbed hard at his cock but he could not come.

There must have been something in the oils, he thought. They've kept me tumescent. It cannot be the ring, surely? He thought of the erotic torture he had been made to endure and wondered where he was. He heard groans from nearby. He tried the door but it was locked. There was a high, small unglazed window with bars across it. The narrow bed was the only piece of furniture. He put his ear to the wall, which was made of some sort of hard stone. He heard the groans again.

He called out, 'Are you there? Where are we?'

Nothing came back. The groans stopped.

He sank back on to the bed in despair.

Some hours later he was given food to eat and water to drink. He was splashed with water and oiled again, including his private parts. The oils soothed his sore anus and his straining cock.

'Can't you remove the ring?' he asked the masked guard.

'No-one can remove it except by order from The Powerful One.' The guard massaged the oil into the handsome prisoner's cock and balls, then wrapped the loincloth around the youth's loins. His own erection was obvious under the cloak he wore. It stuck out and prodded the cloth. The guard rubbed it surreptitiously.

Adam noticed the movement and realised he was aroused.

'Let me out of this penis ring and I'll relieve you,' he begged.

The guard drew back from him, afraid of his own weakness, and said, 'No! The Powerful One will punish me terribly.'

He dragged Adam out to the lustful woman again, and again he had to submit to her will. This time he was made to kneel at her feet while she sat, legs wide on the chair, her anus penetrated by the specially carved knob. She was naked from the waist down. Her pubic hair was black and curly, shaved to a small patch high on her mound. Her wide swollen lips opened like a full-blown rose, pink and fleshy. Her breasts were this time held up by a corset-like silk garment which circled her several times and crossed over between her breasts, holding them apart. Her prominent nipples were decorated with pearls. She still wore a mask of silver covered in white feathers, her wide, cruel mouth and red tongue showing beneath, her dark, narrow eyes gleaming at the slits.

Her feet and legs were wrapped in white ribbons, criss-crossed up to her thighs.

Adam wondered what he would have to do to satisfy her this time, but he did not have to wait to find out. His face was pushed into her crotch and she ordered him to start licking. He could not help but examine the sex parts of the woman in front of him. The outer labia were black and wide apart. The inner labia were black on the outer edges but bright pink inside, and her bud was erect, the hood drawn back. He licked the bud slowly.

'Good,' she said. 'Do it more slowly, and harder, and suck it.'

Adam did as he was told, wishing he could hold her too, but his hands were again tied behind him. His cock strained under its loincloth. It had grown even bigger, he was sure, and he felt the ring tighten on his root.

He licked and sucked the swollen sex parts and her juices slid over his mouth and tongue and chin.

'Keep going,' she said.

He was aware of her spasms soon after he had penetrated her with his long tongue. Then the guard dragged him to his feet and shoved him on to the bed, which was a low bamboo structure. He lay there on his back, helpless still, as the guard untied his loincloth and laid him bare. The Powerful One leant over him, her arms either side of his perspiring chest, and took his purple-brown penis into her long fingers and rubbed her gold rings down its length. He groaned.

'Why are you doing this?' he said. 'I could please you more if my hands were free.'

'I don't need your hands, boy. Just your fat cock.'

She lowered herself on to his exhausted cock and writhed furiously. Her thigh muscles contracted and she stiffened her body. Her orgasms came in sharp flutters, and she held tight to his cock. He groaned in agony. He could not come. He felt as if his balls would explode.

Three days later, he had still had no release, but he had got used to it now. He admired his own erection; he was sure it was bigger than it had ever been. He had decided to control his sex urge so the torture of having intercourse with the insatiable woman would not be so dreadful. If he thought about something else, not her plump sex lips or her bouncing breasts, he would survive. He had to think of an escape. He heard the groans of his neighbours. He felt sure there were other prisoners going through the same procedure as him. Once he had heard a heavy door open and close and a young man's voice. The guard who looked after him was a powerfully built man, Adam could surmise, even though he always hid his body under the cloak. His chest was broad and his arms and shoulders were strongly muscled. His arms were tattooed as far as Adam could see up the wide sleeves. Adam enjoyed the cleaning and massaging he had from this guard. His broad hands took Adam's balls and cleansed them carefully, wiping between his legs and washing his bottom hole. He was even more careful with the youth's cock, treating it with great care.

'It's the best one she's had for a while, I can tell you that,' he said.

'What is?'

'Your big fat cock, my boy. You're her favourite, no doubt about it.'

'Why do you say that?'

'Oh, I know her well. She likes you. You're a lucky boy.' He rubbed Adam's cock with the scented oils, lifting the foreskin and moving his fingers into the folds of flesh.

'I like you,' said Adam. 'What's your name?' The guard carried on with his work but stopped talking. 'Tell me your name, please,' said Adam. 'There'll be a big reward for you if you help me get free.'

'Oh yes, what reward would that be? Who would pay to get you back?' The guard laughed, unconvinced, and this time dressed Adam in his own uniform.

Adam felt better wearing his leather kilt. He felt more like himself, although he still didn't know how long he had been held prisoner or where he was.

'I mean it. I have friends in high places – the palace of Isle de Paradis, to be exact.'

'Never heard of it,' said the guard, his erection gone down and his interest in the youth clearly diminished.

'You will hear of it,' said the angry young man.

He steeled himself as he was taken back to his torturer, who today wanted his leather thongs between her legs as well as his throbbing cock.

Chapter Nineteen
The King's Flies

O n Isle de Paradis, life continued at its usual unhur-
ried pace. Hari was becoming stronger and more
athletic due to his military endeavour. He missed his
wife, of course, but his nightly trips to the Forbidden
Apple did much to console him. Ric was happy without
his wife's suspicions and enjoyed nightly whippings
which he felt were a just punishment for his enjoyment.
Jezebel was satisfied by the young Tom Cat. Samson was
happy growing prize-size beans, potatoes and arti-
chokes. Bartolem was winning much admiration for his
wonderful cooking at Jezebel's popular establishment.

At the palace the queen was enjoying the regular
company of young Joshua and his sister, and she looked
younger and sleek, like a prize mare. The king also
seemed younger. His paunch had disappeared and he
had the swagger of his younger days.

One morning, Trixie-Jane took a handful of the queen's
collection of feathers from the special, long, flat box
covered in porcupine quills. She placed them inside the
folds of her sarong and skipped off to find the king,
knowing exactly where he would be. He was surf fishing.
He stood on the sand, his loincloth slightly unravelled

so his buttocks were exposed, and held the long bamboo rod in both hands. There was a tripod of sticks set up on the beach for him to rest the rod on, but he preferred to feel the tug of the fish himself. The breeze tugged at his hair, which was held back from his face with a wide bandanna, tied behind. He looked very handsome, thought Trixie-Jane, as she drew close to him. He smiled as he noticed her arrival. She had a bundle of food steamers with her, and she put them down on the sand, using the cloth which held them as a tablecloth.

'Have you caught anything?' she asked.

'Oh, yes, look in the bag.' He nodded towards his fishing bag.

She lit a fire and soon they were tucking into a picnic of fresh, spiced steamed vegetables and rice with little fish grilled on sticks stuck into the fire. They licked their fingers and drank the starfruit juice she had prepared.

'Thank you, dear child, that was delicious.'

'Shall you rest now?' she asked shyly.

'Rest' was her euphemism for 'fuck'.

'Yes!' said the king, and they gathered up their belongings and shovelled sand over the embers. They sauntered off towards the forest and his work shack. Once there, she showed him the present she had brought him.

'More feathers for my flies!' he said, delighted.

'Only if you use them on me first,' Trixie-Jane said determinedly.

'Take off your little dress, then,' he said, holding a long curved black feather in one hand and running it over the palm of his other hand as if it was a cane.

'No,' she said petulantly. 'I want to keep it on.' She lifted her short skirt, which barely hid her private parts. He glimpsed her pink, bare pussy and she drew it down again.

'Oh, you naughty girl. Come here and let me spank you.' He tapped the feather on his palm again. He sat on a low stool, unwrapped his loincloth and she sat on his

134

lap sideways on, both feet on the floor. He quickly turned her over and upside down on to his lap. He lifted her skirt over her head and patted the little bottom tenderly. He tickled her anus with the feather and she squirmed.

'That tickles!' she giggled.

His penis rose and prodded her belly. He rubbed against her and she squirmed some more. He dropped the feather in order to spank her delectable behind, and she raised herself so her buttocks stuck up high. His open hand came down hard on her flesh, which reddened fast, and she cried out in mock horror. He spanked her quickly, his own excitement clearly rising. His rod swelled and throbbed. He rubbed his big hand over her swollen pubis, watching the little lips splay out at his touch. The pink bud was peeping out of her inner lips. He stroked it and slapped playfully at the whole tender area. She groaned in encouragement. His penis poked at her bare flesh and she wriggled on it.

'Don't forget the feathers,' she said.

King Aristide chose a small feather and began to caress her with it. He drew it slowly over her private parts, tickling the outer lips and perineum, then swishing it faster and faster over her flesh. Then he chose another, a blue feather of about five inches, which was stiffer than the first. He flicked it in and out of her anus and she squealed with delight. His hands were kept busy, spanking her when she squirmed too furiously. He held her tightly so she could not move, but she was terribly aroused and needed more than a feather tip to grip on. She struggled to free herself from him, and he eventually let her up. She sat on his lap, facing him, impaling herself on his stiff, engorged cock. He closed his eyes in bliss as she fell on him. Her thighs enclosed his cock. She rose and fell slowly, standing as she rose so he nearly came out of her. They both watched the purple head emerge from her pink tunnel, and they held their breath as it plunged again. She waited until he was close to his climax, then let herself plunge fast up and down on his stem. He called out, and she felt her own orgasm singing and throbbing for many seconds.

On Monkey Island, things were not so happy. The continued mystery of Adam's disappearance had perplexed them all at the Kelidora Dance Academy. It had been nearly a week and there was no news of him.

'Perhaps he has drowned,' sobbed Angeline, remembering how Trixie-Jane had had to rescue him from the waves.

'Perhaps he has been kidnapped,' said Gertrude quietly to Kelila. Gertrude could never forget how, several years before, she and Clementine had been kidnapped by pirates and taken to a slave island before being rescued by a war party led by King Aristide and Prince Hari, which included the very brave Angeline, Kelila and Isadora.

'No, it is not possible,' said Kelila, though she looked at Isadora questioningly.

Isadora had sent spies all over the island to try and find out where the bodyguard had gone. No-one had seen him.

Gertrude sought consolation and sympathy with her pearl diver, whose name was Jax. Although he spoke no English she now understood more than a few words of his language. One afternoon, after their initial passionate embrace and his present to her of a twentieth pink pearl, she asked him if he knew anything of the disappearance of the princess's bodyguard.

He told her he knew nothing, and began to poke at her with his half-erect cock.

He looked sly, she thought.

'There is a reward for his safe delivery back to the princess,' she said, lying.

'What reward?' he said.

136

'Gold,' she said, then seeing his lack of interest, she added, 'and a night with the lovely Princess Angeline.'

The pearl diver looked more interested, and his cock stirred against the curve of Gertrude's belly. She rubbed his cock with both hands, twisting her fingers and kneading the fleshy rod. He murmured encouragement.

'She is very young and pretty, the princess,' he said, grinning.

'Yes, and her skin is even whiter than mine,' urged the chaperone.

He pushed his cock into her eager slit and it disappeared. He moved slowly, his cock waggling inside and touching every part of her.

'How do you do that?' she marvelled, as he wriggled his cock as if it were an independent muscle, keeping his legs and buttocks still. 'Oh, that is so clever!' she exclaimed as she came.

'Tell me about the princess. Is she a good fuck?' He licked his lips.

'Oh yes, a delightful girl; very ripe and juicy, I assure you. But first you must take us to the bodyguard.'

The powerfully built diver held down the English chaperone in the bilge of his canoe and fucked her thoroughly. When he had had enough he let her go. She was dishevelled and happy and her limbs felt as if they had melted. She was bruised and grazed on her back and legs, but it had been worth it. He was so virile. He stood above her, his cock hanging heavily on his brown thigh. She daydreamed of how handsome he would look in the uniform of the bodyguard.

The diver decided he would tell the white woman where to find the youth. He knew of the missing youths of Monkey Island. He had seen the boats leave in the dark of moonless nights, from the shores of the Lake of Lost Love. He guessed where they were bound. It had been a threat his mother had given him when he was naughty as a child. 'The Powerful One will get you if

137

you are naughty,' she had said, throwing a gourd at him. 'She will eat you. She will suck you up and blow you out in bubbles.'

'Sounds fun, Mother!' he had cheeked her and run away.

It had been a myth for so long – the powerful woman who kidnapped young men and used them for sexual gratification. His father said he had friends who had disappeared. Jax had been raised on tales of this sexually insatiable amazon. He and his friends had fantasised about her, wishing they could be kidnapped and used erotically as her sex slave.

But the young men who occasionally disappeared on Monkey Island did not reappear to tell their tales. It was generally assumed they had drowned while fishing or diving or had been eaten by wild beasts while hunting, though there was never a clue found.

He talked to his mates, telling them about the reward of gold for the princess's bodyguard, but failing to mention the other reward – the night with the princess. They were bored with their everyday mundane dangers and keen for new adventure. They made a plan.

Gertrude, meanwhile, had told Isadora and Kelila about the diver and his interest in Adam. Isadora and Kelila had of course heard of the myth of The Powerful One. They were not disbelieving, even though the stories of her sexual prowess had lasted for decades.

'She must be a hundred years old, if she's a day,' said Isadora.

'No, don't laugh, Isadora. It is not funny. This woman exists, I tell you. Everyone believes it. She is indestructible.' Kelila looked worried, her lovely face crumpled in a frown.

'All right, there is a female who does not age or die, and she takes the best young men for herself,' said Isadora. 'Sounds OK to me! She sounds like she's got a good thing going. If you like that sort of thing.' She cuddled her lover to her, stroking her strong arms and admiring the glossy copper sheen.

'What can we do about it?'

'I'll go and see this diver,' said Isadora decidedly.

'I'll come with you, darling. We better send word to King Aristide, I suppose,' said Kelila, questioningly.

'No, I'll see if we can manage on our own first. We have enough clout between us, you, me and Angeline. We have fought together before,' said Isadora.

'Yes, but we had the king's army behind us, darling,' reminded her lover.

'Yes, you are right, my love. We better get word to him. I'll tell Angeline,' said the tall redhead.

Chapter Twenty
Rescue Party

The news had at last got to Isle de Paradis. Canoes had been sent with crews of the fastest oarsmen to get there as quickly as possible, with a purse of silver for the winning canoe. The race had taken three days, the rowers taking turns to rest. When King Aristide had news of the canoes' imminent arrival he went with his retinue of soldiers to greet them. He sent out his own welcome guard in boats to greet them and show the way through the reef. There was a huge crowd waiting for the racing canoes to land and a cheer went up as the first crew leapt into the waves. Helping hands took the narrow craft and dragged it safely above the water line, and the exhausted crew sank to the sand. But the captain of the winning crew staggered up the beach to where the king stood.

'Your Majesty, I c-come with b-bad news,' he stammered.

Joshua gave the man a drink and held his arm as he struggled for breath.

'Tell me, man,' said the king, thinking Angeline had been taken ill or worse.

'The princess's bodyguard is missing, believed kidnapped,' the man blurted.

'Adam!' exclaimed Hari, disturbed. Hari was very fond of his manservant-cum-bodyguard. He was concerned for his safety. And who was looking after his wife?

'We will prepare to help find him. Come, bring your men to the compound and rest. Fetch food and drink for these men,' the king commanded.

At the palace the queen was distraught when she heard about Adam's disappearance. The unlikely story of The Powerful One was passed from native to native until the whole island was buzzing with rumours.

At the Forbidden Apple there was great sorrow. All the soldiers' leave was cancelled and the men had to leave for extra training at the barracks. The only business that would be done was with the fishermen, who at least were happy to have the girls to themselves.

When Trixie-Jane heard about Adam, she was desolate. The queen found her sobbing, naked, on the king's bed.

'My poor child, what has happened?' asked the queen, worried that her husband had overdone the spanking and really hurt the girl. He had been known to scar a smooth bottom, as Clementine herself was living proof.

'I love him!' the girl sobbed.

'Who do you love, dear girl?' asked the worried queen.

'Adam, I love Adam. I don't want him to be eaten by a sex-crazed woman!' She threw herself into the comforting arms of the queen.

'Oh, you poor child! She won't eat him.' He'll just get sucked to death, she thought to herself.

'Can I go with the search party, please, Your Majesty?' Trixie-Jane begged.

'We'll see, dear child, we'll see.' The queen hugged the distraught young girl.

Back at Monkey Island, preparations were being made by the pearl diver. He had watched every night and seen

what he needed to know. Gertrude had returned to his
embrace daily and reinforced her promise on behalf of
the princess. She thought she could face that problem
when and if Jax found the guard. She made him excited
with talk of the princess's erotic dancing. She had
watched her at her lessons with Kelila and Isadora and
related the experience to the diver, showing him her
own version of the writhing, undulating dance that
Angeline had perfected. She turned before him, lifting
layers of silk – exposing her belly, then her buttocks; her
breasts shaking like jellies, her thighs trembling. He
watched, entranced, his cock in his hand. She moved,
snake-like, and writhed towards him on the sand, her
plump thighs and round arms shifting the sand in
smooth tracks. She was still undulating and writhing
when he dragged her into the lake, grabbed her buttocks
and thrust into her.

Isadora had followed the chaperone on her visits to the
pearl diver, and watched now as the couple made love
in the water. She was impressed with the older woman's
energy and enthusiasm. Jax was a good-looking man,
she thought – for a man. She preferred the buxom charms
of the chaperone who, though she was blowsy, was a
handsome woman and had a flush about her that was
very attractive.

She was loathe to interrupt but she chose a moment
after an orgasm to pretend to arrive at the lake edge.

'Oh, excuse me,' she said. 'I hoped to find you,
Gertrude.'

The Englishwoman covered herself in a wet wrap of
silk. 'Oh, Isadora! We were just swimming.'

'Yes, so I see. May I have a word?' She walked off
with the pearl diver.

Gertrude followed closely but could not quite hear.
She was still embarrassed about being caught *en fla-
grante*. So she dried her wet hair with the sarong and

went and sat at the water's edge while Isadora and Jax talked earnestly.

'Take me to this Powerful One and I will make sure you have proper reward,' she said.

'What reward, exactly?' he asked.

'The king of Isle de Paradis will be very grateful,' she said.

'And the queen?' he said.

'I can't speak for the queen.'

'Will you be grateful?' he asked, eyeing her with lust.

'I will, but not that grateful. This youth must be found. You will be given a purse of gold by King Aristide, who is your ruler. Maybe more, I cannot say.'

'I want to see the dancing,' said Jax.

'That could be arranged,' said Isadora, amused.

'I will take you to The Powerful One,' he agreed, and they spoke quietly for a while, while Gertrude brushed her hair and put it up in pins again.

Adam, meanwhile, was close to collapse. He was wearing the penis ring again. The Powerful One found him pleasing and made more use of him than the other youthful slaves. He found that he was asked to perform cunnilingus on her several times a day and he had to endure her lustful advances and her harsh caresses on his sorely exhausted member. He dreaded yet craved her touch. He needed to spill his seed. His desperation reached a pitch one day and he broke down, sobbing, kneeling at her feet and begging her to give him relief.

Instead, she ordered the hooded, masked guard to masturbate him in front of her. Adam was chained to wooden beams, his legs pulled apart. The masked man threw cold water over the youth's genitals and the penis shrunk for the guard to remove the penis ring, though with some discomfort to its wearer. Adam sobbed in relief, then groaned as the guard, with no finesse, rubbed and squeezed the hard-worked organ. Poor Adam, after a week of giving pleasure and receiving none, spurted his pent-up semen into the air, where it fell to earth and disappeared. His head dropped on to his perspiring chest, and he sobbed silently.

'Now, clean him and bring him back to me,' she ordered. He was to get little respite from her demands, it seemed.

After he had slept, Adam was again taken to the chamber of The Powerful One. She never removed her white feather mask so he still hadn't seen her face. She was taller than any woman he had known, but perfectly formed with strong muscles and shining dark hair. Her blue-black skin gleamed like polished bronze.

She had his rucksack.

'What is this?' she asked.

'It is a corset, O Powerful One,' Adam replied.

'Is it yours?'

'Yes, no, I mean, yes. It belonged to a lady but she said I could have it.'

'Why do you want it?'

'It was for my model. I am an artist, O Powerful One.'

'An artist? I see, and you paint pictures of women wearing this garment?'

'Yes, that's right. I had found the perfect model, and then I left Isle de Paradis, so I took my artist's materials with me. I was going to ask another lady to model for me, but I never got the chance . . .' He petered out, aware that he had said too much.

The Powerful One looked bored with his story.

'I will wear it. You will paint me,' she ordained. She might be The Powerful One but even she was vain enough to want her portrait painted.

Adam was happy to paint her; it would be a restful change from satisfying her insatiable demands.

Next day the paints and canvas had been found for him and he was freed from his bonds. His wrists and ankles were still sore but it felt marvellous to be dressed normally – and without the penis ring.

The Powerful One was attired in the corset which, although she was much taller than the original model, fitted her well. It clasped her around her narrow waist and exaggerated the curves of her hips and the rise of her succulent, pomegranate-like breasts.

She still wore the mask, of course, but her limbs and genitals were naked. Her pubic hair was shaped carefully and did not hide her sex lips, which had been rouged and looked like another lewd mouth, slightly open. Her long nipples had the giant pearls at their tips. She looked magnificent, thought Adam, and he began to work enthusiastically. He covered the canvas quickly, with bold strokes, using the paint as if he was spreading cream on a sponge. He enjoyed his work, and his model stood still for half an hour before she suddenly shifted her position and stopped posing.

'I will rest for an hour. Come to me in my bedchamber,' she said.

Adam sighed. Damn it, does she want sex again? he thought to himself.

He resignedly cleaned his brushes first before going into the adjacent chamber, where she lay on the silk sheets, the corset still compressing her belly and waist and pushing up her marvellous breasts. Another youth, a powerfully built native of Monkey Island, was caressing her. He held his thick cock in one hand and rubbed it over her belly. His cock too had the torturous ring on it. This ring had hairs attached to it – monkey hair – which would obviously tickle the female parts successfully. Adam became erect at the vision, surprising himself at his continuing virility.

'You are late. How dare you keep me waiting?'

A hooded man with a whip appeared and tied the sorry Adam to rings in the wall. He attached bands of metal around his ankles and wrists, having stripped him first. Adam was humiliated in front of the youth and The Powerful One, who carried on their lewd caresses while he suffered. His penis was shackled again by a penis ring and the masked guard masturbated him to stiffness. He groaned and writhed in frustration and misery, all the while aware of the erotic scene in front of him. He had to watch while the young man penetrated The Powerful One. He saw the hairy penis ring touch her intimately, her scarlet sex wide open. Her breasts wobbled and shivered on her rib cage. The youth was dragged off her after half an hour and several orgasms later. He, of course, did not have any release of tension. He sobbed as he was led away and he looked sympathetically at Adam.

'Right, bring him to me,' she demanded of the hooded guard, and Adam's heart sank.

Chapter Twenty-One
The Legend of The Powerful One

Jax rowed his canoe to the headland and alighted, helping Isadora to step out on to the rock. He pointed to the far shore of the lake.

'There! It is over there – the land of The Powerful One.'

'Who is she?' said Isadora, drawing her cloak about her bare shoulders. The evening air was cool and the breeze from the lake was building up to a strong wind.

'Some say she is ten feet tall. She is black as charcoal and strong as a gorilla. She has six breasts and three vaginas.' His eyes bulged as he spoke.

'Have you seen her?'

'No, any man who sees her is lost for ever. He is consumed with lust for her and can never leave her.'

'Wow! I'd like to see her!'

'She is immortal; she is a hundred years old,' said the pearl diver.

'So, how *are* we going to rescue Adam?' asked Isadora later, when she was back with Gertrude, Angeline and Kelila. 'Any suggestions?'

'Well, we must obviously wait for the king to send help from Isle de Paradis. It is his problem, finally. These islands are part of his territory,' the princess said.

'Haven't you heard of this sex-crazed giantess before?' asked Gertrude.

Kelila nodded her head. 'Well, yes, of course, one has heard of all sorts of weird and wonderful legends and myths.' She sniffed.

'But young men have been disappearing for years, have they not?' said Isadora.

'Yes, that is true. Maybe they are still alive, living in her power,' said Gertrude.

She felt quite envious of The Powerful One. To be able to call on any number of vigorous lads at any time of the day or night! She sounded like a very clever woman.

'Your fisherman friend seems to know exactly where she is, anyway,' said Isadora.

'The pearl diver? Yes, he is eager for a reward,' said Gertrude. She fluttered her fan.

'While we wait for the king's soldiers to arrive we can prepare our dance concert. Your diver will be invited to be in the audience with the king,' announced Isadora.

'Oh, do you think Hari will come?' said Angeline, excitedly.

'I am sure he will not be left out of the rescue party,' said Kelila, patting the princess's arm. 'Come, we will practise some of our more arduous routines.' She took Angeline's hand and led her away.

'Do you really think Adam is all right?' said Gertrude to Isadora.

'Are you fond of the boy?' asked Isadora.

'Oh no, not really. Only he is a likeable lad and good company.' Gertrude fanned herself, hiding her blushes behind the long pink feathers. 'I will go and tell Jax the news about the dance concert,' she said, and swept out, leaving Isadora busy drawing a map of the Lake of Lost Love, based on what the diver had told her.

148

On the lake, egrets, cranes and tall white herons all rose as one from their daytime territories and flew to one broad-spreading acacia tree right on the bank. They settled in the branches, hundreds of them jostling for position. Their combined weight weighed down the acacia so it was like a Christmas tree laden with gleaming white baubles. Their raucous cries filled the lake. The moon rose and Venus was held in the palm of her hand. The birds became silent and put their heads under their wings and slept. In the lake, large fish rose to the surface and plucked insects from the rippled surface.

In the land of The Powerful One came the cries of young men suffering the torments of unsatisfied lust. Adam was dressed in Gertrude's corset, laced tightly so his pectorals swelled above the emerald satin. His naked loins gleamed with oil and his balls and cock were encased in a silk pouch held on with satin ribbons. He wore silk stockings to his thighs. He was chained to a bed, spreadeagled. Two other young men were masturbating over him, but they wore restraining rings on their erections and could not release their semen. They were, in their turn, held on leashes by masked guards. This nightly pantomime went on with all the captives taking turns to be abused by each other. It was another erotic torture. The Powerful One strode into the chamber where Adam lay. She was magnificent in black leather, her nipples peeping through the holes left in her upper garment. Her triangle of pubic hair and exposed sex shone in the gap of her leather-clad thighs and legs. The gussetless trousers left free her proud buttocks too. She held a whip and cracked it loudly. The two youths stopped their masturbation as she entered but she flicked their bottoms with the whip and ordered them to continue.

Adam was beside himself. He wanted to be back in Isle de Paradis with Trixie-Jane, painting her. Life had been so simple at home. He had played at being a soldier and enjoyed the company of the young royals, and he had had the freedom to do as he wished, more or less. He desperately wanted to be free of this ridiculous torment. Did anyone know where he was? Did they care? Had they missed him? What about Gertrude? Surely she had been suspicious when he was not at their trystingplace?

He tried to think of anything except his own present ignominious position. The Powerful One was whipping the other youths now and he watched as their buttocks turned red. They seemed even more aroused, if that was possible, and their tumescent organs grew like cucumbers on the vine.

The Powerful One masturbated herself with her whip handle and Adam yearned to press his cock into that glistening pouch of flesh. Her red slash of sex flashed as she raised one leg on to the bed. He could see into her fleshy tunnel. The whip end rammed into her, coming out sticky with her juices.

He writhed and his eyes bulged. His balls felt as if they would burst. Suddenly she reached over to his cock, held it in her long fingers and impaled herself on him. She cried out in her twentieth climax of the day.

The young prince was ready to fight for the life of his bodyguard. He swaggered into the Forbidden Fruit to show the bar girls and Jezebel how handsome he was in his battle dress. His hairless chest was criss-crossed with shiny leather straps and his kilt swung on his bare thighs. His balls and cock were cupped in a sling of softest chamois – winter uniform because storms would hit the islands for the next few weeks. He wore daggers and a pistol and bow and arrows. He looked like a young god. Sylva stroked his chest and pinched his nipples while Cherry-Ripe fondled his balls, weighing them in her sly hands. Petite Gigi kissed him tearfully.

'Oh, come back safely, Prince Hari. We will all give you a free fuck when you return.'

150

'No you will not, not on my time, you won't,' cackled Jezebel, picking her teeth with a feather quill. 'My, doesn't he look pretty, though,' she noted.

Joshua had volunteered to join the army in order to help rescue his friend Adam. His little sister, Trixie-Jane, was distraught over his disappearance, and the soft-hearted Joshua wanted to make her happy.

The queen was loathe to part with the lad, even for a few weeks. He had become necessary to her well-being, and now she would have to start all over again with a new lad, teaching him exactly what pleased her. It was such a nuisance. There were not many eligible youths around, either. They had all decided to join up to see some action.

Tom was leaving for the promised excitement and battle, too. Jezebel was very annoyed with him.

'You young men don't know when you are well off,' she said. 'Here you are, your life before you, a good woman to care for your *every* need, and you throw it all away for a bit of excitement. Huh! You might die at sea, be eaten by shark; you might perish at the hands of this legendary figure's army. She might imprison you, keep you for her supper.' She heaved her wobbling bottom up from her wicker seat and pinched his cheek. 'Well, don't come crying to me if she tears your balls off. You'll be no use to anyone then.' But she was secretly saddened at the loss of this young lover. How boring it would be for her with only Samson and Bartolem for bed company. Ah, well, she would just have to find her amusement with her girls. Or she could fire them all and have a holiday. Or they could all have a holiday. She was undecided as to what to do. There would only be the elderly fishermen to service and the boys who were too young to join the army.

Bartolem and Samson had talked together and both had come to a momentous decision. They, too, would join the king's forces to make the hazardous journey to the Land of The Powerful One.

Poor Jezebel!

Angeline was dressed in a little slip of a mauve silk dress, which showed one of her budding breasts over the top and was split at the sides to show her naked hip bones. Her bottom and pubis were only just covered. She had ribbons tying her blonde hair back from her heart-shaped face. Her face was contorted by the effort of standing on her points. She was practising hard for the dance performance she and Kelila and Isadora would give to the war party when it arrived. Several other students would also perform. She had made friends with the girls who wanted to be dancers. They were simple native girls from Monkey Island and the smaller islands nearby. Their parents had sent them to the Kelidora Dance Academy and paid for their food and accommodation on Monkey Island for the duration of their studies.

Angeline had a particular favourite among these students. Her name was Delilah. She had thick black hair which flowed in waves down her straight, narrow back like a dark river. Her eyes were narrow; foxy-brown pools of mystery. Her little nose was turned up and pert. Angeline admired this girl more than the others because she was charming to behold. She moved like a small cat, writhing and twisting as if her spine was rubber. Her every movement was poetry. Luckily, Delilah felt the same way about Angeline. She knew she was a princess and so she was in awe of her, but Angeline's natural manner and good nature towards her relaxed her, and she soon became Angeline's inseparable companion.

Gertrude was pleased her charge had found a friend of her own. She was too involved with Jax to be much company for the princess.

'Delilah, show me how to do that movement again.

You know, where you move your hands in that clever way and your neck,' said Angeline one afternoon.

The reed-slender Delilah turned her little body into a pretty contortion of snake-like form and her long-nailed fingers jutted and twisted and drew pictures in the air. Her head, with a heavy headdress of silver and gold, remained facing forward as her body seemed to turn inside out. It was a mystery to Angeline how she did it.

'I'll never be able to do that,' she said.

'Of course you will. But it takes years of practice. I have been doing it since I was a small child, you see. That is why it is easier for me.'

'Oh, you are so charming, Delilah. Come, let me kiss you,' ordered the princess. The dancer took off her heavy headdress and lifted her silver-threaded pleated skirts and sat next to Angeline on a wooden seat. Angeline leant close and kissed the girl on the lips. The girl blushed. Then, shyly, she returned the embrace.

'Come to my room and I will show you something,' said Angeline, getting up and dragging Delilah by the hand. They crossed the little dirt road where chickens and goats and piglets wandered freely, to the house that Angeline shared with Kelila, Isadora and Gertrude.

Once in her room, Angeline stripped off her flimsy dance dress and, unashamedly naked except for her ballet shoes, searched for her erotic volume, which she kept in a sandalwood chest by her bed. She leant over, her bottom poking out, while Delilah sat on the bed, waiting for the princess to find the anatomy book.

Her eyes grew wide at the sight of the illustrations. She had clearly never seen such things as were depicted in the hand-coloured pictures. Men with huge members, purple and swollen, pushing them into female and male orifices. Lascivious young ladies holding male genitals in their naughty mouths. There was a picture of two young ladies doing things to each other.

'Oh, look at that! Let's try that, shall we?' suggested

Angeline. She was missing Gertrude's tender administrations. Her chaperone-cum-handmaiden had been lax in her duties lately.

Angeline carefully undressed her friend, kissing her all the while to keep her excited. She uncovered Delilah's pretty little breasts, apple-like in their roundness. The tiny brown nipples, like the stems of the fruit, were stiff to her touch. She kissed them and sucked them gently.

'There, isn't that pleasant? You must agree that it is,' she insisted.

'Oh yes, Princess, indeed it is, but is it not unnatural?'

'Of course not, don't be silly. Look at these pictures! Nothing is unnatural; anything is allowed by nature.' She turned the pages and pressed her hands into the girl's intimate parts. Delilah was passive and soft and then eager as the caresses became more urgent. Angeline was hot with desire and wished for her friend to be more aggressive in her love-making. She released herself from the girl's eager lips and opened the sandalwood chest again. She brought out a silk-wrapped bundle of dildos.

'Oh, what are those strange things?' said Delilah, giggling as she obviously realised what they were.

'I'll show you,' said Angeline, and chose a monkey-hair covered, slender and short dildo. 'Open your legs darling,' she said, and the innocent girl complied.

Chapter Twenty-Two
Delilah and the Dildos

*A*ngeline had been missing the company of her very best friend, Clementine – Queen Clementine – as she was now. Since her childhood companion had married her father-in-law, Angeline no longer shared little intimacies with her. They had shared the king's bed, time and again, but Clementine and Angeline had other duties and their marriages took over. They became more involved in matters of state and less dependent on each other for friendship.

Sylva, the bar girl on Isle de Paradis, had looked like a charming companion to the bored princess, but the High Priestess Viva had disapproved and put a stop to the liaison. On the voyage to Monkey Island, Angeline had enjoyed the company of her handmaiden and chaperone, the mature and voluptuous Gertrude, but even she was preoccupied with a man now it seemed.

Angeline was sincerely sentimentally attached to the dance student, Delilah. She was very like Angeline, almost a mirror image, except that Delilah was dark. Her slender shape was as androgynous as the princess's form. Her heart-shaped face was as charming and pretty.

Their pert bottoms had dimples in the exact same places, they were to discover.

Delilah went each day, after the morning lessons with Kelila or Isadora, to Angeline's room. There they would kiss and cuddle and the older, more experienced Angeline would show her new friend all the tricks of love. They experimented with the dildos Angeline had brought with her. Little had she thought that she would be sharing these with such a charming partner. They pored over the erotic illustrations each day to fill themselves with feelings of warmth and readiness for love.

'Do you see what he is doing to her? Isn't it interesting?' said the princess on one of these occasions. 'Shall we try it?' She strapped on to herself a thin dildo made of tightly woven leather, on one side of which was another thicker dildo. She inserted the thick dildo into her own vagina and left the thin one sticking up from her thighs, looking all the world as if it was a real cock she flaunted. Delilah lay back passively and bent her knees the way Angeline had told her. Angeline embraced her friend passionately and inserted the thin dildo carefully into her virginal sheath. She pressed herself on the dancer's belly, causing both dildos to push into their fleshy purses. Delilah cried out in anguish and excitement as the dildo found its target. It came out of her and she pushed against it so it disappeared into her pink shell again. Angeline's face grew pinker. Delilah sighed and moaned in appreciation. Her hips undulated and writhed prettily under Angeline's tender administrations and the two young friends found instant release from the tensions of the day's dance routines. They seemed to have renewed energy after this initial simulated copulation. They tried other positions and other dildos. They kissed and caressed and invented their own positions and their own love games.

'Tickle me with the peacock feather, please, Delilah. You know which one I like best.' Angeline squirmed and spread her legs to give the other access. 'Pretend you are a nurse, examining me.'

'Very well, Princess, I am your nurse, and now you must do as I say.' Delilah tied back her stream of hair and put on an apron around her naked body. Her little breasts could just be seen as she leant forward, at gaping sides of the apron bodice. When she turned away to pick up the feather, Angeline was given a fine display of firm, muscular, dimpled buttocks, a very narrow waist and long legs. The crisp, white linen apron looked well on the copper-toned flesh.

'Oh, nurse, please help me,' Angeline said. 'I have an itch in my tummy.'

'You poor thing, let me look,' said the nurse. 'Where is it? Is it there?' She pressed the princess's tummy button.

'No, much lower than that. Quickly, scratch it for me, before I go mad.'

'There?' Delilah moved her long nails gently down the princess's belly on to her pubis.

'Between my legs, nurse. Scratch between my legs.'

The obliging nurse scratched her nails down the proffered pink slit and with the feather opened the swollen lips. She both scratched the itch and caused more irritation with the long feather. It was a sensual torture for Angeline. First she was frustrated, then satisfied. The feather fluttered on her flesh and licked her moist tunnel. The long fingers moved on her private parts in a truly artistic way. She flung her arms above her head and abandoned herself to the dancer's hands, then she became aware of another element. A moist, long tongue was dancing inside her sex lips, tuning her little bud, vibrating it and making it sing. Her whole body shivered in bliss at the dancer's love-making. Her thighs were on fire. She saw nothing, she heard nothing, she felt nothing but Delilah. Then Delilah kissed her mouth and she tasted herself on the dancer's lips and tongue. The saltiness of her sex; the musk. She was filled with love of herself. Oh, how she was beautiful! She came again in blissful joy of how lovely she was, and how very desirable.

Then she remembered her partner, and roused herself from the aftermath of an orgasm to gently begin to make love in return. She turned the girl over and kissed her buttocks and thighs. She wrapped her slender waist in white ribbons and tied her thighs with the yards of silk. She tied Delilah in an erotic bandage and slipped the ends over the wooden bedhead, tying them so she could not escape. She lay next to her captive and caressed her thighs. She tickled her bottom hole with a feather and the girl begged for more ardent caresses. Angeline pressed a monkey-hair face powder brush into the crevice and stroked her anus.

'That tickles, Princess!'

'I know it tickles, silly.' She slapped the upturned buttocks playfully with the flat handle.

'Ouch!'

Angeline was pleased at the marks that formed on the dusky flesh. She repeated the blow.

'Ouch!'

'It doesn't really hurt, does it?' she asked, innocently.

'Yes it does. Well, it did – it doesn't now,' said Delilah. She was moist between her legs and instinctively lifted her hips to give Angeline better access to her private parts. Angeline kindly complied, easing her fingers up into the other's moist pink tunnel. Delilah had only a little, fine pubic hair, but Angeline wasn't used to seeing any at all.

'Shall I shave you later, darling? Would you enjoy that?'

'Yes please, Princess. I would love to be as smooth as you. My hair grows so quickly.'

Angeline kissed her captive's pretty quim with enthusiasm and pressed fingers inside to feel the wetness envelop them. She smacked her clitoris softly, then harder as the dancer opened to her touch. Delilah called out in a muffled cry as she orgasmed. Almost immediately, Angeline caused her to cry out again. It was a wonderful game that they had evolved, and their partnership was as creative as their dancing.

Later, as promised, Angeline prepared her friend for her first shave. Delilah sat on the bidet, facing Angeline. A bowl of warm water was at hand, as was a monkey-hair shaving brush and the razor blade. With one hand Angeline smoothed lather all over the pubic area and between Delilah's legs. Even this was arousing to both friends. Angeline wore the apron and was acutely aware of how naughty she looked in it, her bare bottom peeping out the open back under the long white ribbons. She smoothed the lather all over and then expertly shaved the fluffy dark hair. She went all around the girl's sex parts with the sharp blade but the girl did not flinch. The lather was removed, and the flesh was rinsed clean. Delilah sat, leaning back on her hands. She looked down at herself.

'There, you are all finished,' said the princess, turning away with the bowl of water to empty it. 'Look at yourself – how lovely you are!' She gave Delilah a large hand mirror and the dancer admired her newly bare pussy.

'Let's try it out, shall we? See if you feel different.'

They slid on to the fur rug on the floor and entwined their arms and legs and caressed each other.

'Yes, that is an improvement. I would not have believed it, but it is delightful. I can feel so much more. It is wonderful!' Delilah announced, and they spent a happy afternoon's siesta playing naughty games.

'I want the big dildo this time,' said Delilah bravely.

'No, it's for me. I am a married woman, you forget. I need a bigger cock than you.' She ran after the naked Delilah, who brandished the eight-inch leather-bound

159

wooden cock in her hands. It was curved to resemble a banana-shaped penis and ridged along the under edge.

'I'll give it to you,' giggled Delilah. 'Only let me insert it and wiggle it about for you.'

'Very well, but only do it when I say,' ordered Angeline. She bent over a low leather stool and presented her buttocks to the dancer. Her vagina was pinkly swollen and opened to the first caress. Delilah first smoothed oil into the opening, as Angeline had taught her. She patted her long, articulate fingers on the open flower and parted the petals wider. She pressed the oiled penis substitute gently into the opening, and it slowly disappeared into the princess's eager purse. Delilah pushed more firmly, and Angeline groaned and writhed prettily. The apron was tied at the waist and her white bottom gleamed under the bow. Angeline moaned for more.

'There is no more, darling, you have it all inside you,' said the admiring Delilah.

'Oh, wiggle it out a bit and then push it in,' ordered her teacher.

Delilah did as she was told, learning more about female anatomy in one afternoon than she had hitherto learned in all her eighteen years. She was ready for more intimate interference by Angeline by the time the princess had been satisfied. And so they continued. It was a time of day when they should have been resting from the arduous dance practice, and instead they were exhausting each other in passionate embraces. But they showered and dressed for the evening as if they had slept all day, so renewed and refreshed were they.

'Angeline,' said her friend, thoughtfully, 'wouldn't it be wonderful if someone invented a dildo that vibrated?'

'They have,' said Angeline. 'A man!'

Chapter Twenty-Three
To the Rescue!

On Isle de Paradis preparations were made for the voyage to the Land of The Powerful One and the newly recruited men were being made into soldiers as quickly as possible. They were marched up and down and taught how to use a sword and dagger, if they did not already know how to use them. They were run off their feet every day, up hills and across deep sand. They climbed trees and swung from tree to tree using liana roots as ropes. Joshua, Tom and Prince Hari, along with his friends Arturo and Jimi, were expected to be fit for the battle within a week. They had known each other all their lives and trusted each other with their lives. Samson and Bartolem, older than these lads by ten years or more, were keen to show their superior strength. They had lived a soft life in recent years and needed to lose weight and build muscle. They worked hard under Ric's command.

On the last night before the voyage they were given leave to visit home or wherever they wanted to go. With hardly an exception the battalion visited the Forbidden Apple. It was overflowing. The food was basic because Bartolem had not been able to organise enough provisions, but the fishermen had come up trumps and provided dozens of sailfish, kingfish and tuna. The scent of charcoal-blackened fish, roasted peppers and sweet potato filled the humid night air. The girls were bathed and scented and dressed in their best. Jezebel was helping Bartolem do the cooking, but she had time to see to Tom between courses. After the feast, and a generous consumption by all of banana wine and manioc beer, Cherry-Ripe was thoroughly fucked in all her orifices by a grateful platoon, as were Petite Gigi and Sylva. The haughty Lana had her work cut out cracking her whip and spanking the boy soldiers. Ric was in his element, showing off his sexual prowess to the new recruits. The orgy continued almost until dawn, when the traditional conch was blown – the call to arms – to mark the embarkation of the army.

The king and queen were at the beach to wave the troops goodbye. King Aristide embraced his son Prince Hari on both cheeks, and so did Queen Clementine.

'Be careful, Hari. Look after yourself,' said the queen, squeezing his arm.

'Bring Adam back with you,' said Trixie-Jane, tears pouring down her face.

'And give our love to Angeline,' said the queen, as an afterthought. She had not been able to say goodbye properly to Joshua and she was cross, but she was pleased that the king was not going with this war party. He wanted to stay and look after her, he had said, and she preened herself, thinking that maybe her married life was not dead after all. And she had kept Trixie-Jane to comfort her.

The men took their places in the war canoes, and Hari and Ric went on ahead in the royal yacht with a chosen few good men. The yacht had been armed with a large gun on the forward deck. Captain Barnabus, long since recovered from his unfortunate accident on the way to Monkey Island, was in charge again. The weather was probably going to be a problem for the canoes – it was the time of year when storms and even hurricanes could strike suddenly. Some of the canoes were loaded with provisions: dried fruits, coconuts, for eating and for the milk, bananas, rice, maize and water. The soldiers sang the old chants of Isle de Paradis as they paddled. Their brave voices rose above the sound of the waves and the rising wind. Ric and Hari, high above their men in the relative comfort of the yacht, steamed ahead to Monkey Island.

When they arrived there was a large group of islanders waiting to greet them. Angeline leapt up and down on the pier when she saw that Hari was on board. When the gangplank was lowered she ran up, the first to board the boat, and flung herself into his arms. He kissed her enthusiastically. They disembarked and he and Ric made their greetings to Isadora, Kelila and Gertrude. Ric looked delighted to see his wife. She had lost a little weight (with all the athletic sex she was enjoying,) and looked as sleek as a brood mare. They embraced. Gertrude was aroused, as always, at the sight of her husband's strong arms and thighs under the straps and leather of his uniform. She smiled over Ric's shoulder at the ship's captain, also handsome in his white duck uniform.

'Is the king not with you?' asked Isadora.

'No, he decided to stay and look after things on Isle de Paradis,' said Hari. 'Ric and I are in charge of this operation.'

They went to the house of Isadora and all ate lunch together.

'We must reconnoitre this Land of The Powerful One,' said Ric.

'I have a map of the Lake of Lost Love,' said Isadora, showing Ric and Hari the drawing she had made.

'What is this lake?' asked Hari.

163

'We must go to the lake to get to the Land of The Powerful One. It lies on the furthest bank,' said Isadora.

'We have made friends with a pearl diver who says he knows how to reach The Powerful One,' said Gertrude demurely.

'You must take me to him,' said Ric.

While Angeline and Kelila showed Hari the Kelidora Dance Academy, Ric and his three soldiers went with Gertrude and Isadora to find Jax.

'There he is!' said Gertrude, and waved at the pearl diver, who was dozing in his boat. Jax swam to the bank and pulled himself out. He greeted Ric and the others and they squatted on the sandy bank to discuss the map and what they were going to do to rescue Adam and the other youths. Ric explained that his war party would arrive later and that they perhaps should wait until they had more troops. The fisherman was worried about his reward, but Ric assured him that if he showed the way through the mangrove swamps and other obstacles to the Land of The Powerful One, he would be royally rewarded.

Hari held Angeline's hand, clearly delighted at the sight of her lithe little body in the skimpy outfit in which she had chosen to greet him. It consisted of nothing more than a large silk collar which circled her neck and fell over her shoulders to end just above her nipples, and another frill of material which skimmed her hips and buttocks and ended just above her bare pubis. Her charms were on view, and Angeline knew he wanted to make passionate love to her. But first things first. Hari had to meet the other dancing girls – including the charming Delilah, who was dressed exactly like his wife. Her darker charms were titillatingly displayed, too. As soon as they had shown Hari the dance academy, Angeline and Delilah took him by the hands and led him to Angeline's room.

'I am sure you need a lie down, darling, after your voyage,' said the princess.

'Well, yes, I suppose I am in need of a rest,' he agreed, trying to walk with his erection pushing his leather kilt straps apart.

'I didn't say you could rest,' said Angeline, and she pushed him on to her bed. The two dancers threw themselves on to the young prince, tugging at his kilt and exclaiming over his fine erection. Delilah was a little shy, but Angeline had insisted that this was what she the princess desired, and who was Delilah to complain?

'Oh, Hari, what a pretty pouch you are wearing!' admired Angeline, stroking his balls through the chamois leather.

'It is winter uniform,' said the prince.

'Please show my friend your hidden goodies, Hari. She has never seen a man before.'

'Really?' said Hari. He obliged his wife and stood up, undoing the straps which held his testicles and cock in the chamois pouch. He threw it off in a gesture of arrogance and stood, his hands on his hips, his cock pointed at the dancers. They sat together on the bed, their arms around each other, tenderly caressing each other's breasts. Hari was left in no doubt that his wife had found consolation in his absence in the delicate embrace of this charming native girl.

His cock twitched as he watched them kiss each other. He held his cock and waved it at them.

'Don't you want some of this?' he joked.

'Mmm, in a minute,' said his wife, enjoying too much the tender caresses of Delilah, whose long fingers were between her legs.

Hari watched the dancer's fingers part his wife's labia and he knelt nearer to see the moisture wet her thighs and buttocks. Delilah slipped to the floor and put her dark head between the princess's open thighs. Delilah's succulent buttocks were too tempting a fruit to ignore, and Hari grabbed them hungrily. He placed his stiff cock between them and rubbed it where he could. The dark cleft held his swollen cock in a comforting vice. He came immediately.

'Oh!' said Delilah. 'Was that it?'

'Oh! Poor Hari often has that problem,' said Angeline apologetically, as she saw what had happened. 'Don't worry, we will let him sleep a few minutes, and then he will be able to begin again.'

While they waited for Hari to have his cat nap, they continued their gentle caresses, kissing each other in all the most sensitive places. They still wore their provocative garments, their sex parts and breasts easily accessible. They had spent hours preparing each other's bodies that morning. The ritual depilation; the oiling of parts; the brushing of hair; the plaiting in flowers and shells. Delilah had gold bracelets around her ankles and wrists. She always wore them, so proud she was to have these love tokens from the princess. Delilah had painted rouge on Angeline's private parts, exclaiming over the pretty design of her shell-like labia, which were more prominently displayed than her own. Delilah's sex parts were further back than Angeline's; closer to her bottom hole. She had had to lift her legs up higher and bend her knees to her chin for Angeline to paint them.

Their nipples were left their natural colour so as not to spoil the cream silk of the frilly collar.

Delilah was curious as to the workings of a real cock and she asked Angeline to show her what to do with it. Hari slept on, snoring lightly. Angeline told Delilah to lift his kilt and look. Delilah took a strip of leather and held it up. Hari's flaccid cock lay curved on his thigh.

'Oh, it has shrunk!' said the alarmed dancer.

Angeline laughed. 'Yes, darling, unfortunately that is the male member's usual state, until we cause it to grow sufficiently for our own satisfaction. Unlike our wonderful dildos, we have to work hard to stiffen the real thing.'

'Take it in your hand, like this,' Angeline showed her.

Delilah silently did as she was told and her brown eyes narrowed as she watched the cock grow in her fingers. She rubbed it more quickly and could not believe the size it reached.

'It is so much softer than our dildos, yet so firm, as if a bone grows inside.'

'Yes,' whispered Angeline, 'a wonderful bendy bone. It is better than a dildo, darling. Just wait until it goes inside you and pumps hard. It is a delightful sensation, I assure you.'

The prince stirred, and his cock grew under the pressure of four hands. His balls tightened as they weighed them in their soft palms. He kept his eyes closed so he didn't know whose breasts pressed against him, whose hot thighs rubbed his. He licked his lips and felt the gentle pressure of a bottom pressing on his face. He obligingly stuck out his tongue and foraged with it. He heard gentle moans and felt the writhing bodies wrap themselves around him. He began to move his hands over the two warm bodies. He felt the softness of their flesh, the firmness of young muscles. He smelt the sweet salt perfume of their hot bodies; tasted the melange of love-juices. His cock was sucked and handled firmly, slapped on firm flesh. His mouth was invaded by stiff nipples. His tongue was tired from licking faster as they begged for more. His cock ached. He needed to find a soft, warm nest for it; a moist channel to tunnel into. He suddenly felt his cock being sucked into just such a warm, wet purse, and hands grabbed his buttocks and thrust his hips forward to meet the eager flesh. He thrust firmly, again and again, and felt hands stroke his testicles, his anus invaded by little fingers, his mouth covered in kisses. He heard the thankful cries of Delilah as he felt his own orgasm peak. His seed burst from his proud cock into the depths of the dark beauty, and he fell back, exhausted again.

Delilah was surprised at the amount of liquid that dribbled from between her legs.

'It's so messy!' she said, alarmed at the sticky stuff covering her legs, bottom and belly.

'Don't worry, darling, that's perfectly normal, especially since it has been so long since Hari has made love,' said Angeline. 'The juices build up and need to be released.'

Hari had to endure several more tests of his virility before the girls allowed him to get up and shower. He looked down at the bed where his wife and her new friend lay and smiled at the sight. They were prettily dishevelled and happily exhausted by the orgasm-filled afternoon. Angeline's pink buttocks were sticking up and her head was under a pillow. Delilah was lying with her legs open, her dark red sex displayed like a split fig.

Delightful! he thought, and hoped the war party would not arrive too soon.

Chapter Twenty-Four
A Performance of Dance

*R*ic admired his wife's string of pink pearls.
'Are they new?' he asked.

'Goodness, no, I've had them years,' she said, shifting her weight so her thighs were wrapped around his loins and her bottom was poised over his genitals. The pearls hung in a long rope from her neck and tickled his chin. He took a pearl into his mouth and dragged her head down to his face. He kissed her red lips.

'You look well, Gertrude. The air suits you here. The lake air is particularly fresh, I think.' He slapped her bottom playfully and she wriggled it tauntingly.

'Fuck me, Ric!' she commanded, and his thick organ slipped into her sex mouth. She shuddered with the force of the embrace. He burrowed into the warm flesh, his penis filling the fleshy tunnel. She moaned and writhed on him. He slapped her plump bottom cheeks and the loud sound excited them both. She held his cock at the base and stroked it lovingly.

'Have you missed me?' she said.

'Of course, my flamboyant flower,' he said. 'But I'd rather show you than tell you how much.'

She laughed and moved up and down firmly on his

stiffness. She raised herself so his cock nearly came out of her, then hung there briefly before plunging again, filling herself with his hardness. She leant back on her heels and her flushed breasts fell out towards her armpits. He grabbed them and looked down towards her open crack. It was spread open on his belly, his cock swallowed by the red gash. He felt himself flood with tumescence and his cock started to throb. He was at the moment of no return. His sperm hit her cervix and she thrust down hard on him, coming too.

Afterwards, they cuddled and kissed as they had done in the first days of their marriage.

'You must go on holiday more often, my darling,' he said.

'Yes,' she agreed. 'Perhaps I will.'

The king's war canoes had met with trouble. The wind had gradually risen and the waves were mountainous. They had lost two of the provision-filled boats and both crews – gone to the bottom of the sea. They struggled on in the fifteen foot high waves. They were terrified of capsizing, and their arms were tired after hours of paddling.

They had seen sharks thrashing in the sea. The fins were with them for many miles, following them, hoping for their canoes to fill with water and sink. The men had not slept. Samson and Bartolem were exhausted but struggled on, as did Joshua and Tom. Unfortunately, they were in separate boats so could not support each other.

The voyage was dreadful in every way. Men were seasick; others collapsed at the oar and slumped into the bilge. Suddenly, the lead boat saw land.

The call came, 'Land ho!'

'Hurrah!' came the answer from all the surviving crews.

On Monkey Island, the prince and princess and their

new companion ran down to the sea and joined other islanders and soldiers to help bring in the canoes and carry the exhausted men up the beach.

It was late that night before the stories had been told of the dangerous trip and the six lost men grieved for by their compatriots. After a good meal of fish and spiced vegetables, washed down with banana beer, the soldiers were housed in a temple building as the weather had become even worse, and as well as the high winds there was heavy rain to deal with. They settled down for the night with blankets provided by islanders.

Next day the storm had not abated, so it was decided that they would sit it out. There was no point in making plans to sail across the large lake, which had waves as high as the sea. Instead, the men rested and regained their strength.

'We'll do the dance concert now, shall we? That will help pass the time, as well as entertain the troops,' suggested Isadora.

'Good idea. I'll give the girls a dress rehearsal,' said Kelila.

Angeline and Delilah were practising anyway, determined to have their acrobatic act perfected by the time they had to perform, but Kelila was happy with all the dancers' ability and enthusiasm. They all went through their paces, with only Isadora as audience. She clapped loudly at the end and said to Kelila, 'We'll do the performance tomorrow.'

The soldiers were merry with wine and beer and full of satisfying food. They lounged in the temporary auditorium in the centre of the village. The wind blew hard and the tree trunks leant and bent, but there were huts all around to keep off most of the wind from the centre stage, and a tarpaulin was erected over the top. Musicians played flutes and stringed instruments, and two boys hammered loudly on a large and a small drum. A bell was struck and the show began.

First Kelila gave a solo performance. She was decorated as if she was a snake, with zig-zag stripes all over her naked body and face. Her hair was tied tightly in tiny plaits which were close to her head and her eyes were enlarged with kohl. This dance was what she was famous for throughout all the islands of the King of Paradis. The cheers were tumultuous as she finished with a swirling, leaping, twisting dance which had the crowd gasping in astonishment, so like a snake was she.

One of the young dancers, a girl called Grace, was next. She danced on her hands only, moving around the circle of soldiers slowly, to give each a private view of her bare privates. Her short transparent skirt was over her head, hiding her lovely face, but her sex was naked and smoothly shaved. Her genital area and bottom had been painted to portray a face whose mouth opened and closed, smiled and pouted, according to her leg movements. The soldiers loved it. They wanted more. She came out on her hands again and bent right over so her belly was uppermost. The crowd grew quiet at the sight of the young girl's glistening sex parts. The music grew to a crescendo and she leapt to her feet and threw out her hands in triumph.

'She is good, isn't she!' said Angeline to Delilah. 'I haven't seen that routine before. I must learn it for Hari.'

Isadora performed next. In America she had been an exotic dancer and an actress, or so she had told Angeline when they met on board the ship that was to be wrecked on Isle de Paradis and so throw their lives together. Angeline had always admired the woman's athletic prowess and her long straight limbs and large breasts. Isadora's red hair was in fiery ringlets down her back. Her dramatic, black leather, loose-legged knickers hung from her narrow waist to her thighs. At every high kick her pink pussy was visible at the sides. Her breasts were almost hidden by a black leather corset, but her long stiff nipples were allowed to peep out the middle. Straps held the breasts high. She wore long boots to her thighs and a black mask over her eyes and nose. She wielded a long whip and cracked it in time to the drums.

The men drew back from the barrier, afraid of the instrument she held.

'I want a volunteer,' she said.

No-one moved except away. Then one soldier – Ric, no less – stepped forward.

'I volunteer,' he said, and stepped over the rope that served as a barrier.

Gertrude gasped. He had made love to her several times since his arrival and she thought he must be exhausted. He threw down his sword and dagger and stood there, unarmed, an interesting bulge under his kilt.

'Very good. A willing victim for Madame Whip, I see,' said the husky-voiced Isadora. 'We will see what you are made of, Captain Ric.'

His men cheered as the whip flicked at his kilt, lifting it and revealing his bulging chamois pouch. The whip end went so fast no-one could see it undo the laces that held the pouch. It slipped from him as the whip licked it off and threw it on to the ground. The cheers grew louder. Ric did not seem frightened of Isadora or her whip, but he had suffered similar torments from Lana – although she wasn't as proficient as Isadora. He stood stock still and allowed the dominatrix to undress him with the whip. It was a clever trick, interlaced with erotic writhing from the dancer, one leg lifted high for a glimpse of secret flesh. The men yelled with excitement. Ric was soon standing in his boots and nothing else, clearly proud of his stiff manhood. Isadora leant forward and wrapped the thin tail of the whip around his penis, then drew him around the stage by his cock. She tugged on the whip gently, dancing meanwhile, and he had to run or walk to keep up with her undulations. His cock was near bursting. Isadora called Kelila, denuded now of her snake make-up, to deal with his problem. The dusky dancer fell on her knees and tugged at the leather plait-covered cock. She left a ribbon of leather wrapped around it and sucked gently on the head. The soldiers cheered. Kelila then played with him, taunting him with her tongue, and he tried to thrust himself into her. The audience was in uproar. Suddenly, with a quick pull of the whip, he had spurted his white gobs of juice on to the sand.

'Oh!' The soldiers obviously felt cheated, as did Ric.

But before they could show their displeasure, Kelila and Isadora had fled from the arena. The lights dimmed and the drums rolled. A sudden flare of flame illuminated the next two dancers, Angeline and Delilah. The latter stood on the other's shoulders. They were dressed as schoolgirls, exactly the same in short, white tunics and their hair in ribboned plaits. They wore no underwear, but long white stockings held up with ties above their knees. They each sucked their thumbs. The soldiers cheered. Delilah slid down next to Angeline and the two dancers were like mirror images, moving in exactly the same way, echoing each other's steps. It looked as if there was only one schoolgirl, watching herself in a mirror. The soldiers were stunned and amused. The girls stood on their hands, did cartwheels, skipped with ropes and leapt over each other, their legs wide. It was a thoroughly moving performance. Unfortunately, before it could reach any sort of climax, the wind had blown out the flares and torn down the canvas roof that had protected them from the worst of the rain. The audience and performers fled to the relative safety of the huts and the temple.

'You were wonderful, darlings,' said Isadora to her girls.

Hari was waiting for the princess in her room, but Ric

appeared and said his men were expecting him to be with them at the temporary barracks. The soldiers left together and Angeline and Delilah had to console each other.

'Didn't Kelila look gorgeous as a snake?' said Delilah.

'Yes, and wasn't Isadora terrifying with her whip?' said Angeline.

'Yes! And isn't the captain a handsome man!' said the younger girl. 'So big and strong.'

'Isn't his cock big, you mean!' giggled Angeline.

'Yes, I do. Let's get the dildos and play at being Isadora and the captain, shall we?' suggested Delilah.

And they did.

Chapter Twenty-Five
Lake of Lost Love

*A*dam was one of six youths being used by The
Powerful One. He was dressed in the corset he had
with him when he was captured – Gertrude's emerald-
green velvet and satin corset. It was hardly recognisable
as the captain's wife's garment any more, so stained and
torn was it. It had been worn by The Powerful One, and
by Adam, and the other youths had masturbated over
its silky softness. The ribbons that laced it were tattered
and shredded, but still it managed to hold a fetishistic
place in their imagination.

Adam's coffee-coloured thighs and buttocks shone
with oil. His pectorals, deltoids and abdominal muscles
were defined by the shine. His cock, erect as required at
all times, was trapped in a fine leather string which
wrapped his rod like a cricket bat handle.

His balls were hanging tightly, nudging the root. He
was not blindfolded today, but he was restrained from
moving far. A leash was attached to a broad leather
collar around his neck, and one of the hooded, masked
guards held on to it. The other five slaves were similarly
restrained. One had his cock poking out of a pair of
ragged shorts. It looked somehow obscene, purple-

headed as it was, sticking straight out of the scout's shorts. Another was strung up from the ceiling on a chain, and he swung round in a meandering circle, naked except for ropes that encircled his chest, thighs and buttocks. Adam could not watch him without feeling dizzy. Another lad was trapped inside a sort of basket contraption, his cock and balls hanging down through a gap in the basket, the less useful parts of him tucked away. The last youth was upended over a leather stool, his bottom up high. He was tied to restraining rings in the floor. He wore a skirt which was pulled up over his head. His anus was oiled and had obviously been used several times recently.

The masked guards were silent. They each held a small, heavy whip which they used unmercifully if any of the youths disobeyed the commands of The Powerful One. Adam had never seen the faces of any of the guards or the formidable woman who held them in her power. It was a good name, he thought. She seemed like some sort of evil goddess; indestructible. He dreamt of her every night, and his erotic subconscious could not imagine the deeds she actually performed. He wondered if perhaps she was just a figment of his fevered imagination. He hoped so. He wanted to be back leading a quiet life; fishing with Hari, playing music, painting. Most of all he wanted the undemanding, sweet-natured Trixie-Jane to hold him in her arms. He had only kissed her once, but he had built up their relationship in his mind. He loved her more than any other woman he had met.

His captive cock was suddenly tugged by someone. He was back in the present, his sex organ being toyed with by a merciless, insatiable, inhuman female fiend. Some men would pay good money for this, he thought, as the guard dragged him closer to the seated Powerful One. Her position in the centre of the group of youths enabled her to touch each one of them easily. Youthful flesh surrounded her. She wore a black, one-piece garment of animal skin, which left her erogenous zones uncovered. Her nipples were painted orange, as were her nails and lips. Her sex mouth, too, was orange under the triangle of dark hair. She wore the white feather mask, only her flashing eyes visible, and today they had an orange fire in them. She pressed sharp high heels on the buttocks of the lad who was upturned and dug them in slightly, marking his nut-brown flesh with a purple bruise. He made no noise. She whipped his tender bottom cheeks and he flinched. Her next desire was to see him buggered. Adam was dragged over to the youth and made to kneel over him. His leather-entwined erection was positioned by the guard and he was pushed forward. His cock went into the puckered anus a couple of inches and the youth's groans were loud. The Powerful One whipped Adam across the buttocks and he thrust further in, past the sphincter. It felt good, he had to admit – it felt wonderful, the tight hole holding him. She breathed heavily very close to him, but he could not see what she was doing because he was too involved now in the strong sensations which racked his belly. He knew he would have no relief until she ordered it, but he buggered the youth vigorously in spite of himself. He had no self-control; only he was under her control.

The youth beneath him groaned as his thrusts got stronger. Behind him he heard other youths moan. He could well imagine what she was doing to each of them. How long had he been captive? He had lost count of the days. Each night was endless. He would be imprisoned in an endless fuck, for all time.

The Powerful One had milked each youth with her hungry cunt until they begged for mercy. Her orgasms were like animal cries, fierce yowls and screeches that tore the humid air. The silent guards, their hoods over their masked faces, looked like allegorical figures of Death.

Later, in the relative peace of his narrow bed, Adam lay exhausted, planning his escape. He was an artist, not a prisoner, he told himself. He was a soldier, too. He must be brave and creative. He had a plan.

Next day at dawn, his captor had all the youths dressed in aprons and made them scrub the floor on all fours. Each youth scrubbed with a wet cloth and as he moved his hands and knees, his duster-covered cock dried the clean area. This was a bizarre entertainment for The Powerful One, who ate her breakfast of fried monkey heads as she watched.

'You have missed a bit!' she screamed and threw an empty monkey skull at the offending youth's head.

'Your humble pardon, O Powerful One,' whispered the terrified youth. What punishment was in store for this foul deed? Adam wondered. He didn't have to wait long to find out. The guards carried him to the seated Powerful One and placed him over her naked lap. His duster was taken from him. She spanked the youth firmly with her open hand, digging her long nails into his anus as she did so. His scrotum was spanked and she took his erection between her thighs and rubbed herself on it. Her own satisfaction was loud. He whimpered and begged for release from his torment. She spanked him all the more and his agony was obvious.

The erotic spanking was having a detrimental effect on the other cleaners, and their enlarged cocks dragged on the clean floor, drying it faster.

'Good! Now I want to see that one on his own.' She pointed to Adam.

The other youths beat a hasty retreat and left Adam, standing now in his ridiculously short, frilly apron, with a feather duster in his hand. He remembered his feverish dream of last night. The Powerful One had allowed him to have an orgasm.

Perhaps his dream would come true. Then he remembered he must try to escape.

'O Powerful One,' he said quietly, smiling at her masked face.

'What is it you dare to say to me?'

'Would you like me to finish the portrait of you? You are so magnificent, I would give you a picture that would last for ever and show your beauty to every man who ever will live. It would be a monument to your greatness,' he finished. It sounded ridiculous to him, but her orange eyes glinted at the flattery.

'Oh, yes, the painting. I forgot. You were doing a painting of me in that old corset, weren't you! All right. You will paint me. But first tickle my parts with the feather duster.'

Adam did as he was bid, pushing the long, fluffy feathers between her legs, amazed as ever at her wetness, her scarlet sex mouth gaping between the orange-painted plump lips. She orgasmed to the delicate touch of the feathers and told him to fetch his paints and the unfinished portrait.

Two hours later, he was still painting. She was a remarkably patient model and could hold a pose with no discomfort, except that every half an hour she demanded a rest, which involved intercourse or titillation or masturbation of some description. Gertrude's satin corset was stained and split, but Adam ignored its imperfections and painted it as if it were new. He remembered with longing the corset that Trixie-Jane had modelled – the queen's corset. Oh, would he ever see her again? He remembered her saving him from the sea; saw again her skinny arms and legs thrashing; saw her swim with the dolphins. He tried to concentrate on the fearsome woman before him. She stared with her emerald eyes at him. Surely her eyes had been light brown earlier? Maybe she really was a mythical beast, the best and worst imagined sexual fantasy of all the youths. He wanted very much to see her face. Her hair was a tangled mass of long dark curls, or was it sleek and smooth? Her dark limbs swallowed light. Her sex was wide and glistening, the swollen lips like some awful sea anemone, waiting to swallow its victims. He painted her as if she was some sort of giant, with legs that went on for ever. Her breasts were unclimbed mountains, her loins and buttocks like undulating sands of wide deserts. But her eyes were all colours to all men: they were like deep dark seas, they were volcanoes of erupting fire. He looked again, more carefully, wanting to mix the exact hue. He drew closer to her. She was seated, her legs apart, her arms folded over her breasts. He did not look at her sex; he only wanted to see the truth in her eyes. She turned her stony gaze on him.

'It is time for another rest,' she said, and took a clean paintbrush from a jar.

Adam wore a loincloth. She tore this from him. She pushed him on to the couch and used the paintbrush to tickle his scrotum. His erection was held as usual by a ring at the base of his cock. The Powerful One told him to do the same to her. He tried not to look at her gaping sex, but as usual he was hypnotised by the moist slit. He pressed closer, wanting to penetrate her. She lay back and he mounted her, desperate to surround his cock with her sucking flesh. She moaned uninhibitedly, and Adam's face and chest flushed. The Powerful One's legs stiffened with an impending orgasm. Her cries were like a wild creature in agony. Her limbs shuddered and were still. He carried on with his caresses, as he knew he must. She came again at his delicate touch. He pressed the heel of his hand on her open sex and she came again. He was still unsatisfied, of course, but he was used to that, so he controlled himself and withdrew. He looked again at her eyes. Now they were a pale blue-grey, milder than he had ever seen them before. Why? Was she made serene by the orgasms? Did this mean that she was vulnerable at these times? Her orgasms were always multiple and she had at least 35 every 24 hours. Could he take advantage of her quietened state, perhaps, after she had a particularly strong chain of orgasms?

He went back to his paints and pretended to be totally immersed in the business of painting her again.

The painting was beginning to take on a life of its own. There was not one woman in the image, but many. This portrait was not only of The Powerful One; it was of Adam's mother, his sister, Trixie-Jane, Queen Clementine, Princess Angeline, Gertrude, Jezebel, and every woman he had ever wanted, loved or feared. He was frightened of The Powerful One no more. He knew he had found the secret of her power. He was determined to escape.

The youths were regularly allowed relief from their semi-permanent states of lust. The masked guards would gather them together, drench them in freezing water and when their cocks had withered, they removed the penis rings. The youths plunged into a hot spring that bubbled up between flat rocks, and there they behaved outrageously, masturbating each other and slapping each other's buttocks. They had competitions to see who could spurt their semen furthest. The weekly holiday was enjoyed by all of them. They rested. What did The Powerful One do for entertainment on this rest day? they wondered.

On the Lake of Lost Love, the pearl divers worked. They had paddled out in their small canoes to a new oyster bed, further from the safety of the shore they knew than they had been before. They had dived too much in the usual oyster grounds and so had to take more chances. It was a dangerous business. The lake was dark and deep and full of unknown hazards. There were dangerous currents; thick weed that wound around and dragged on unsuspecting limbs; shoals of fresh water fish with sharp teeth that could tear flesh from bone. There were also crocodiles.

182

Jax had not dived much lately, so involved had he been with the white woman who had bewitched him. He had sold her many pink pearls, but at a greatly reduced rate as she had been so obliging with her charms. Now he was hungry and needed money. Perhaps if he found The Powerful One for the soldiers he would be rich, but the soldiers were not ready to make the journey across the lake. The weather was still bad, with storms ruffling the water and building high hills across it. So for now he had to dive. He pushed out his small boat, with two other men helping him launch it into the surf, then he was on his own. He paddled hard for half an hour and then let the boat drift. He placed a long thick bamboo stalk into the water and peered through it. After he had searched the area and was satisfied that there were oysters on the lake bed, the diver threw out the anchor. He put his shoulder bag over his head and his knife between his teeth. He dived overboard into the darkness of the water.

When he did not return to the lakeside beach that evening, his friends were concerned but not too worried. Jax was a strong swimmer and an experienced diver. He would have gone for shelter somewhere close to where he dived if he was late finishing and knew he could not make it back to his home. They sat around a charcoal fire in the communal hut they used, trying to keep their food dry. They ate their meagre meal of shrimps and mussels, drank rice wine and told yarns that had been passed down through the ages.

The most repeated story was of The Powerful One who lived on the far shore of the Lake of Lost Love.

Many divers had gone missing over the years. Some had drowned, their legs tangled in the writhing weeds; others had been taken by crocodiles or eaten alive by flesh-eating fish. But some had disappeared mysteriously under strange circumstances.

'There were the four divers camping on the far side of the lake after diving. They did not come back.'

'There was the case of the twin divers who went out together in their boat. They found a new bed, with clear water. They gathered several dozen oysters and were preparing to come home. One went down for a last dive. He did not return. His brother dived to look for him. The water was clean and he could see for a long way, but he could not find his brother. He had gone. Completely vanished.'

'Yes, and there was the case of the lad who was asleep in his boat at the lakeside, and he vanished into thin air. His father woke to find him gone.'

'But he could have run away – got bored with the life and run off.'

'No, no-one ever saw him again. He was taken by the masked men.'

'What masked men?' asked a new diver.

'The Powerful One's masked guards. They wear black hooded cloaks and have no faces under their masks.'

'Have you ever seen these masked guards?' asked the new man.

'Yes, I have seen them. Out of the corner of my eye, I have seen them.'

'Me too,' said another.

The divers huddled together, frightening themselves.

'And have you ever seen The Powerful One?' asked the new diver.

'No-one sees her and returns to tell the tale,' said the oldest oyster diver.

Chapter Twenty-Six
The Pearl Diver

Jax was bound hand and foot. His eyes were covered with a cloth and he found he was gagged. He was being scrubbed by several hands, and he could not think what had happened to him. He remembered only the dive, a strong current which pulled him away from his boat, and being exhausted. He had tried to swim back to the canoe but could not find it straight away in the high waves. It must have been in a trough when he came up from the deep. He swam, pulled down by the heavy bag full of oysters. Suddenly he was scooped out of the sea by unseen hands. After that, nothing. Now he was being dried by a towel. He tried to call out, but could not.

The Powerful One was waiting to see the latest captive. The pearl diver was pushed into the chamber, still bound by the wrists and blindfolded. He walked with difficulty but was not injured as far as he could tell. His head was very sore and he was dizzy. He could smell turpentine.

'Let me see him,' ordered The Powerful One.

Someone undid his loincloth and it fell around his ankles. He felt terribly vulnerable, but strangely excited. He must be in the presence of The Powerful One. He felt his cock twitch and endeavoured to show it off to her, even though he was her captive. He stood proudly, his fine physique displayed to her. He had always been content with the size of his organ. He had never had any complaints, anyway. He puffed out his chest and pulled in his already flat stomach.

'Yes, he'll do,' came the verdict and he was led off.

Adam, who was painting The Powerful One, recognised the latest captive as the pearl diver. He did not say anything, but carried on applying paint to canvas. He was quietly planning his escape – and perhaps the diver could help.

Jax was given a bed and then chained to it, and his blindfold was removed. He found himself in a darkened chamber of stone, like a cave, with a small chink of light at one end. He tried to move but the shackles held him. He soon became accustomed to the gloom and saw that there were other men in the cave. There were about six youths, all natives of Monkey Island, he thought. They too were chained to their narrow beds. He felt indescribably tired and he closed his eyes and slept.

Angeline and Delilah opened their eyes and saw each other. They had fallen asleep after making love and had slept peacefully all night. They leant towards each other and kissed.

'It must be time to get up,' said Delilah.

'Time for love first, then we'll bathe and depilate each other,' said Angeline. She kissed the girl tenderly, causing her nipples to harden and her skin to soften. Delilah's dark eyes became darker and her legs opened wider to the princess's delicate caress.

'Oh, darlings! I do apologise for interrupting,' said Gertrude, who, without the company of her husband, was bored and had risen early. She was delighted that the princess and her friend did not leap up but stayed, their slender limbs entwined on the dishevelled bed. 'Do not let me disturb you, pray; I only wanted company.'

Princess Angeline felt sorry for her chaperone.

'Oh, poor Gertrude, do come over here and join us if you want.' She patted the bed between them and made room for the voluptuous woman. Gertrude did not need to be asked twice. She removed her red and green kimono and, naked but for a chiffon petticoat and a corselet of pink satin, demurely stepped into bed, as if it was the most natural thing in the world to do.

Delilah was enchanted with Gertrude's clothes, as she was with anything new. She exclaimed over the corselet. Gertrude's plump breasts rose like white moons over the top.

'Oh! How I wish I had breasts,' she said.

'Silly child, you have charming breasts,' purred Gertrude as Delilah examined her.

'No, I want big breasts, like yours. May I suck them?'

'Well, all right,' said Gertrude, glancing at the princess to see what she thought of this development.

The princess nodded encouragingly. 'Go on, darling, taste her breasts. They are charming, are they not?'

The copper-skinned native dancing girl delicately caressed the swelling bosoms, licking the cleft of her cleavage. Gertrude sighed happily. Angeline, meanwhile, pulled up the chiffon skirts of her chaperone's slip and slid her fingers into the gap between her plump white thighs. Gertrude sighed the more. She allowed her own fingers to caress the dusky dancer and found her willing to be touched. Delilah opened her legs and let Gertrude's hands press and fondle.

Gertrude's female companions made gentle love to her, and she delighted in the sweet touch of four hands, the natural perfume of hot bodies, the melange of sexual scents. Her mouth was invaded by sex-scented fingers. Her sex was penetrated by flickering tongues, and so was her anus. Her buttocks were spanked soundly and her sex lips swelled and opened.

'Time for the dildo, I think,' said Angeline quietly to Delilah, and the dancer reached over to pick up a long thick rod of rubber, which was shaped like a monstrous, ridged penis. All around its root were spiky baboon hairs tied in a ring. There were even mock balls, made out of rubber, attached to the base. It was a dildo the girls had played with and taunted each other with, but could not accommodate. It was huge.

Gertrude winced as the oiled rod was inserted slowly into her vagina by Delilah.

'Oh, my goodness! It is big. It is bigger than Jax. It is even bigger than Ric,' she sighed.

Delilah's eyes shone as she pushed the dildo into the older woman. It was attached to Delilah's waist and thighs by leather straps. She had the other end inside her own vagina, which was a much smaller version of the other. She sighed as she performed a pretend copulation with Gertrude. Angeline played with herself while she watched, content to simply stroke the smooth bellies of both partners and occasionally touch their private parts. Her own orgasm was reached by means of her own experienced digits. Gertrude and Delilah trilled their delight and moaned out loud as their spasms erupted and swept over their bodies.

Captain Ric and Hari were poring over the map that Isadora showed them. It showed the shape of the Lake of Lost Love and the sort of terrain that surrounded it. The landing stage where the pearl divers moored was indicated and the far shoreline known locally as the Land of The Powerful One. Behind the beach there were heavily forested hills with many hidden caves. It was here that the slaves were probably kept.

'We must carry our canoes from the beach to the lake. How long will that take?' asked Ric.

'Not long,' said Isadora. 'Half a day.'

'Will this stormy weather continue?' he asked her.

'It could last for days,' she said.

'Well, it can't be helped,' said Ric. 'We can't hang around for ever. We'll make a move tomorrow.'

'I'll find the diver who seems to know where to find The Powerful One,' said Isadora.

'I'm sure my wife knows where to find him,' said Ric.

Hari sighed and thought of Angeline. He wanted only to be with her again, and perhaps the little Delilah.

'I'll tell the men we are going into action on the morrow,' he said. 'They will be pleased to be doing something positive. This rain and wind is getting them down.'

Ric accompanied Isadora back to the dance academy and watched for a while as Kelila taught the students how to leap and twist and twirl fast in the air. Then he wandered back to where he thought he might find his wife, but she was not at the house. He supposed she was visiting her pearl diver.

Gertrude was indeed trying to find Jax. She had set off early, after her little dallying with the princess and Delilah, and was worried that he was not there. The waves were crashing on the narrow beach and the other divers were in the rough shelter, drinking a hot beverage.

She dared to enter, and asked where he was.

'Actually, he should have returned last night, but he did not,' said one man. 'It's bad on the lake. We're staying here.'

'Oh, dear me! What can have happened to him?' The men looked silently at her and said nothing. 'Well, I better be going,' she said, and hurried back through the storm, her disappointment turning to indignation then anger, then fear.

* * *

Next day, the king's army carried their canoes across the beach and through the forest dripping with heavy rain, the sorry sound of toucans clacking above and cawing crows black in their funereal feathers. They reached the lake shore and put their craft down in an orderly row. The divers, still shore bound, came out to see the soldiers.

'Where is the diver who is called Jax?' asked the captain.

'He is not here,' said a diver.

'Where is he?'

'We do not know, captain. He has disappeared. He went out diving two days ago and has not been seen since. It is not good.'

'Damn!' said Hari. 'He was to be our guide across the lake.'

'I will give gold to whoever guides us to the Land of The Powerful One,' said Ric, holding up a small chamois pouch of gold.

No-one moved or said anything.

'Come on now,' he cajoled. 'Don't you want this gold?' He opened the purse and poured the gold pieces on to his palm, where they glistened. No-one moved. 'Are you all cowards, then?' he taunted. 'Afraid of a woman?'

'Yes, we are,' said the oldest diver. 'And you would be, too, if you had any sense.'

The other divers laughed and shuffled back to their hut and their pipes and their banana wine.

The storm had not abated. Instead, the wind howled, sending the waves into mountainous peaks as far as they could see. The rain was coming at them in horizontal spears.

'We will go anyway,' said Ric. 'All right, men, launch the boats.' They heaved and shoved the heavy craft into the waves, then leapt aboard and started to paddle furiously. Hari was in the lead boat and Ric followed in the next craft.

* * *

190

Jax was being masturbated by a masked man in a hooded cloak. He was not shocked at what was happening to him, but he wished he could use his own hands to join in. Instead his hands were tied to a wooden beam above his head. His ankles were chained to rings in the floor. He was naked, having been bathed and oiled. His organ was distended and he was almost ready to ejaculate. Suddenly he realised that a metal ring had been placed at the root of his cock, and it was holding his organ in a vice-like grip, which meant that he could not come. The masked masturbater stopped his erotic torment and left the diver hanging and unsatisfied. The Powerful One opened the heavy door and stood immediately in front of Jax. He gulped. Never had he seen such a beautiful woman. Her blue-black skin glistened. Her thick curls surrounded a masked face. Only her wide mouth was visible. Her dark violet eyes gleamed through the narrow slits in the white feather mask. Her bare shoulders and full breasts rose above a garment of cream chamois which fitted her like a tight glove. It was laced in front from her crotch to her breasts, but had gaps where the laces were. Her hip bones and thighs gleamed with oil. Her buttocks were naked but for a thong of chamois, and her sex parts were visible through the gaping sides of the crotch part. Her long legs were encased in thigh-length, white leather boots. He could not help but stare at this vision of sexuality. She was like a dream creature, not real. Her body was perfect. She had in one hand a long whip.

'So, let's see your balls jump,' she said, and set about his thighs with the whip.

He was shocked at the suddenness of the attack and his flesh reddened as she struck. He stared at her heaving breasts. He saw the gap between her legs widen and glimpsed her sex parts. His eyes narrowed and his cock grew.

She grabbed his scrotum and fondled it. His cock stretched towards his belly.

'Good! He has vitality and vigour. Cut him down and bring him to me,' she ordered the guard.

Jax was unshackled and led into her presence in the next chamber, where she lounged on a low couch. Her gaping chamois drawers revealed her rouged sex lips. Her regal peaks rose above the bodice and the nipples poked out, stiff and rouged.

'Come here and make love to me,' she ordered.

'If you say so,' he agreed.

This was a bizarre slavery, he thought, and began to enjoy himself. He slipped his hands under her bodice and pulled out the luscious fruit, which he sucked and nibbled. She pushed him down between her legs and he sucked the proffered sex mouth each side of the chamois strip that divided the lips. His tongue slipped into her folds and curled around the proud clitoris. She shivered and came for the first time with him. He tried to untie the laces that hid her, but she would not let him, slapping him hard. He understood and turned her over, pressing his hand under the chamois strap to touch her bottom hole. It was a puckered, black cave, and his fingers probed. She came again. She turned over and took his erection – a purple-brown rod of hard flesh – into her. Her sex mouth held him tighter than any woman had held it before. He groaned as she sucked on his cock with her powerful muscles. He felt as if his cock was being pulled off. He yelled, but she did not stop. She came again, his cock deep inside her, before pushing him away. Then, realising his awful fate, he began sobbing. She laughed.

'Take him away and wash him,' she said, 'and bring me the other one – the artist.'

Chapter Twenty-Seven
Hidden River

The storm had abated and the sea was again calm and the colour of a kingfisher's feathers. The sun shone.

The royal yacht, and its gun, had been abandoned by Ric and Hari because they had understood the lake could not be reached by sea. Instead, the yacht's captain had it moored close by the pier where they had originally disembarked on Monkey Island. Gertrude found herself on the pier, the day after her husband and his army had sailed, dressed in her best blue gown, with her white corset tightly laced and her neat ankles showing under the frothy petticoat.

'Oh, captain, you are still here!' She pretended astonishment.

'Will you come aboard, ma'am?' he asked politely.

'Please.' She lifted her skirt, showing him her white-stockinged calf.

She remembered their dalliance on her trip over with Angeline and she demurely smiled as he took her hand.

'Will you take some refreshment in my cabin, ma'am?'

'Mmm, thank you, captain.' Her arm brushed his immaculate white uniform and her heartbeat quickened.

She was soon semi-naked, her skirts above her head,

her white-stockinged legs thrashing. He obliged her twice, and afterwards found that his uniform was ruined. She had insisted he keep it on, and his and her juices now decorated the trews.

'That was charming, thank you, captain,' she said.

Next day, it occurred to her to ask him if he could take her and her friends on a trip around the island. After all, there was nothing they could do to help the soldiers, and they were fidgety, just hanging around, with no men to entertain them.

So it was that Kelila, Isadora, Angeline, Delilah and Gertrude accompanied the yacht's captain on a voyage around Monkey Island. He was pleased to have the opportunity to show off the royal yacht's superior speed. Angeline and Delilah sat on the gun barrel on the foredeck and watched the shoreline.

'What's that?' asked Angeline, looking through the yacht's telescope.

'What? Where?'

'There,' she pointed. 'It's a river mouth, I think.'

The captain steered the yacht towards the narrow opening in the mangroves.

'Yes, it *is* a river,' he said.

'It might lead to the Lake of Lost Love,' said Isadora. 'Shall we try it?'

'If it gets no narrower or more shallow, we might make it,' said the captain.

The yacht nosed its way through the narrow channel, breaking roots and lianas as it did so. The trees closed in over their heads, and monkeys screeched at the big white beast invading their territory. The ship's company – all female except for the captain – were excited and exhilarated at the idea that they might have found a way to get the yacht and its powerful gun to the scene of the impending battle. They fanned themselves with coconut leaf fans and drank coconut milk.

'We should have brought more provisions. Shall we go back?' asked Gertrude anxiously.

'No, we must continue,' said the intrepid Angeline. 'The men need the gun.'

So the slow push continued through the thick overhanging branches and the tangling roots and weeds. Twice the screws stopped, completely tangled in weeds, and twice Kelila and Isadora leapt into the green water to cut it free. The captain was clearly impressed with the females' strength, ingenuity and courage. They were as good as any men he had had as crew, if not better.

Suddenly, the yacht was stuck in much thicker weed and could make no headway again.

'What shall we do?' asked Angeline.

'The only thing to do is to get out and pull it through,' said the captain.

The four women – Gertrude stayed in the boat to steer it – and the captain removed their clothes, climbed over the side into the muddy water and half swam, half walked, pulling and pushing to get the boat through the unyielding weeds. When they at last got the yacht through to a wider, more weed-free stream, they climbed back, filthy and exhausted.

'Oh, goodness me, what is that on your leg?' Gertrude pointed in horror at Angeline's bare, muddy thigh.

Kelila said, 'It's a leech.'

'Ugh!' said Angeline. 'Get it off me!'

'Oh, no, I have them all over me,' said Kelila.

'We all do,' said Isadora.

At the captain's instructions, Gertrude lit matches to heat the leeches so they released their hold on the delicious flesh and fell off. The crew dried themselves and dressed again to fortify themselves against the mosquitoes.

'Have some whiskey, ladies, it's the best thing,' said the captain, opening a bottle of single malt. 'That and a smoke will keep them off,' he told them, offering his cigarillos to the suffering women.

The river widened at last and the yacht slid through the dark, slimy waters faster now. They saw crocodiles floating like logs and shuddered at the thought that someone might have to go into the water again to fix the jammed rudder, but the journey continued without mishap. Green and pink parrots whistled from high branches; loud insect noises filled the humid air. The five friends had taken off most of their clothes again, so hot was it. Gertrude's bosoms glistened and she kept dabbing her cleavage. Kelila and Isadora were stripped down to their panties. Their breasts were proudly bared, with leather straps criss-crossing their upper bodies. Delilah and Angeline had little cotton slips barely covering their breasts and pubes. They sat on the gun barrel, their little legs either side, their bottoms showing. The captain was surrounded by heavenly bodies and he hummed happily to himself. The whiskey had worked its magic on the females and they were relaxed and leaning seductively against each other.

'What weapons do you have on board?' asked Isadora, already planning ahead.

'Apart from the gatling gun, do you mean?'

'Yes.'

'Well, there are several cutlasses and daggers and a musket.'

'Good. Fetch them, captain, and we will clean them and make them ready in case we need to use them.'

The captain complied with her demands, hypnotised by her swelling pectorals and her fine breasts. The redhead was magnificent, he thought.

'Show us how to use the gatling gun,' said Angeline.

'With pleasure, Princess, but I think, if you allow me to suggest it, that perhaps Mademoiselle Kelila and Mademoiselle Isadora would be better able to handle it, if the occasion arises.'

'Nonsense!' said the offended princess. 'You will see that we are not purely decorative.'

Gertrude was the least useful member of the female crew, not knowing how to clean a musket or sharpen a knife, but she kept the crew happy with cups of black tea and fresh fruit plucked from the trees they swept past. The voyage continued through the meandering stream, which was sluggish in its flow. They saw crocodiles edging into the water from the banks. There were howls of wild beasts coming from the forest on each side. The trees were thick and dense, and there was as yet no sign of the Lake of Lost Love.

Meanwhile, the king's army still paddled in the flotilla of canoes across the now more calm lake. Then, suddenly, they found the pearl diver's abandoned canoe, floating upside down.

'He could have drowned in the storm,' said Hari.

'Maybe,' said Ric.

They took it in tow and carried on. The map that Isadora had drawn showed a spit of land covered in low scrub and acacia trees. Beyond that was the shore that marked the beginning of the Land of The Powerful One. The spit was reached and passed. The men were silent as they paddled, oars muffled, to the steep sloping beach. They pulled the canoes up on to the lakeside, and armed with knives, daggers and shields, they crept forward into the dark forest.

The royal yacht, its shiny paint scratched from the long thorny branches that dragged at it from either side, pulled slowly through the narrow channel. Suddenly, there it was, widening out before them – the Lake of Lost Love.

'You were right, Princess, this is it,' said Kelila. 'We are on the side away from our village, the uninhabited shore.'

'Is it the Land of The Powerful One?' whispered Angeline.

'Yes, we are there.'

Night was falling and with dusk came the mosquitoes, biting every bit of exposed flesh. The friends quickly donned their discarded garments. They did not light the yacht's lamps. Instead they followed a course set by the captain along the coast, close in, but not too close. They kept their eyes peeled for a sight of the war canoes or any sign of life.

Adam was in The Powerful One's arms. His poor, tired cock was pummelling inside her belly, and she rode him without rest. He sighed with exhaustion.

'If you are tired, I shall fetch another youth,' she barked.

'Please do, O Powerful One. I need to pass water, among other things.'

'Take him away,' she ordered a guard, 'and fetch another.'

Adam was unceremoniously removed from her presence. In the urinal cave he was drenched with cold water to lose his erection and he relieved himself. The guard who had brought him back to the cave had left him alone, unchained. He looked out of the urinal cave and saw that the guards were talking animatedly and were not watching him. He slipped out silently into the darkening forest.

The pearl diver was once again between the long legs of The Powerful One. He lapped at her juicy private parts, parting the lips with his tongue and nibbling the erect bud. She held his hair in a knot and yanked on his head. He was rubbing himself, though he had learnt that he could not ejaculate until she allowed it. Other slaves sucked her breasts. Her bottom hole had a slender prick inside it, attached to which was a swarthy youth. His penis was exactly the shape she required in her anus;

long and curved slightly, like a long banana, and not too thick. Jax could feel its pressure on the outer side of her tunnel with his tongue. His fingers were on her pubis, slapping at the swollen flesh. She was having multiple orgasms, her legs stiff, her face and chest flushed. Her wide, red mouth opened and her throat was an endless dark tunnel.

Adam was totally in the dark. But he was free! He crept slowly from tree trunk to tree trunk, looking for a liana root to climb. He found one and began his ascent, hand over hand, up into the tree, using the swinging root as a rope. He thought of his little Trixie-Jane and climbed higher. A baboon howled with anger at the interruption and leapt away into the dark. Adam rested in the vee of two branches, frightened, his heart banging in his chest, his cock sore. He listened and heard shouts. The guards were yelling something but he could not catch what it was. He supposed it was to announce that he had escaped. He jammed himself more securely into the narrow space. An hour later, the sound of shouting was fainter, but he could still hear men's voices. He slept briefly, but awoke to find a large, thick snake slithering over his arm. He froze, unbreathing. It slithered slowly over him and away. The forest was dark. The high, thick canopy hid even the gleam from the stars.

Ric's canoes were hidden in the low brush of the lakeside beach. They nearly missed them, but Angeline's sharp eyes caught the glint from a mother of pearl handled oar – it was Hari's canoe. She had given him the oar as an anniversary gift.

'There! Our men are there. Look!' The captain hove to.

'Be quiet, everyone,' said Kelila. 'Listen.'

They listened. All they heard was the hoot of tree frogs crooning and the screeching of insects. Monkeys hallooed to each other and a fox yowled.

'I'm frightened,' said Gertrude. 'What are we going to do?'

'Do not worry, ma'am, I will allow no harm to befall you.' The captain took her arm protectively.

'Can you get us in any closer?' asked Isadora. She had heard a splashing in the water and did not fancy the swim ashore in the dark.

The captain threw a lead line over the side and drew it up again. He moved the yacht forward a little using paddles and tried the lead line again.

'It's no good, we're going to get stuck on the mud if we go in any closer. I ought to take it out a bit further from the shore. If we see the enemy we need to take aim from further away.'

'All right, captain, you do that,' said Angeline. They helped push the yacht into deeper water with the oars. 'We shall wait and see when we are needed,' decided Angeline. 'We certainly don't want to be in the way.'

'No, absolutely not,' agreed Gertrude gratefully. She went below to make some tea.

Chapter Twenty-Eight
King Aristide Has a Little Problem

On the Isle de Paradis life went on without the menfolk. At the Forbidden Apple Jezebel had to do her own gardening and cooking. She had given most of her girls leave to go home and told them only to come back when they had notice that the men had returned. She kept Sylva with her to help with the everyday running of the establishment and to deal with the fishermen, her only customers.

'Sylva, go and dig up some potatoes for our dinner,' Jezebel bellowed.

'Get them yourself, you lazy old bag!' Sylva said under her breath, but took up the fork and did as she was bid.

It was dull work, these days, at the Forbidden Apple, with only the drunken fishermen to service. She missed the excitement of having different men every day. She enjoyed being flattered and petted by Ric and the soldiers. She wondered how they were all getting on. Had they rescued Adam yet? She was gathering the waxy white vegetables into the basket when she saw Trixie-Jane running towards her.

'Sylva, where is Jezebel? They need help at the palace.'

'What is it? What's the matter?'

'The king is sick. The high priestess has been to see him and says he needs extreme measures to cure him.'

'What on earth does that mean?' said Sylva. She took the anxious handmaiden to the kitchen. 'Trixie-Jane is here, Madame Jezebel.'

'Hello there, poppet, what can I do for you?' The slatternly brothel keeper wore a tattered sarong around her waist. Her large bosoms flapped on her arms and got in the way of her food preparation.

'Madame Jezebel, it is the king. He is sick. The High Priestess Viva needs your help to cure him.'

'My help?' Jezebel wiped her hands on her soiled sarong.

'Will you come now and see her, please? She asked me to fetch you.'

'Wait, I better wash and change first,' Jezebel grumbled. She was curious as to what Viva wanted her to do.

Trixie-Jane and Sylva chatted about the missing Adam, and Trixie-Jane was in tears when Jezebel reappeared, looking slightly less untidy. Her hair had been bundled high. Her face was covered in pink powder which did not tone with her olive complexion one bit and her lip rouge was smeared badly, but at least her clothes were clean. She wore an elaborate tight-waisted gown of bright green, its skirt in flounces and covered in bows. Her bosoms had been encased in a boned corset, which pushed them up almost under her chin.

'Carry on with the cooking, Sylva, there will be a rush for lunch soon,' she said, and went off grumbling with the unhappy Trixie-Jane.

At the palace, Queen Clementine sat by her husband's bed. He was lying, looking very miserable. She looked anxiously at Viva, who was waving her hands and moaning strange incantations over the king. The high priestess stopped her rituals and sat down.

'When did this problem arise? Tell me again,' said Viva to the queen.

'Well, we have been having successful marital relations for some time now, due to the helpful contributions of a handmaiden and a youthful manservant.'

'You mean Joshua and his little sister?'

'Yes,' said the queen, dabbing at her eyes. 'But poor Aristide seems to have lost interest again. Nothing we do seems to arouse him.' She sobbed quietly.

'Pull yourself together,' said the high priestess. 'Blubbing won't help him or you.'

The guard let in Jezebel and Trixie-Jane to the king's private bedchamber.

'Oh, Jezebel, I am in dire straits,' moaned the king.

'I'm sorry to hear that, Your Highness,' said the soft-hearted whore. 'What can I do for you?'

'Viva seems to think I need special stimulation to get my pecker up,' said the king, sadly. 'I can't do a thing with it.' He lifted the white Egyptian cotton sheet to reveal his sad, droopy penis, shrivelled up smaller than it had ever been.

Jezebel leant forward to get a better look. 'Yes, I see what you mean,' she said.

'Can you help?' said the high priestess, disdainfully. Viva had never approved of the brothel keeper or her bar girls, and she had insisted that Angeline should not associate with Sylva. But now she realised that the king probably needed the special talents of Jezebel to give him back his virility.

'I'll give it a try. What is it worth?'

'Your reward will be the knowledge that you helped the man who gave you freedom,' said Viva, sternly.

Jezebel did not need to be reminded of her debt to King Aristide. He had forgiven her past activities as a slave-mistress and had allowed her to live in peace on Isle de Paradis, and even set up her establishment with

Samson and Bartolem. He was a good, kind ruler, she knew, and she was grateful.

'You are right, Viva, I am sorry to have even suggested it,' she said. 'So, what exactly do you want me to do?'

Viva took Jezebel into the antechamber to talk privately and they were there for some time.

When Jezebel got back to the Forbidden Apple, Sylva was hot and bothered from all the cooking she had had to do on her own. There were five fishermen sprawled around the yard table drunk already. They had eaten the rabbit stew and potatoes that the girl had provided and now they wanted sex.

'All right, give me a chance,' said the harassed bar girl. 'Madame, thank goodness you are back; I need help with this lot.'

'No, I haven't got time for mere fishermen today,' said Jezebel, sweeping by in a swirl of dusty petticoats. 'I have been summoned to make love to the king.'

'Oh, really?' said the disbelieving Sylva. 'Do you mean I have got to service all these alcoholics on my own?'

'I do mean that,' said the brothel keeper.

She went to her bedroom and found the equipment she needed for her royal duties.

'I'll be back as soon as I can cure his malady,' she said to the astonished Sylva.

'What malady has the king got?' asked Sylva.

'His Highness cannot keep it up,' said Jezebel, 'but don't tell anyone.'

The fishermen catcalled after the blowsy woman, blowing her kisses and suggesting very rude things.

Sylva threw the pot at one of the men. 'Blast and bugger!' she raged.

It was two hours later before she could call her time her own again, and she was exhausted.

'It's not fair,' she said. 'Angeline has gone off on a dancing trip; Trixie-Jane has got a jammy job at the palace. Jezebel doesn't do a thing around here, and I get all the rubbish and mess to clean up, as well as the riffraff to entertain. It isn't fair!'

Back at the palace, Jezebel was given a chamber of her own in which to wash, dress and prepare herself. She was even lent the queen's handmaiden to help her. Trixie-Jane was fascinated by the madame of the brothel. She had heard all sorts of stories about her, of course. Now she was in a position to find out if they were true.

'Trixie-Jane, my armpit hair needs combing, dear. Will you do it, please? And then my pubic hair.'

Trixie-Jane had helped bathe the plump woman's arms and legs, her heavy buttocks and her private parts. She had been shocked at the amount of pubic hair there was between her legs. It was a vigorous growth of black curls and it extended up her belly and down her thighs. And then there was the tattoo at the top of her right thigh. It was of a dragon. Trixie-Jane had heard from various people that Jezebel had a tattoo and now she admired it.

'How did you get this tattoo, Madame Jezebel?' asked the cheeky handmaiden.

'It came with the job, dearie. I was for two years a slave-mistress on a slave island. It was badge of office, so to speak.'

Trixie-Jane took ages over Jezebel's bouncing breasts, fascinated by their size.

Then Jezebel said, 'I think I should trim my pubic hair a bit. What do you think, dear?'

'Well, the queen is usually depilated completely,' Trixie-Jane said, by way of suggestion.

'Oh, no, we don't want anything the queen has got. That is just the point. The king needs something different.'

'I see,' said the handmaiden. She had been rather sad lately that the king had not been able to get an erection. Her games with him in the forest hut had come to an end. He had no enthusiasm for anything she had to offer. She was worried that she would lose her very easy and delightful position as royal handmaiden if she did not please the king. Queen Clementine had had her hands full with Joshua, and was not too interested in her either. Trixie-Jane had been preoccupied lately, ever since the news that Adam had disappeared. She was desperately unhappy without him and she had not given of her best to the royal couple. She felt sorry for the king. He had always been kind to her. She particularly enjoyed the spanking sessions when she bent over his lap and he spanked her firm little bottom and stroked her swollen sex parts, calling her a naughty girl. She grew warm now at the thought of his big hand on her privates.

'Come on, girl, find the scissors. I want a trim, just a little trim. Cut it in a heart shape, will you. Do you think you can manage that?' Jezebel had let herself go lately, since her menfolk had gone to war. She had always been a slut, and now she had every opportunity to indulge her carefree style of dress and toilet. Her nail polish was always scuffed. Her fingernails were dirty and snagged.

Trixie-Jane could see that she had her work cut out to clean up Jezebel and make her presentable for the royal bed. She scraped and buffed, varnished and shone, cut and shaved, scrubbed and polished, until, at last, Jezebel was transformed into a softly shining, still fat, of course, but wholesome-looking whore. Her hair was tied into becoming curls on her head, her make-up was subtle and her pubic hair was a perfect heart. She refused the scent that the handmaiden offered.

'I prefer my own perfume, thank you all the same,' she said, 'and you will learn, young miss, that men prefer your body scent to any artificial stimulation.'

'Really?' said the girl, eager to learn any tricks. The queen was a good employer but not very knowledgeable when it came to subtleties. Her idea of dressing up for the king in bed consisted of wearing her corset and stockings. He had not complained, of course, but it certainly wasn't doing anything for him lately, was it?

'Oh, I could teach you a thing or two about men,' Jezebel said, smiling wickedly.

'Would you, please?' said Trixie-Jane, mindful that one day, if Adam, the love of her heart, ever returned safely, she would need to know how to woo him, win him and keep him.

'I didn't say I would, only that I could, and I've got important matters to deal with.' A sad look appeared on Trixie-Jane's face. 'Come now and watch if you want – if the king doesn't mind,' she offered in a softer voice, clearly regretting her harshness.

'Oh, thank you!' cried Trixie-Jane gratefully.

The brothel keeper now had to dress. Jezebel had brought a large bag of strange garments with her. They had them all out on the floor.

'What is that?' said the innocent handmaiden.

'It's a little number I made for special occasions. Let me have it.'

Trixie-Jane helped the matronly Jezebel climb into the arrangement of black leather straps and a buckled corset which left her sex parts bare and her bottom sticking out. It was tightly laced up the back. Jezebel's amazing breasts were teased into the straps, so they were held high and pressed together, the cleavage deeply defined. Most of her flesh was disguised under the leather, but the interesting bits were not left to the imagination.

'You look wonderful, Madame Jezebel,' said the hand-maiden, standing back and admiring the impressive figure.

'Yes, I need boots now. Get them, child – and the whip – then all will be ready.'

'A whip, madame?'

'Yes, dear, hurry. The poor king will be waiting.'

Trixie-Jane found the bull whip coiled up like a sleeping snake in the carpet bag. She handed it to the magnificent figure before her. Jezebel looked blowsy and sluttish no more. She looked powerful, formidable, terrifying, yet ultimately sexual. Her dragon tattoo seemed to writhe its tail as she moved slowly, tottering on the high heels of the thigh-length boots.

'Will this outfit cure the king, do you think?' asked Trixie-Jane, who was quite damp between the thighs.

'Let's say it will help things along a bit,' laughed Jezebel. 'Come on, dear, let's see what we can do for the poor old thing.'

Adam had decided he had to move from his tree-top hideout. Dawn would come soon and he would be discovered if he left flight till then. He clambered down, spearing himself on spiky branches and tearing his loincloth to shreds. He dropped the last few feet to the ground and crouched there for a moment, listening. He could hear distant voices still, but they seemed to be going away rather than getting nearer. Which way to flee? He needed to get to the lake and find a way of getting across it. He had not had a chance to talk to the diver, so he did not know if his canoe was on the shore. But he assumed that there had to be boats in the Land of The Powerful One.

He started to run from clump of bamboo to tree trunk, finding shelter where he could but moving in one direction, he hoped. Adam was weary but desperate for freedom. He blundered on through the forest, treading softly, his eyes straining for signs of movement.

In another part of the forest the king's army eased their way silently. They were camouflaged with black and yellow stripes of paint on their faces and bodies. They merged with the forest foliage. Birds began to call; herons and snowy egrets stirred. Soon it would be dawn.

Chapter Twenty-Nine
Jezebel Proves Her Worth

Jezebel and the handmaiden knocked on the door of the king's bed chamber.

'Come in, do, Jezebel – and you, dear,' said Clementine, who still looked concerned. She wore her best negligee, a lacy, black swirl of frills. The king sat, morose and drooped over a chess board, where the queen had been showing her superiority yet again.

'Oh, hello there, Jezebel. I say, you do look smart,' he said, smiling, as he saw her interesting ensemble.

'Do you want me here?' said Clementine, who had been desperate to get to bed and play with herself, but when she had seen the brothel keeper's bizarre outfit had changed her mind and rather wanted to be part of whatever was about to happen.

'It is up to the king, I suppose,' said Jezebel, in a non-committal way.

'Oh, I don't know . . . Yes, Pumpkin, do stay. You might be able to help.'

'Might learn something, you mean,' laughed Jezebel, stroking the king's knee.

'Well, it's a sad pass when my pecker won't stay up

for my beautiful wife, isn't it!' said the king, patting the queen's hand.

'Don't even think about it, King Aristide. We'll soon have you begging for it,' said Jezebel.

'Really?' Queen Clementine raised an eyebrow. She was impressed with the transformation of the brothel keeper. Trixie-Jane had certainly done a marvellous job.

'Will you stay, too, child?' asked the king.

'Yes, please, sire, I think it would be good for my education,' said the handmaiden.

'Come and sit by me then, my little one,' said the queen, making room for her on the couch. Jezebel continued stroking the king's knee through his purple silk kimono.

'I think a blanket bath would be a good start. Fetch water and sponges and towels. Chop, chop!' Jezebel clapped her hands to Trixie-Jane and the girl ran to obey.

'She has been a useful handmaiden, then?' asked Jezebel pointedly.

'Oh, yes,' said Clementine, blushing. 'She has been very helpful, up until recently.'

'What happened recently to change things, do you think?'

'Well, the men went off to war and Adam's disappearance has worried Trixie-Jane immensely, hasn't it, dear?'

The handmaiden nodded sadly.

'What about you, King Aristide, what has upset you?'

'Can't say, really, I wish I knew. Total lack of interest in our usual fun and games, I'm afraid.'

Jezebel had all the while been stroking the king's legs and thighs, slipping her hand inside the hem of his kimono. His prick remained soft and flaccid, leaning sadly on his thigh like a moping dog, curled up and miserable.

'Dramatic action is needed,' said Jezebel. So saying, she stood, then ordered the queen and the handmaiden to tie the king to the wall chains.

'Strip him first, will you,' she said.

'Oh, darling, do you mind?' the queen tentatively asked her husband.

'I am in charge now. Do as I say,' ordered the madame.

'Better do as she says, Clem,' said the king.

He was stripped of his royal dressing gown and strapped ignominiously, his legs apart, his belly almost touching the sharp coral wall. His arms were above his head.

Jezebel stood a few feet away from him, magnificent in the black leather, cracking the whip.

'Oh, no, Jezebel, don't beat me,' he whimpered.

'It is for your own good, Your Highness. You have been a naughty boy.' She struck the first blow, a light lick of the whip end on his right buttock. It flew so fast the queen did not see the whip move.

'Aagh!'

'Naughty, naughty, naughty!' Jezebel got into the swing of things and found her target each time.

The royal bottom was marked with red lines, like a noughts and crosses game written on his flesh.

Clementine held Trixie-Jane close to her bosom. She was aroused, even if the king was not. He still had a good figure for a man of his years. His buttocks were firm, tight bundles of muscle. His skin was a dark honey colour, clear of imperfections, apart from the whip marks. He had one long scar down his side – a battle scar from many years ago, which only made him more attractive in the queen's eyes. He had not run to fat, as many men did in middle years, but was nicely made and had a flat stomach. She had not examined him coldly, like this, for a long time. She saw that he was still a very attractive man. If only he could retain an erection, she would be happy. Clementine hugged the girl to her and casually played with her breasts.

Trixie reciprocated, as was usual, with a tender caress of her royal highness's titties. The two women were therefore happily entwined while the poor king suffered the torments of Jezebel's punishment. She struck him on the legs and thighs and back, but mostly kept the whip end aimed at his bottom. He flinched at every stroke, but had stopped complaining.

'Better turn him around so he can see what you are doing,' ordered Jezebel.

Clementine and Trixie-Jane turned him and chained him again. His cock was, interestingly enough, slightly swollen. It still hung on his thigh, but it looked thicker.

'Stand back, or go and carry on with your *tendresses*,' encouraged the dominatrix.

Clementine thankfully returned to the couch with the handmaiden, who was undressed completely now. She sat on Clementine's lap and allowed herself to be caressed between the legs. King Aristide watched the loving couple. His cock grew longer and twitched.

Jezebel whipped him on the thigh, close to his balls. A red mark appeared immediately. Jezebel took a blindfold from her belt and tied it around his eyes.

'You are having naughty feelings, you bad boy!' She whipped him again. His cock swelled and rose. The queen was aroused by the sight of her husband, helpless; and the fierce figure of the erotically attired woman, her nipples sticking out of the leather cups. Jezebel's body was getting hot and her perspiration began to flow. Her heady sweat filled the chamber. It was an aphrodisiac, as she had said, and not only to the king but to the two tenderly kissing women, clasped in each other's arms.

They were pressing hands on to each other's pubic bones and fingers had disappeared into dark, secret places.

Jezebel drew closer to the king and took his stirring cock in her leather-clad hand. Her sweat filled his nostrils. He could see nothing but he was aware of her breasts and belly pressed against him. Her tongue was on the end of his cock now, her hands still pulling and squeezing. His balls were licked and stroked by leather. His cock was in her mouth, being tugged, almost swallowed. His buttocks and thighs were on fire. Suddenly his cock was abandoned, and he was left, desperately eager to finish off what had been started, but helpless.

Jezebel took off his blindfold and allowed him to watch the two affectionate females on the couch. His wife had her legs in the air and Trixie-Jane was kneeling between them, her dark head buried in her groin. Clementine sobbed in ecstasy.

Aristide saw his wife stiffen and tremble all over.

Jezebel oiled the king's organ and rubbed hard with her leather gloves. His cock lengthened and stiffened. His wife and handmaiden roused themselves in time to see the still-helpless king being milked by the erstwhile slave mistress. He was enjoying it, that was obvious, and they watched as she expertly brought him to orgasm.

'You see,' said Jezebel later to the queen, 'you mustn't always let him have his own way. You must be in control of things sometimes – make him feel how powerful you are and let him be the weak one. Men like to be dominated in bed – most men, that is.'

'I see, yes I do see,' said the queen, 'but I am not terribly good at being dominating, Jezebel. Do you think you could help me do what you seem able to do so well?'

'We'll try tomorrow, shall we? I need food and drink now,' said the ex-slave mistress, back in her old persona. She strode off, her back straight and her breasts proudly sticking out before her, rock-like. Her big bottom swung and shuddered under the black leather corset.

Next morning, Jezebel made use of the handmaiden again to help with her toilet. She had to agree that Trixie-Jane was very good at massage, bathing, rouging and dressing hair. She thought maybe she could train Sylva to do the same for her at the Forbidden Apple. It was wonderful to feel pampered. She enjoyed dressing up with the help of the handmaiden. Today, she wore a red satin boned corset which drew in her waist and pushed her bosoms up high so they bulged over the lacy top. Her suspenders held up black stockings, leaving inches of soft olive flesh swelling at the thigh. Her knickers were of red satin too, and crotchless, her black pubic hair visible at the slit in the shiny fabric. She wore impossibly high-heeled black boots, laced to the ankle.

'My hair is a mess, dear. What can I do with it?' said Jezebel.

'It is odd, isn't it?' said the handmaiden, consolingly. 'I often have bad hair days, and I just have to wash it and start again.' The kind-hearted Trixie-Jane washed the heavy mane of black tangled curls and dried it with a soft towel before combing in coconut oil scented with jasmine. The result was stunning. Jezebel admired herself in the mirror. Her usual 'dragged through a bush backwards' look was replaced with a sleek, smooth, shiny crown.

'You are a gem, darling, you are really.' She hugged the girl. 'How would you like to come and look after me instead of the royal couple?' It was a fine joke, and they both laughed.

They reported at the royal bedchamber before breakfast.

'Middle-aged men often have good erections first thing in the morning,' said Jezebel knowingly.

But the king had no such thing. His sleeping member sat sad and uninterested as his wife tried to coax it to get up. She had been encouraged by Jezebel's performance the day before and was hopeful of an immediate change in developments, but poor Aristide could do nothing with it.

Clementine took the limp member into her hands and rubbed hard.

'Oh, it's like a schoolboy's little prick,' she said endearingly and kissed it.

But the king took the innocent remark as an insult, and became, if anything, even softer.

She put the prick between her warm thighs and rubbed herself on it. It brought to mind her childhood when she had played with a boy cousin. The naughty thought excited her, but still Aristide was bored.

'Come in,' said Clementine, and the brothel keeper entered, followed by Trixie-Jane. The handmaiden wore a fetching little shift of white silk chiffon, which left very little to the imagination. Her hair was wreathed in flowers freshly picked from the royal garden, still damp from the dew.

'Ah, Jezebel!' The king perked up immediately. 'What an interesting ensemble you are wearing this morning.'

'Thank you, sire.'

'And you look charming too, my dear,' he said to Trixie-Jane, who had jumped on to the bed and kissed the king and queen fondly. He patted her little bottom, lifting the short hem to get his hand on her flesh. She snuggled into his embrace, enjoying the big hand so close to her private parts.

'Your Royal Highness has broken my first rule,' said Jezebel imperiously.

'What's that?' he asked.

'No touching unless I give permission. You will be punished for that.'

'Oh, really, then I'll touch a little more if I'm to be punished for it, and get good value,' he laughed. So saying, he stroked the handmaiden's newly shaved pussy, admiring the softness of the skin and the smoothness leading to the slit in the peach. She lay back across the bed, her face close to the queen's, while the king toyed with her bottom half. Queen Clementine kissed Trixie-Jane and cupped her little breasts and the handmaiden dutifully stroked Clementine's melon-like bosoms.

'All very pretty, but you must be punished, both of

you. If you will not follow my instructions you cannot hope for a lasting cure.'

The three women chained the king to the wall rings as before and then Trixie-Jane and Jezebel strapped the queen to the wall in a similar manner. She was clearly aroused at the feeling of helplessness; her intense feelings showed in her erect nipples. She wore only a pair of loose pantaloons, with a gap in the middle, which hid her dimpled knees and full belly but showed her small waist and her plump pussy. Her breasts, heavy and proud, were held up by straps across her chest, attached to the wall rings. She was unable to move. She and Aristide faced their tormentor.

Chapter Thirty
The King's Cure

The erstwhile slave mistress was enjoying herself again. She had not had this much fun for a long time. Here she was in the royal palace, dressed to the nines, having the time of her life. She was eating food that was even better than Bartolem prepared. She was hob-nobbing with the royals, and she had her own handmaiden. If only she had some men! The king would have to do. She had not yet fucked a king. She would make the most of this golden opportunity.

Her whip was raised and she struck – first the queen's thighs and then the king's. They cried out in instinctive terror. The whip she used today was a shorter version of the other. It had several knotted strands coming from the main stem, all plaited and shiny. The strands of leather stung in tiny pin-pricks of pain. The queen's white skin reddened quickly. Her knickers were torn by the whip and hung in rags from her fair thighs. Her sweat made the cotton cling to her round belly and delineated her cleft peach. Her bosoms heaved and swelled under the restraint of the leather straps. The king's organ grew with every stroke of the whip on his wife's thighs.

'Yes, sire, you are coming along well,' said Jezebel, her sweat spraying as she lifted her arm yet again.

The room was full of the scent of the three women and the male, a sweet, sour melange. Trixie-Jane had been ordered to play with the king's member if it looked like flagging, but it didn't. However, that didn't stop her enthusiastically tugging the swollen head between her little fingers and rubbing his brown balls whenever she got a chance. She was also given a long peacock feather to tickle the privates of Queen Clementine. Her hips writhed and her belly strained towards the trembling feather. She came twice in this manner, but the king had not got near his climax – although his erection was solid.

'Now, I want to try a little experiment,' said Jezebel. 'Let us see if the king can service all of us, one after the other. Me first.' She drew close to the king and pressed herself against his belly. The truth was she was so frustrated, she needed a cock inside her as soon as possible.

She took his royal rod in her hands and rubbed it on her satin corset. She leant over him and pressed the cock between her big breasts. It grew harder. She inserted it between her legs and pushed against him, holding the chains that held his hands. Her legs wrapped around his waist and her feet pressed against the wall. His cock withdrew and glistened before plunging between the red-rouged lips. Her pubic hair shone with their juices.

Trixie-Jane tickled faster with the feather and Clementine squirmed passionately. King Aristide called out in a sob of satisfaction and Jezebel writhed and cried.

'Is it my turn now to have him in me?' said the queen, after a rest from the feather.

'Look at him! I think not – not yet,' said Jezebel. 'You'll have to wait a good while, Your Highness.'

'Perhaps next month, Clem?' said the king, hopefully.

* * *

Back on Monkey Island the army was surrounding the caves. Several guards had been slain, and not one of them had seemed to be prepared for attack. But one man they had kept alive. When Samson offered to tear out his arms and legs, he was suddenly eager to talk and tell them what they wanted to know. They tied his arms behind him and kept him to the front, so if any arrows should come their way, he would be the first victim. Hari and Ric led separate squadrons of men. Joshua and Tom were with Prince Hari, their faces hidden under the mud-coloured make-up. Samson and Bartolem were part of Ric's squadron.

Adam, meanwhile, was heading away, he thought, from the Land of The Powerful One. He had been walking, or stumbling, along, torn by the long thorns of thick bamboos, for hours. The sun had come up and low rays pierced the gloom of the forest where a tree had fallen. He was still searching for the lake, where he hoped he would find a way of escaping to another shore. He rested for a moment on a log and examined his wounds. His loincloth came in useful as a bandage for his thighs, which had been sorely cut, and his chest, which was pitted with small abrasions. Leeches had attached themselves to his flesh and he could not get them off. He had no salt or matches with him. He had nothing with him to help him survive, and he was fast becoming exhausted. He needed water – and soon.

His head sank thankfully on to a mossy branch and he closed his eyes, just for a moment.

Ric and Hari and their men crept through the jungle on two fronts. They knew they could not be too far from the cave where the slaves were kept. The captive soldier grew nervous and warned them of the hooded, masked men, who were indestructible, as was their mistress, The Powerful One, or so he said.

The Paradisian army closed in on the cave where most of the captive slaves were held. They stormed it, slaying the masked guard outright, even though he brandished a huge sword which shone and gleamed its sharpness as it flashed through the air. But when they pulled aside the mask and hood to see the face of the guard, there was no-one inside. He had vanished into thin air. This event terrified all the soldiers who had witnessed it and they began muttering among themselves.

Ric and Hari ordered their anxious men to free the chained slaves within the cave who were crying in happiness at being found at last by their own people.

'Adam is not here.' The sad truth was admitted at last, when all the youths had been unshackled.

'Then where is he?' said Hari.

Each youth was questioned, and each gave a different story as to the physical appearance of The Powerful One. Some named her the fairest creature in the world, others said she was dark as nightmares. Some said she was tall as a pawpaw tree and had six breasts, like a bitch. Some said her hair writhed on its own, with no wind blowing it, and her clitoris grew like a man's penis. And her breasts were bigger than water melons. They all loved and feared her; hated and desired her.

'Is Adam with her?' asked Hari.

'She is with the pearl diver,' said one.

'Jax? So he is here, too; not drowned?' said Ric. 'Gertrude will be pleased.'

'He is as good as drowned, poor man; he is being sucked up by her and blown out in bubbles,' said another brawny youth, whose cock was sore and swollen.

'You speak with feeling, my man,' said Hari.

'Is she so terrifying, this Powerful One?'

'Yes, indeed, she is more than that. We are in her thrall; in her power for ever, I fear.'

'And do you not have loved ones to return to?' asked the prince.

'Yes, we do, O Prince, but we will never forget the demands of this she-devil.'

'Show us where we might find The Powerful One,' demanded the prince.

The youths were first put out of their extreme discomfort by drenching them in water to cool and shrink their cocks, and they were able to remove the rings that kept them stiff.

'I never want another erection in my life,' said one youth, rubbing himself.

The prince and Ric chose three of the most intelligent-looking youths and made them lead them to the palace of The Powerful One.

Jax was close to exhaustion. He was fucked to within an inch of his life. He sobbed for mercy and at last she was bored with his thick member.

'Take him. I cannot stand the rolling of his eyes into his head. It is off-putting,' she said. 'Bring back the artist and one or two others.'

The masked men carried the diver away, his legs dragging under him, his still-erect penis purple and swollen.

When they were halfway to the cave they were surprised by Ric's soldiers, who captured them with no trouble and took the weight of the exhausted pearl diver.

When Jax recognised his saviour he smiled wanly.

'Where is the prince's manservant, do you know?' asked the captain.

'I was to be replaced by him now. He should be in the cave,' said Jax.

'No, he is not there. Maybe he has escaped.'

'What about The Powerful One? Shall we go back for her?' said Hari.

The men were still fearful of the legend, and they now held tight to the captured masked guards, too frightened to tear off their hoods in case they too disappeared.

'No need, if Adam is not with her,' said Ric.

'We'll spread out and search the forest for Adam.'

The two hooded men were tied up and left under a tree. No-one had dared lift their masks.

The forest was in a perpetual dusk as the sunlight hardly ever penetrated the thick growth of ferns and bamboo, lianas and immensely tall trees. No animals moved on the ground and no butterflies glimmered. All life was higher in the tree tops, in the sunny canopy. Here on the dark, humid ground only the men slipped like shadows, and the dark-loving beetles and ants and creeping, crawling, blind beasts.

When they found Adam he had been cocooned in a spun web by a flesh-eating spider. He was untangled from its sticky threads and given water to sip. He was hardly conscious. He only knew he was safe, or he was dreaming that he was safe, which was the same thing. He had also dreamed that The Powerful One had carried him back to her lair, and had gathered him into her warm arms and was hugging him tight. He woke with an erection. He was being placed in a canoe.

Angeline and her companions were bored. They were hot and cross with anxiety and inaction. Gertrude and the captain had gone below to discuss some matter or other, and Isadora and Kelila were dozing. Delilah was doing extravagant things with Angeline's hair, knotting it tight to keep her neck cool. No-one was on watch.

Gertrude and the captain were intimately entwined, their lower limbs bare of clothes.

'Quickly, before anyone comes below,' begged Gertrude.

'I am going as fast as I can, ma'am. I only need another thrust or two – aah!'

Gertrude had had her satisfaction and was politely awaiting his. Now she moved to adjust her clothing. Just then came an uproar from the shore.

A hundred masked guards brandished swords and muskets. They fired on the Paradisian canoes which were leaving the shore with soldiers and freed slaves trying to clamber aboard.

The female crew leapt into action. Before the ship's captain or his perspiring partner could find their clothes, the gatling gun had started to stutter its retort. Princess Angeline and Delilah had mastered the machine in practice and now showed their prowess. They aimed at the masked horde who were wading into the water after their soldiers. Another danger awaited the struggling men who were attempting to board the canoes. Crocodiles! Like a raft of grey logs they moved inexorably towards the canoes. The soldiers paddled for their lives. Some men still had not clambered aboard, and the water around them burst with gun fire. Panic had set in, and the yacht's crew could see the disaster unfold as they watched. The crocodiles thrashed their long tails and the men plunged into the dark water, unknowing.

'Quick!' shouted Angeline. 'Kill the crocodiles!'

The gatling gun was turned quickly away from the hooded horde on shore to the flotilla of killers who swam towards their men. Rat-tat-rat-tat-rat-tat! The belt of ammunition was threaded expertly by Delilah as Angeline took aim again. Then she turned back to the masked guards, who were wading in deep to get a better aim at the canoes. In the massive swirl of muddy water, two crocodiles survived the bullets and swam towards their prey. The soldiers had helped each other into the boats. They had seen the yacht and their probable salvation. Ric cheered them on as they rowed and paddled as fast as they could away from shore. A few men had fallen from their canoe in a panic which had upset it. One was Prince Hari. He was hit on the head by one of the ornately carved oars which his wife had given him on their anniversary.

The hooded men fell to the crocodiles jaws. They were grasped in the long fierce jaws, held under the water to drown, then the massive beasts twisted and writhed, over and over, and disappeared beneath the muddy churned waters to their lairs, their dinner in their jaws.

'Hari!' called Angeline. 'Hari!'

She dived overboard, Kelila at her side, and they swam to the prince and the other two men who were still in the water. Two lifebelts were suddenly thrown into the water beside them and with Angeline and Kelila's assistance the prince and his men were safely dragged back to the yacht.

'Adam, dear boy, how are you?' said Gertrude. 'And you here too?' she said to Jax. The yacht was steaming ahead of the canoes, showing them the way out through the narrow channel.

'Yes, Gertrude, I saved your diver for you, but don't ask me why!' laughed the indulgent Ric.

'Oh, Ric,' said Gertrude, hugging her husband. 'You know you will always be my favourite man in uniform.'

Chapter Thirty-One
Homeward Bound

A ngeline had her husband in her arms again. Ah, such bliss! *She* had saved him. Never would she be unthinkingly cruel to him again. Never would she entertain thoughts of unfaithfulness. Ah, young love! She would display her love for him by allowing him to play with her favourite dancer as soon as they returned to the Kelidora academy. But they still had to navigate the strong currents and dangerous waters of the river before they could find their way back to safer shores.

The ship's captain was in command again. He shouted orders. They were followed by his female crew, while the prince leant in the bow with the lead line, checking for shallow water and the danger of going aground. The Paradisian canoes followed the yacht, anxious eyes watching for the sudden dart of a crocodile. The waters were muddy and brown, and debris ran swiftly by the boats. They had to struggle to keep the craft moving forward against the flooding tide, away from the Land of The Powerful One.

Back at the palace of that she-devil, pandemonium had broken out. The female creature who was the subject and object of men's wildest fantasies was mad with unleashed lust. Her guards had fled in terror, and she had no-one to fuck. She sucked her own breasts, biting the huge brown nipples and stretching them to long peaks. She put whole cucumbers inside her orifices. She writhed and bucked in continuous orgasms. The palace crumbled around her, and the earth shook. She did not notice the earth move.

At the other palace, on Isle de Paradis, the king was disconsolate. Not even Jezebel, it seemed, could get his cock to stay up long enough to please more than one of his womenfolk at once. Viva was called. She made up more potions – of monkey brain and aloe vera this time – and rubbed them on his withered member. She sang incantations. Her young company of virgin novices danced around him, lifting their saffron habits and showing him bare pudendas. They came closer and closer to him, so their sweaty perfume surrounded him, and he inhaled their musky fragrance. His senses reeled as he was aware of twenty young bellies swaying; twenty bared sexes rubbing him all around.

'Stop!' Viva called the pack of excited nuns away. It had worked. The royal erection was hearty and solid.

'No, Viva, don't take them away, the dear little things. Let them see their sovereign's rod. They may stroke it if they wish.' He stood, his arms clasped over his head, his silk robe open but tied at the waist by a plaited leather rope. His stiff cock poked out of the robe and jutted at the enthralled gathering of young females.

'No, King Aristide, they are virgins, and must remain so, as well you know.'

'Yes, yes, I know that, but at least let them play with me and let me play with them,' he begged his late first wife's sister.

Viva sighed in supplication and sat down to watch, with Trixie-Jane, the queen and Jezebel. It was a bizarre group. The king was at once set upon by three or four of

226

the young nuns, who giggled and simpered and stroked their king's eager member.

He sank on to his couch and put two girls on his knees, stroking their budding breasts through their thin cotton habits, feeling the ripening nubs. They wriggled and squirmed. His prick stuck up and poked them in the buttocks. He moved around to enjoy the sensation of two ripe bottoms pressing on him. Then he turned one girl over his knee and lifted her skirt to bare her plump buttocks.

'Look at that lovely little melon,' he said to his wife. 'Smack it, dearest, while I play with the other one.'

Clementine obliged, giving the girl resounding slaps which gave the king much pleasure. The other little nun stood by the king and let him fondle her under her voluminous skirt.

'Lift it up more and tie it; it is in the way,' he ordered Trixie-Jane.

'Yes sire.' She tied the offending clothing up from the girl's rounded thighs and belly, so she was all the more available to his caresses. He slapped her bottom. Trixie-Jane drew closer to Jezebel who took the initiative and calmly began to caress her intimately. Trixie-Jane swooned in the older woman's musky arms, and pressed her lips to the large nipples which were offered. Viva watched the king carefully. He was enjoying the parade of lithe young bodies pressing close. He spanked each young novice in turn, admiring the pink roundness, the shallow breathing, the pressure of breast and belly. They caressed him and kept his cock stiff. They kissed and fondled. He was in his seventh heaven. Clementine occasionally pushed herself forward and stroked his wonderful erection, remarking on its marvellous girth and length. He smiled proudly.

'Let us borrow a few of your little nuns, Viva, my dear high priestess,' whispered Clementine. 'You see how wonderfully he is up. His prick is bigger than I have ever known it. With the nuns' help we will keep it that way, I feel sure.'

Viva nodded silently. She could see the sense of the queen's request but she was concerned that the king would forget himself and deflower the virgins. Their future careers could be jeopardised. Deflowered, they could never become priestesses. They would have to be concubines. Viva had of course been the king's consort for many years after her sister's death, so she was not a virgin. But she had changed the rules since she had been made a high priestess – it was one of the perks of her position.

'Will you promise me that my students will not be violated by your husband?'

'If it is in my power to stop him, I will,' the honest queen allowed. 'He has not despoiled our handmaiden, you know. Trixie-Jane is still a virgin.'

'I did not know,' said Viva, 'but I am delighted to hear it. All right, I give my permission for five novices to stay with you for a period of three months, then we'll look again at the royal problem.'

'Thank you, High Priestess, thank you!'

Trixie-Jane was swooning in Jezebel's experienced arms. The voluptuous whore fondled the handmaiden expertly. She brought her close to climax, and then withdrew her caresses. She stroked and pressed the tender, silky flesh, moving slowly to her own satisfaction as she did so.

'Darling girl, put your hand there – yes, there, and press with the flat of your hand. Squeeze the lips together. Yes, yes, like that. Mmm! Now kiss me!'

The state of undress of all those attendant on the king's pleasure was similar. All his womenfolk were naked apart from a strip of silk wrapped around their limbs and bosoms. Their eyes gleamed and softened as they reached the height of pleasure, and their sighs filled the air like a gentle breeze from the aquamarine sea. The king happily obliged his queen, and then she smacked and gently chastised the little novices as he commanded, so raising his prick again to its former glory. He was proudly rampant. He was the king of paradise.

The Paradisian canoes, led by the triumphant royal yacht, reached the river mouth at last. No-one had followed them and no challenge had been made. The Powerful One was so self-absorbed and delighted with her own body and its pleasure that she had no time to chase the poor devils who had escaped her clutches. Her obsessive self-love was all embracing, all consuming. The masked, cloaked guards were, like The Powerful One, figments of man's imagination. They disappeared when challenged.

The Powerful One needed men's desire to keep her alive. Without them she was nothing. She would sink into the mire of time and myth until she was needed again.

Adam's memory of The Powerful One was dimming already. Had she been tall? Was she dark skinned or fair? Did her hair curl or sweep in a waterfall on her long back? Had she really treated him badly? Had he enjoyed her tortures?

The men were subdued and talked little about their adventures. Each one had doubts about what had happened. Was she real – this horror, this sex-crazed virago? They could not wait to get back to their quiet, sweet, undemanding wives, who put up with their pleas of tiredness, their drunkenness, their snores, their occasional limpness. Oh, they were so lucky to have such wonderfully understanding wives!

On the yacht, Captain Ric was down below, making use of one of the state cabins to make love to his willing wife. His leather straps were between her legs, rasping her soft flesh. His chin was buried in the cleft of her full breasts. He breathed in her musky scent. He took a long hard nipple between his teeth. She sighed and encouraged his fierce embrace. Her plump legs held him in a vice-like grip. Her buttocks shook and trembled and he grabbed them and pinched them firmly. His hands were under her bottom, feeling the moistness of her sex parts, which were gaping wide. She welcomed his caress, kissing his head and writhing on his thick cock. He sucked her nipple and bit it. He churned inside her, feeling the fleshy silk of her purse. His excitement was rising to a crescendo and she knew the signs. His mouth was a grimace; he looked grief stricken. His chest and neck were suffused with a dark glow. His legs stiffened and Gertrude rammed her bottom down hard on his belly so her clitoris was stimulated in just the right way by his hardness. His hands were still under her, now pushing into her vulva, now tickling her anus. She came with a rush, and came again as he spurted into her, her limbs melting into his.

'That was the best ever fuck, my darling wife. The very best!' He unceremonially sat her on the table on which they had been leaning and withdrew his emptied member. She pulled her garment demurely over her plump knees and smiled beatifically at him.

As they went up the companionway, Prince Hari and his wife, Angeline, were on their way down.

'Ah, Ric, keep an eye on things for a while, will you?'

'Yes, Prince, of course, Your Highness.'

Hari picked his little wife up in his arms and carried her over the threshold of the cabin. He sat next to her on the narrow bunk and kissed her tentatively.

'Oh, Hari, darling, do you love me?' she asked prettily.

'Who could not love you, you darling sweet thing, and you so brave, too, to swim to save me in crocodile-infested waters?' He kissed her upturned face, which was like a damp flower lifted to the sun.

They folded each other into their warm limbs, wrapped each other in loving caresses, merged into one being in the intensity of their love-making. Her mouth enfolded his sturdy cock, his tongue tunnelled into her other mouth. They sighed and sobbed and their bodies knew each other totally.

'Oh, Hari, that was wonderful,' said Princess Angeline. 'Let's do it again.'

'You'll have to give me a minute or two to recover, sweetness.' He paled at the thought of having to perform again so soon.

'Let me call Delilah – she will help,' said Angeline, and without waiting for the prince to acquiesce, she ran up the short companionway and called to her bosom pal, the little dancer. 'Delilah, dearest, come and play with us. Your prince and princess need you.'

And Delilah obeyed the royal command.

Her heart-shaped honey-brown face peeped around the cabin door. She was wrapped in a sarong. The wind had risen and they had come to the mouth of the river and were sailing across the lake to safety. Captain Barnabus and Kelila and Isadora were getting on with steering the boat. Ric and Gertrude were in the ship's kitchen making hot drinks. Delilah was delighted to be summoned to the bed of her best friend and her husband.

Hari was sprawled across the table, on his belly, naked. He was almost asleep and not really up to the challenge of two ardent females. However, he roused himself sufficiently to turn over, and pretended to be asleep while they tied his wrists to the available furniture. They did the same with his ankles, using their own flimsy clothes as ties. Naked, they sat on him – one on his face, the other on his belly – facing each other. Angeline spread her legs over her husband's thighs and rubbed his flaccid cock on herself. Delilah's open legs hovered over Hari's open mouth, and she lowered herself gingerly on to his lips. He sucked greedily at her sex lips, his tongue slipping in and out of her sheath. His cock rose, not surprisingly, and jutted proudly at Ange-

231

line's soft underbelly. She stroked his stem softly. He wriggled and insinuated his cock into her private parts while she still held it tight in her hand. Delilah heaved up and down, riding his mouth. She was flushed and her eyes had narrowed. Angeline leant forward slightly to kiss the girl. Their lips met and they gave each other their hands. They caressed the small breasts; two white, two brown. They stroked and slyly pressed fingers into each other's sex, feeling Hari's wet mouth here, Hari's throbbing cock there. He was in a veritable daze of lust, the dancers writhing on his belly and face. He sucked and licked, nibbled and thrust – with his hands and feet tied, he was helpless to do much else. Angeline felt his imminent release and checked it quickly.

'No, my Princeling, we need you hard a while yet,' she whispered. She held his cock at the base firmly between her fingers and thrust herself on him. When her cries had ended, she shifted position with Delilah, so her little friend had the pleasure of Hari's stiff rod invading her soft parts. Delilah moaned appreciatively and spent herself on his silky cock. Only then was Hari allowed to have his orgasm. He was caressed by both dancers simultaneously; four small delicate hands stroking him and bringing him to ecstasy. The three lovers kissed and thanked each other sweetly for the enjoyable experience, and then cleaned themselves in the little wash basin and bidet that were cleverly tucked away in the cabin. When they went up on deck, they were surprised to notice how the wind had risen. In their passion they had not noticed the waves.

The canoes battled behind the yacht, fighting the waves, rising over the top of a mountain and falling into a deep cleft. Gertrude looked green.

'I must go and lie down,' she said.

Isadora and Kelila had thrown ropes over the side and these were taken by the warriors and made fast to the canoes' high prows. Samson and Bartolem could be seen hauling away at the oars in the leading canoe. Samson looked years younger. He was leaner and more muscled than he had been for years. Bartolem, too, looked very fit. Angeline could see Joshua and Tom in another craft. She thought of Trixie-Jane.

'Hari, how is Trixie-Jane?' she asked.

He blushed as he remembered his adolescent fumbling with the artist's model.

'Did you know she is my parents' handmaiden now?'

'No, I didn't know. Adam, did you know that?' she said.

'No, I did not know, Princess. I was painting a picture of her.' He sighed, remembering the lithe naked girl in the constricting corset. He grew hot at the thought of her.

'Yes, I tried to paint her too, but I am no good at it, no good at all, dear boy. I'll have to leave the artistic talents to you,' said Hari, smiling indulgently at his friend and manservant.

Angeline smiled smugly to herself.

Chapter Thirty-Two
The Storm

The canoes were still battling through high seas, and it was now clear that there would be loss of life unless the crews were transferred to the yacht. Isadora and Kelila organised the rescue. They hurled themselves into the wild waters of the Lake of Lost Love, ropes tied to their waists, then they attached the ties to each canoe and drew each craft deftly to the yacht's side to allow the men to climb aboard. The boats were drawn close together and tied so that they made a tight raft. In this way the canoes were carried safely next to the sturdy yacht, like a foal tied to its mother. The men crowded on board the yacht and thankfully drank the tea which Gertrude, who had dragged herself from her sickbed, had brewed for them. Isadora and Kelila looked magnificent, their wet hair streaming down their straight backs, their muscular limbs shining and gleaming and their nipples stiff on their firm breasts. The men were impressed by the females' strength and mercy. After the horrific experiences that some of them had endured at the hands of The Powerful One, they were thankful for the care these lovely females were showing for them.

The yacht, heavily loaded, wallowed dangerously in

the waves, and it became necessary for some of the men to get off the vessel and cling to the exposed canoes. Captain Barnabus was busy steering the overloaded yacht through the troughs of the stormy waters. Ric and Hari organised the men into squads. Twelve men would jump off on to the raft of canoes to stop the yacht from sinking under the excess weight. After a while, another twelve men would take their place, then another. In this way they all survived the storm. Even the females took their turn on the canoes – except Gertrude, who was thought too feeble to withstand the experience. The princess and her friend Delilah, with Kelila and Isadora, clambered down the yawing hull and clung to the war canoes, which were creaking and straining under the strain of the big waves.

'Oh Isadora, if you were to die, I do not think I would want to live,' said an emotional Kelila, as they clung together, the horizontal rain burning their faces, the dark waves bursting on their semi-naked bodies. Isadora wallowed in the drama of the occasion. She was enjoying it. She felt like she was a warrior, a veritable heroine. She wanted to be wearing a horned helmet.

Meanwhile, on the Isle de Paradis, Jezebel was not pleased. She felt she had been usurped in the king's chamber by Viva and her little novices. Was she to go back to the brothel? Was this the end of her usefulness to the royal house? But she need not have worried. The king's problem was complex and needed several and various remedies. He enjoyed the attentions of the lively virgins, but he tired of their youthful exuberance very quickly.

'Viva, we still need help with the king's erection,' said Clementine, sighing deeply.

'Well, I don't know what to suggest. He is beyond help,' she answered.

'Nonsense!' said Jezebel. 'Give me one more chance.

But I'll need paying this time. I'll get Lana back. That'll give him something to rise for.'

Viva, Clementine and Trixie-Jane waited in the king's bedchamber, playing chess with him and letting him win to keep him cheerful. The tidied-up brothel keeper, still magnificent in black leather with holes in convenient places, swayed in, carrying her weight well. The king glanced up and smiled at her.

'Goodness, Jezebel, who is that you have with you?'

'King Aristide, meet your mystery mistress and her slave.' She held the door open wide and in came the bizarre pair – Lana and Sylva. Sylva was naked but for a saddle of leather which was tied around her body and knee and arm leathers to protect her from the hard ground, as she walked on hands and knees. Her face was hidden behind a soft black mask so that only her mouth showed. Her eyes glinted through tiny slits in the cloth. Her buttocks were naked and round, shining with oil. Straps holding the saddle on to her went between her legs and buttocks and above and beneath her breasts, which hung like dugs and swung as she moved across the floor of the chamber. She moved like a large wild cat, a sinuous writhing of hips and buttocks, her arms and legs gleaming. Around her neck was a broad leather collar attached to which was a chain. The queen, the high priestess and the handmaiden gasped at the vision. The king smiled broadly and tipped up his chess king.

Behind Sylva, holding on to the chain that held her tight, was the magnificently attired Lana. Her hair was hidden under a close-fitting helmet of white leather. She wore a white leather mask over her eyes. Her exposed nipples and shaved sex were painted bright red, and the rest of her was covered in softest white chamois leather. She wielded a white whip, made of plaited leather strips, which she cracked on the raised buttocks of the 'slave'.

'Ouch!'

'Shut up!' She struck the cheeky girl again.

The king sat up straight, as did his twitchy organ. 'Oh yes, I like this display of lewdness and naughtiness, my dear.' He held his wife's hand over his swelling organ. 'You see?'

'Yes, dearest, I do see,' she said.

The bizarre duo pranced and writhed, with the slave being thoroughly punished at each sign of weakness.

'Let her do it to me, dearest,' said the king.

'What? You want to be in harness under the whip, Aristide?'

'Of course he does, Your Highness,' said Jezebel. She helped the king from the bed and together with Trixie-Jane undressed him completely and transferred the saddle and straps from the disgruntled Sylva to the king. He looked ridiculous but he clearly did not care. He wanted to be punished by the lovely Lana, the fearsome dominatrix. She complied, haughtily, not deigning to change her expression. Her cruel lips half smiled as the whip found its target. The king's bottom was soundly thrashed. The straps of the saddle dug into his flesh, separating his balls and buttocks. His cock hung down, thick and swollen. He tried to press it on the floor, but he was punished with more strokes of the whip.

'Trixie-Jane, mount your king, my dear,' ordered Queen Clementine. Trixie-Jane did as she was told, fearful of the whip which Jezebel cracked and frightened by the threat of the white whip which Lana flicked.

'Take off your garment, dear,' said the queen, helping the girl to lift her sarong from her shoulders.

Trixie-Jane sat on the king's back on the leather saddle, squirming on the hard pummel which fitted neatly into her pussy and rubbed nicely. She smiled delightedly at this new pleasure. The white whip fell on her behind, licking it with a fierce kiss. She yelped and it happened again.

'No, no, not her. Give it to me,' begged the king.

Meanwhile, Jezebel had taken off her black leather suit

and helped the queen to put it on. The queen was soon dressed in the dominatrix outfit. It fitted her well, like a soft close glove. She and Jezebel shared similar curves and bulges. Their breasts were large, though Clementine's were younger and firmer. Her nipples and sex bulged through the indiscreet slits and holes. Her plump legs were encased in long black boots, which had high spiked heels. She looked magnificent. Jezebel slipped on a loose kimono of red silk and showed the queen how to flick her wrist properly so she could use the whip to best effect.

The king was unaware that his wife was about to punish him. He thought it was the white whip that licked his privates so deliciously. He yelped and whimpered and the whip came down on his thighs and anus.

Lana withdrew quietly with Sylva, and Viva left too with Jezebel. The king, on all fours still, with the handmaiden leaping up and down enthusiastically on the erotic saddle on his back, enjoyed the torture of the whip leather. His cock leapt at each stroke, and the rider reached down under his belly and tugged at it. The whip reached several unexpected places that the white whip had not reached, but he loved it all.

When at last his orgasm threw him to the floor in a state of collapse and the rider was thrown, it was with great surprise that the king turned his head to see his own dear wife with her spiked heel on his naked bottom, the whip in her hand, a smile on her red lips.

'Golly, Clem, that was marvellous! You look charming, my dear. Come here and let me thank you properly.'

'Oh, don't be silly, Aristide, you know you won't get it up so quickly,' she chastised.

'Well, if I don't, my dear, you must thrash me for it.' He kissed his perspiring wife firmly on the lips and pinched her proud nipples.

'Trixie-Jane, dear, go and find the feathers, will you?' said the queen.

'Yes, ma'am, straight away, ma'am.'

The handmaiden ran from the royal bedchamber, grabbed a sarong from a hook in the antechamber and made her way to the hut in the forest because she had removed all the queen's supply of feathers and taken them to the king's hideaway.

On the way she passed the brothel. There was a group of disgruntled fishermen waiting to be fed and served banana wine. Sylva was shouting at them and waving a saucepan. Jezebel was hitting Sylva with a wooden spoon.

'You stupid girl, you should have put the CLOSED FOR ONE DAY ONLY, BY ROYAL ORDER notice up,' she said. 'I told you to do it.' The men laughed at the antics of the brothel keeper and admired her swinging breasts as they fell out of the kimono.

Jezebel noticed Trixie-Jane and called out to her. 'How is it going at the palace? Has the king still got it up?'

'Yes, Jezebel, I think it has worked, your plan.'

'I'll be back tomorrow to make sure,' she said, and thought about her reward.

She wished she had Samson and Bartolem back with her. She missed their muscular bellies up against her rolls of fat. She needed their big cocks thrusting inside her. She gazed sadly at the poor specimens of maleness who craved their banana wine and manioc beer at her door. She had no time for puny men. She thought of the young and enthusiastic Tom. Her randy little Tom Cat. Ah, how she would like to stroke him now! She licked her lips and took a swig of beer from a coconut shell.

Trixie-Jane hurried back to the palace, running all the way, the bundle of feathers safe in a fold of chamois. She had had to discard quite a few, due to their disreputable state. Some were sticky from her juices and should have been thrown away before. She noticed that the hullaba-loo at the Forbidden Apple had died down. The fisher-men were either sprawled outside on the dirt, in their

239

cups already, or were eating a delicious-smelling spiced vegetable and fish stew. Sylva was learning new skills while Samson was away.

'Oh! Oh!' came the sighs from the royal bedchamber.

Should Trixie-Jane enter? She knocked gently and went in. The king was strapped to the rings in the wall, his leather harness still tied between his firmly fleshed thighs, his balls bulging either side. He was gagged and blindfolded. Queen Clementine was stroking his stiff purple penis with a small bundle of artist's paintbrushes. He was clearly enjoying it. His thighs and belly showed signs of recent beating and stripes of dark red criss-crossed his legs. He moaned appreciatively as Clementine slapped at his cock and balls with the bunch of brushes. The king's cock throbbed to the delicate touch.

'Ah, there you are, dear, give them to me,' said the queen, noticing her handmaiden at last.

Trixie-Jane watched as the queen substituted feathers for the brushes. She took the brushes from her queen and thought suddenly of Adam. She ran sobbing from the bedchamber.

'Mmm, mmm, mmm?' asked the king.

'Be quiet or I'll whip you again,' said the newly harsh queen.

'Mmm, mmm!' he agreed.

She stroked his scrotum with the longest, firmest feather. His cock twitched and his balls gathered into a tight knot.

The queen stroked herself with a thick white parrot feather, moving it in and out of her inner labia. She grabbed her husband's thickened prick and pushed it into herself gleefully. He mumbled through his gag and pressed into her softness. She held him tight until she had had her pleasure several times, then she allowed him his release. He spurted on to her leather-enfolded belly and she sighed happily and undid his gag and blindfold.

'Phew, Clem, that was terrific, my little pumpkin! You were wonderful.'

'So were you, dear heart, so were you.' She undid his chains and they kissed lovingly.

Chapter Thirty-Three
Royal Performance

*T*he storm abated as the yacht and its precious load reached the safer shore of Monkey Island. Their coming had been noticed and many Monkey Islanders were waiting to greet them, especially the youths who had been saved from the dreaded clutches of The Powerful One. Families were overjoyed to see their loved ones again. Much sobbing ensued.

Neighbours took food and drink to the house of Isadora and Kelila, and an impromptu party took place. There was much music and dancing, celebrating the homecoming and redemption of the lost youths. They were asked about their experiences, but they seemed anxious to forget. They drank and kissed their mothers, sweethearts, sisters and their wives.

The next day, when the party had recovered from the exhausting voyage, Isadora suggested a dance show for the royal party before they left for the Isle de Paradis.

'Surely my time with you is not over?' sighed Angeline, clasping her friend to her bosom.

'Oh, no, can't I come and visit you soon?' begged the sobbing Delilah.

'Yes, of course she must come soon,' said Prince Hari, who had grown very fond of their little playmate.

The dance academy was packed to the seams with royals and followers. Prince Hari sat in the front row with Captain Ric and his wife, Gertrude. Captain Barnabus pressed on to Gertrude's other side, his hand under her right thigh. Samson and Bartolem were there with Tom and Joshua and their friends from Isle de Paradis. Jax was sitting behind Gertrude, watching her other admirers fondle her. She wore a magnificent string of large pink pearls around her neck.

The dancers were twittering like little songbirds behind the heavy curtain. A drumbeat exploded suddenly and the curtain rose. The audience let out a long sigh. There on the little makeshift stage were the two dance queens of the academy – Kelila and Isadora – draped in white satin, which covered them both together, so they were like one creature. They moved together in a sinuous wave across the stage, then held the satin above their heads, exposing their naked bodies. They wore no body jewels, no item to take away the audience's awareness of the perfection of their erotic movements. Their lithe arms swayed and they swam effortlessly – floated almost – with no imperceptible foot movement. The black body gleamed and shone with oils and the scent of her spicy musk filled the tiny stadium. Her honey skin was coffee, then chocolate, then black silk. Isadora's copper hair swung in a silk sheet from her high-held head. Her fair skin glittered with a sheen of gold. The only colour in this black and white cinematic image was Isadora's hair and the painted sex of both dancers. That and the red rouged nipples. The audience gasped at the beautiful writhing and snake-like undulation of the performers. The drum beat fast and Kelila and Isadora wrapped themselves in the satin sheet, twisting round and round until they were completely hidden in its folds. The curtain fell as they kissed. There was a roar of applause.

243

Next came the troupe of novice dancers, including Delilah and the princess. They all wore little tutus which showed off their legs and bottoms as they went pirouetting and leaping and doing the splits. Their bare bottoms and straining muscles were much admired. They did the dying swan act to loud cries of 'Encore!', and then they obligingly repeated the performance.

Ric was busy watching a particularly plump little ballerina in the front row, mesmerised by her bouncing breasts and the sharpness of her prominent nipples. Her tight flesh-coloured knickers dug into her pudenda so nicely, outlining every crease. Her plump labia were so well-defined, the garment left nothing to the imagination. He was practically salivating. Gertrude, meanwhile, in the dark of the small auditorium, was enjoying more than the spectacle. Her sea captain had several fingers inside her pussy, while behind her, the pearl diver was nuzzling her neck. His teeth nibbled her nape and she shivered. She opened her legs to give Captain Barnabus's blunt fingers better access to her delights. Suddenly, she felt something go. Her necklace had come undone and the pearls slipped silently from her neck, down her satin-encased breasts, into her décolleté. She swore and made a grab for the pearls. Behind her, Jax, the diver, also made an attempt to reclaim his treasure, which he felt she no longer deserved. He was disgruntled that he had not been given the reward he had expected – to share the bed of the princess and a present of gold from the prince. It had been pointed out to him that he had not shown them where to find The Powerful One and that they had found and rescued *him*, but he was still not satisfied.

He fell to the floor and pretended to gather the pearls and give them to Gertrude, but in fact he substituted the precious jewels for some which were quite worthless. Gertrude managed to save a few, however, and in the dark and confusion, she was not aware that anything untoward had happened. She resumed her position as the candles were lit and the curtain fell.

'You look flushed, my dear,' said Ric, noting the rosy glow of her swollen breasts.

'Well, so do you, Ric, darling. It is very hot in here.'

'Shall I accompany you outside to get some air, ma'am?' said the eager Captain Barnabus. He looked particularly dashing tonight, Gertrude thought, in his winter uniform of navy blue, with gleaming brass buttons and gold braid covering his broad shoulders and chest. His plumed cap sat well on his handsome head of black straight hair.

'Very well, captain, that would be delightful, thank you. Will you accompany us, Ric?' she asked her husband. But his mind was elsewhere for the moment.

The princess's chaperone and the sea captain rose and he led her out into the cool night. The full moon was a huge blue coin in the star-spattered fabric of the sky. Captain Barnabus held her close.

'Ma'am, come with me to the water's edge.'

'If you wish, captain. It would be refreshing to hear the waves.'

He led her quickly to the little pier and they bent low to negotiate the wooden struts. Once under the pier he lifted her voluminous skirts and petticoats to her waist. Underneath she wore nothing, of course, in anticipation of just such an opportunity and because the heat of the tropics dictated such sensible habits. She breathed heavily. Captain Barnabus undid his flies and loosed his eager rod. She saw the gleam of purple flesh in his hand. He shoved her up against a wooden post and pushed into her. He lifted her legs and held her up by her buttocks, her legs wrapped around his waist. They clung and fucked hurriedly, eager for the climax. The water lapped around the captain's feet, soaking his boots.

* * *

Captain Ric had removed himself from the auditorium in order to have a smoke and take some air in the interval. He walked around the small wooden building to the back door, which was open to let air into the hot interior. There came the twittering of many dancers, giggling and chattering. He stood by the open door and looked inside. It was a sight to gladden the heart of many an old man – and some youths too. The little dancers were semi-naked. They were changing their costumes; helping each other lift costumes over each other's heads, tying up stockings, dressing hair. Slender arms lifted and little breasts strained high, nipples bobbing like pink flowerbuds. Cygnets bent over and showed him their bare bottoms, wriggling into tights. He searched for his favourite dancer – the plump beauty. There she was, encasing herself in a little pink satin corset, holding it tight to her waist while another girl pushed her foot into her back and tightened the laces. Her short, flimsy chiffon skirt was sitting on a chair waiting for her to slip it on. All that covered her legs were white cotton stockings to above her knees, held up with elastic ribbons. Her plump, pinky-brown pudenda gleamed bare below her little convex belly, which pouted prettily. Her belly button was hidden deep in a dark cave. He felt the urge to touch her between the legs. As if she knew his thoughts, she suddenly lifted one leg on to the chair, giving him a perfect view of her pink folds of fleshy sex lips. Her bud was even pouting from the lips, swollen, he imagined, waiting for his urgent touch. He felt himself, the bigness of his organ, prodding through the leather straps of his kilt. He rubbed himself, luxuriating in the illicitness of the occasion; the enjoyment of voyeurism. His favourite was surrounded by little, fluttering birds, all feathers and frills, budding breasts and flashing bottoms. She was still naked below, while her friend adjusted the corset. Her breasts rose pertly above the close feathered bodice. He almost stumbled into the doorway in his excitement as she turned away from him suddenly and bent over, one foot raised on the chair. She stretched and her buttocks pushed out towards him. Her naked purse bulged beneath her plump little thighs, and he was in heaven.

Under the pier, the sea captain was ready to return but Gertrude was eager to continue the game. She bent to his withered cock and took it into her mouth, while he looked about him uneasily.

'Ma'am, I feel sure that the dance has recommenced. Don't you think we ought to return?'

'Oh, very well, captain, I see you are no longer interested in my attentions,' she sighed, disappointed.

They picked their way back along the little beach and returned to the candlelit dance hall.

'I do beg your pardon, ma'am, I have failed you, I fear. I assure you my ardour will return very soon.' The captain bowed low and let Gertrude proceed.

'Perhaps, captain. We shall see.' She flounced before him and saw her husband at the back door, shaking his still-stiff cock before he moved through the shadows and followed them back into the throng of audience.

The music had started up, the bells ringing and drums drumming. This time the stage was empty except for a cross-legged princess, dressed in a white velvet short tunic which fell in folds over her bare thighs. One little breast peeped over the top of the flatteringly draped bodice, its nipple painted a deep red. Another figure appeared dressed as a boy, with chamois breeches carefully cut to expose Delilah's sex parts. However, instead of the expected slit and pouting purse of female sex, there was a mock penis attached to the girl's thighs and hips by means of thin leather straps. She wore a waistcoat of chamois leather, open to the waist. Her black hair was tied back off her heart-shaped face and she wore a false moustache. The audience cheered. Delilah pranced and strutted like a cocky young man, waving the leather erection at the audience and lewdly at Princess Angeline, who had risen in feigned surprise at the horrid sight of this rude boy. Delilah twirled her moustache and blew Angeline a kiss. Angeline simpered prettily, lifting the hem of her velvet skirt so all in the audience could be thoroughly certain that she wore nothing underneath but red rouge.

The naughty fellow pointed his thing at the princess, who turned away. He danced closer to her and rubbed himself against her side. The audience hooted and clapped. Angeline turned quickly, and took the leather dildo in her hands. She danced around the stage, pulling her partner with her. The audience loved it. Then, as a finale, she turned over and threw her skirt over her head, pushing her bottom up to his prick. As he proceeded to mount her from behind – down came the curtain.

The place was in uproar. Everyone cheered and clapped and whistled for an encore. When the curtain went up again there was a hush. Delilah was actually inserting the dildo into her pretty partner's pussy, there on the stage. Angeline gasped and pressed backward to meet the leather penis. Delilah was poised over the princess, her hands pressed to the base of the dildo. The audience was allowed three seconds' viewing of this blissful union before the curtain came down for the last time.

Chapter Thirty-Four
The Return to Isle de Paradis

*A*fter the success of the finale there was a feast. All the islanders attended and gave the princess a rousing applause when she appeared, still in her dance costume. The prince was so delighted with his wife's new dancing expertise that he gave Isadora and Kelila a purse full of gold to build themselves a proper dance theatre. They were overjoyed. Delilah clung tearfully to the princess, sad that she would have to say goodbye to her on the morrow. Gertrude sat next to her husband, Ric, who had managed to position himself beside the plump cygnet of earlier. She twittered and fluttered her white wings next to him and tickled his thigh with her feathers. After the feast of pumpkin soup with kingfish flakes, melons and pork, lobster tails cooked in coconut milk and fresh kiwi fruit, he sat back, washed his hands in the bowls provided and began his final course. His hands slipped under the skirts of his wife on one side and the ballerina on the other. They both thought themselves blessed by his singular attentions and squirmed happily. Gertrude went to caress her husband's protruding member and found another small hand clasped around it. She added hers to the stem and together they pleasured him.

Angeline and her husband slipped away, the young dancer, Delilah, between them.

'Doesn't she look adorable in those breeches and that wonderful moustache?' Angeline giggled, a little the worse for having drunk rather too many tots of banana wine. But she was excited and exhilarated at her dramatic success. She was a dancer! She led Delilah and the prince to her room in Isadora and Kelila's hut, and they all squeezed into her little bed.

'I can't help grabbing hold of your prick, my dear Delilah,' said the prince. 'It is fascinatingly realistic.'

'It certainly is, Hari. It feels almost like the real thing. Turn over and try it. No, wait a moment. Take off your kimono.' Angeline tore off her husband's beautiful yellow silk kimono, unwound his satin loincloth which was a slightly paler hue, and put over his head her little tutu. She dressed him in white cotton stockings and caressed his cock, which swelled and nudged the flounces of his net skirt.

'Oh! Doesn't he look gorgeous? I could eat him.' So saying, the princess sucked at the prince's thickening cock and admired its purple head and the little drop of moisture that sat in its eye.

He murmured encouragingly to his wife and Delilah churned her hips and pelvis so the dildo moved in a lascivious manner. Then the dancers manhandled him on to his stomach. His lifted his tight little bum up to the firm caress of the dildo.

'Oh! Isn't she rude!' said the princess. 'I must spank her for that.' She spanked her husband firmly with her hand, touching his anus and the sac of his balls as she did so. His cock leapt and shook with each sharp smack. She moistened her fingers in her mouth and massaged his anus. She went in front of him and watched his face as Delilah moved closer to his backside and clasped him around the waist. As the dildo met with resistance, he grimaced. Angeline took his face in her hands and kissed him. Delilah insinuated the false penis in deeper, until he accepted it and it disappeared into him, his puckered hole gripping around it. Delilah felt underneath his bottom and stroked his root, while Angeline sucked the ripe fruit. It was like eating a plum, she thought, sucking and nibbling on the purple helmet. She sucked and drew her teeth along the shaft. Delilah pushed and pulled.

His wife knew exactly when to stop the erotic torture. Now she was on all fours, her buttocks up hard against his cock. He penetrated her swiftly and as she came with the suddenness and violence of the thrusts, so did he ejaculate with the boy/girl behind him. Delilah was too excited to have thought for herself, and she withdrew the dildo slowly and threw it off. But the thoughtful Angeline, aware of her little friend's sacrifice, lay next to her on the narrow bed and caressed her gently. Soon the three tired and happy playmates were asleep, curled up together.

'Goodbye, darlings, goodbye!' The Monkey Islanders were all gathered to wave goodbye to the yacht and canoes. Delilah had been left with a promise that she would visit them soon. Kelila and Isadora waved the bag of gold. Jax waved his bag of pink pearls.

Though the winter waves were high, the voyage back to Isle de Paradis went without mishap. Ric had joined his men on a canoe, and so had Hari. On board the yacht were Angeline, Gertrude and Adam – the same passengers as had made the outward voyage. Captain Barnabus had a little time to make up to Gertrude for his lack of fortitude under the pier, and he made use of every opportunity to please her. Her buttocks were bruised from the hardness of the wooden thwart over which she had been bent. Her breasts were bruised from his rough caresses. Her lips were bruised from his ardent kisses. Her pussy was in a constant state of moistness, ready for his every assault on her person. She was in a state of bliss.

Adam was back in his uniform, the chamois pouch hiding his youthful erection. He admired the princess's satin gowns, her pale flower face. But he knew now that he loved only Trixie-Jane. He could not wait to see her again and tell her of his undying love.

Angeline looked forward to her homecoming. She made plans to carry on dancing, thinking that maybe Sylva could be her partner – she would talk Aristide into it. Delilah would come and visit them next year, when her studies were over. She looked forward to it.

The yacht had let off a loud blast of its horn as soon as land was sighted. On Isle de Paradis the word got round and all the islanders ran to the shore to watch the canoes return. They ran into the waves and helped the boats through the surf. The yacht moored at the wooden jetty and off stepped the princess in her finery, and Adam in his. Gertrude was helped down the ladder by Captain Barnabus, who bowed and kissed her hand.

'Thank you, captain, for a very entertaining voyage.' She smiled at him.

Aristide was at the landing stage, beaming broadly and looking, Angeline thought, much younger. Queen Clementine hugged the princess and said how lovely she looked.

'You look blooming, Clementine,' said the princess.

On the beach were the bar girls and Jezebel, pleased to see the soldiers home again. Samson and Bartolem kissed Jezebel and grabbed her by the waist and lifted her in the air. She squealed delightedly and kissed them both.

'I've missed you,' she said.

At the back of the throng stood a lonely little hand-maiden, not sure of her loved one's state of mind. She greeted her brother joyfully and kissed him. She turned and found Adam standing, his arms by his side, his chest broader than it had been three months ago when he left. His thighs gleamed under the leather kilt and his muscles bulged. He only had eyes for her. He held out his hands and she ran to him and threw her arms around him.

'Oh! Adam! You are safe!'

She was prettier than he remembered; rounder and softer, and her hair was shiny. He held her tight and kissed her on her soft mouth.

'I must go to my duties now, but I'll come to you when I can,' he promised.

Chapter Thirty-Five
Adam and Queen Clementine

*T*rixie-Jane waited on the beach for her lover. She
wore a delightful short sarong of bright blue cotton,
covered in a pattern of small yellow flowers. She kept
untying it and retying it, adjusting her small bosoms so
they looked larger, pressing them together so she had
the hint of a cleavage. Her little body was prepared
specially. She had depilated, washed her hair and
brushed it until it shone like moonlight on the calm sea,
oiled her body with a very light coconut oil, polished her
nails, trimmed her fringe and perfumed her skin with
essential oil of frangipani. In her hair was a fragrant halo
of small white flowers woven in a circlet of lemon leaves.
Around her ankles were similar circles of flowers. While
she waited she passed the time making more garlands of
flowers for herself and for Adam. She envisaged him
dressed only in flowers, his loins and buttocks bare, the
flower garlands covering his chest and around his head.
She made a penis sheaf of leaves and surrounded it with
tiny pink buds. She had quite a pile of garlands surrounding her. She felt dreamily happy and leant back
against a smooth barked palm and slipped into a light
sleep.

While she slept, her lover was trying his hardest to get away from his duties. But the queen had other plans. She too had noticed how charmingly the youth had filled out and grown since she had last seen him.

'Oh, Adam,' she said, 'have you finished with Prince Hari for the time being?'

'Yes, Queen Clementine, I was just going off duty.'

'Oh good, dear boy.' She patted him on the shoulder, caressing the smooth brown skin admiringly. 'Follow me, Adam, I have something for you.' She swayed her generous hips and buttocks invitingly as he followed her, dog-like, not daring to tell her he had an appointment. She went into her private chamber and closed the door behind him.

'You are looking particulary charming, Adam.' She turned and grabbed him roughly. 'I would like you to kiss me.'

He gulped. 'Kiss you?'

'Yes, don't be afraid. I won't eat you.'

He remembered the fearsome Powerful One and her insatiable demands. He moved away from the queen with something like fear in his eyes. Perhaps she would eat him?

'Oh, Adam, let me make you happy, dear boy – a reward for looking after the princess.' She advanced on him, her bosoms straining to escape the confines of their corset prison, her thighs deliciously hot as they rubbed each other under the silky skirt.

'Look, I am wearing a corset, just for you,' she said.

'I-It looks very b-becoming, Your Highness,' he stuttered, admiring her curves for the first time. He had been too anxious to escape and see Trixie-Jane before to allow any thought of another woman. He stared at her breasts and the narrowness of her tightly laced waist. Yes, she was a handsome woman, no doubt about it, and a corset did do something for a female, and something for a man, too, he thought, feeling his erection grow under his leather kilt. He tried to hide it, but she knew what he was suffering. She drew her hands up under her breasts and stroked them, watching his eyes grow large.

He breathed more quickly and covered his bulging crotch. She took his hands and placed them on her breasts. He had to do as his queen asked; to refuse her would be treason, he supposed. So he stroked her heaving breasts and marvelled at their roundness and silkiness. She dipped a finger inside her corset and lifted the nipples clear. He stared at the hard, dark buttons.

'Oh, Your Majesty,' he sighed.

She had her hands on his straining penis, and pulled him towards her gently. They fell back on to her bed, the Egyptian cotton sheets gleaming white, the elephant tusks cornerposts curved over them.

'You like corsets, do you not, Adam?'

'Yes, ma'am.' He nibbled her nipples and pressed his hand on her belly.

She squirmed appreciatively, encouraging his hand to drop below her belly and between her plump thighs. She manipulated his cock, caressingly, expertly, remembering all the tricks that Jezebel had so recently taught her. She used gentle, firm pressure on his scrotum and knew exactly where to press and squeeze. He kissed her large, ripe melon breasts, lifting them over the top of the corset. Her hips flared white from beneath it, her buttocks like two huge pomegranates. He had her skirt off and she lay in all her glory, her pouting pudenda lifted to meet his touch. He lifted his leather strap kilt aside and mounted her, his knees either side of her hips. She raised her arms in supplication and groaned as he entered her. Her scent was of frangipani and flamboyant and the earthy perfume of her sex. Adam breathed it in, inhaling its aphrodiasic properties.

'Oh, Adam, that is good. Your prick is so stiff, my boy; so very thick.' He could feel it stiffen even more as she encouraged his thrusts. 'Do you want to tie me to the

256

bed?' she asked. 'There, the straps are already attached
to the tusks. It's all right, really, I command you to tie
me,' she insisted.

He withdrew from her, noting the juiciness of her sex,
the oiliness of his cock. He leant over her to tie her
wrists, and she grabbed his cock and slipped it into her
mouth, sucking it firmly. He knelt, his cock stretched in
her red mouth. He leant to her side and tied her other
wrist. She still had him by the cock. He withdrew from
her mouth and turned around so his face was over her
stretched thighs and his cock was once more nestled in
her warm, welcoming face. He parted her swollen labia
and looked inside at the coral tunnel. He put a finger
inside and churned it gently. Her hips writhed. He
squeezed her large buttocks, amazed at the quantity of
desirable flesh. Her tongue wrapped around his youthful
erection and lapped. He fingered her little red tongue-
like clitoris and licked it to erection. It was as hard as
her nipples – and as scarlet.

She strained at the bonds that held her, pretending to
want freedom. He felt that he had her in his control,
utterly; his queen was his to use as he wanted. She
moaned and sucked his balls as he withdrew his member
from her moist mouth. Then he used his cock as a gentle
baton, banging on to her genitals with its weight. He
lifted and dropped his cock on her open purse. It slid
inside and slipped out, and again, he tortured her with
its caress, withdrawing just as she became excited. She
thrust up her hips and belly at him, wanting the thick
hardness to fill the aching hole. He let it go inside again
and felt the tugging of her muscles pulling it in. It was a
wonderful feeling; a letting go of all tension, a releasing
of his energy. He pumped into her suddenly, going right
into her, up to the tunnel's end. He felt the limits of her
soft flesh, holding and squeezing him. He saw her big
breasts falling out of the tight corset. He sucked them
hungrily. His cock filled her, growing to fit her fleshy

purse. He pumped harder and his balls hit her raised thighs on the innermost, sensitive flesh. She cried out as her climax overtook her and he too groaned loud as his cock released its spurts of white foam inside her.

Afterwards, they lay together in a haze of satisfaction. She rubbed her sore wrists and turned over.

'Undo my corset, dear boy, will you?' she commanded.

His large fingers fumbled at the strings and he loosened her from the erotic garment. She stroked its warm satin and breathed more easily.

'There,' she said, handing it to Adam. 'Your reward, for looking after my best friend Angeline so well, and for looking after me.'

'Oh, thank you so much, Queen Clementine.' He bent and kissed her hand. 'I shall value it all my life.'

'I have lots more, dear boy. Look . . .' She slipped on her green and gold silk kimono and led him to her dressing chamber – a large cupboard with shelves and hanging space. He looked in amazed appreciation at all her corsets hanging in rows. There were black leather corsets with stiff whale bones keeping their severe shape; there was shiny satin, red and emerald; pearl-encrusted black lace; transparent white lace; blue silk with tiny velvet bows of red. He fingered the desirable garments, his cock twitching again.

'Which do you like best?' she asked.

'I am sure they are all delightful when you are inside them,' he told her.

'Dear boy,' she sighed happily. 'Well, you must tell me which you want me to wear for you next time, and then you may keep it, too, if you wish – if you please me, of course.' She smiled wickedly.

'Oh, next time?' he squeaked. He cleared his throat. 'Of course, ma'am. Your wish is my command.' He bowed and left, moving out of the room as fast as he could without appearing rude.

He looked at the sun. Poor Trixie-Jane would have

given him up. He had said he would be with her an hour ago. Had he really been making love to Queen Clementine all this time? He sauntered off to the beach, the corset wrapped up and tucked under his arm. His cock ached as he walked. It rose and touched the leather strappings of his uniform kilt and aroused him. He thought of how Trixie-Jane would look in the royal garment. He ran.

Chapter Thirty-Six
True Love

*T*rixie-Jane was cross. She had woken and Adam still had not come for her. She looked at the sun. It would be time for her to go home for tea soon. Where was the tiresome creature? She wandered down to the sea and paddled her feet. Her floral anklets got bedraggled. The other flowers were drooping. If there was anything she hated it was being kept waiting. She flung off her halos and garlands and threw them into the sea. She took off her pretty sarong too, and flung it angrily on to the sand. Naked, she walked into the warm, violet-coloured water and plunged herself into the waves. She swam out, powerfully, her strong little arms carving a swathe through the warm water. She met the dolphins, who surrounded her joyfully and leapt and danced together. She touched them in friendship and they smiled at her and clicked their strange voices to her. She swam with them far out, and when she tired, they held her so she could rest. She dived and swam under the water with them, admiring their grace and speed. They waited for her, and nudged her if she hung back.

Adam arrived at the appointed place on the beach, under the tree in which Trixie-Jane had first hidden when they met. She was not there. He was out of breath, hot and bothered and desperate for her kiss. Where was she? He looked around him. Only vervet monkeys grinned from the branches, their babies clinging to their bellies. He sat disconsolately under the tree and unwrapped the corset from its banana-leaf wrapping. It was cool to the touch, having lost the heat of the queen's body. He admired the stitching along its stiff ribs and the velvet ribbons trimming its top and bottom. He remembered Clementine's large breasts tumbling out of it and grew warmer. Where was Trixie-Jane? He did not notice the discarded flowers on the ground, the specially made, now wilting garlands that were to have graced his proud chest and the penis sheath, so lovingly crafted. Instead, he removed his uniform, telling himself he would have a swim while he waited for her. He disrobed and held his half erection between his admiring fingers. He held the corset around his hips and writhed his buttocks and hips, pretending to be Clementine. His slender thighs and taut buttocks churned. His prick, now quite stiff, lifted under the corset and he trapped it under the garment, so it was held close to his belly. He tied the corset tightly in front so he could do up the strings easily. He danced around the deserted beach, the corset holding his erection firmly, rubbing him with its satin smoothness. He rubbed the corset over his cock and tenderly caressed his balls. He pretended he had breasts and pinched his own vestigial nipples, enjoying the unusual sensation. He suddenly fell and got entangled with a liana, and the strings of the corset were caught in its long snake-like branches. The more he struggled, the tighter he became tangled. He could not escape its embrace. His fight was in vain. He rested a moment to recover his strength and work out a way to get out of the ridiculous predicament.

'What on earth are you doing?' It was Angeline, come for a little exercise before she was to take tea with King

261

Hari and Queen Clementine. 'Adam, are you all right?' she giggled, as she saw he was trapped in the corset's strings tangled in the liana root.

'Oh, Princess!' He blushed, unable to hide his nakedness.

'I see you need some assistance.' She knelt, and instead of untying him, she took his stiff prick in her hands and stroked it. 'Are you trying on girl's clothes again? You know what they do to you, don't you? You only get over-excited.' She caressed the growing member, and he lay there, totally helpless.

'Oh, Princess, take pity on me,' he groaned.

Angeline sighed, and lifted her little skirt up to her waist. She wore no undergarments, of course, and her thighs opened to reveal a pale pink sex mouth, uncovered by hair. She slid over his trapped body.

'Of course I'll take pity on you. I can see what a state you are in.' She kissed him and suddenly he felt the slither of his prick inside her. Her tight little pussy, so well loved and dreamed about, enclosed his throbbing rod.

'Oh, Princess, what are you doing?'

'Well, if you don't know, I don't know how you are going to begin to please Trixie-Jane, you big booby!' she said, thrusting down hard on him. 'But you are big, aren't you!'

When Trixie-Jane emerged, dripping and naked from the embrace of her beloved sea, she found her discarded sarong where she had dropped it by the edge of the sand. As she stood she noticed Adam under the tree. He appeared to be sleeping, curled up in the shade.

'At last, Adam, you are here,' she called, no longer upset or concerned as her swim with the dolphins had put her in the best of humour.

She approached him but he did not move. She saw with surprise that he could not rise. He was tied firmly to the tangle of liana root by the ribbons of a corset, which he wore around his middle.

'Oh! What are you doing?'

He could not answer for he had somehow got a ribbon tied around his mouth. His hands, too, were tied together.

His cock and scrotum, however, were covered in the floral leafy penis sheath that she had crafted earlier for him.

He mumbled incoherently.

'Oh, Adam, you do look delectable in that corset. And you found the decorations I made you! They were even prettier earlier, before they wilted.' She knelt beside him, her naked little body still damp and glistening in the sun's low rays. 'Have you been waiting for me long? I went for a swim.' She took up his limp penis in her hands. 'Do you like being tied up? I suppose all men do . . .' She thought of the king and what Jezebel had done.

'All right, I can play this game. What do you want me to do to you?' She did not wait for the mumbles from his gagged mouth. She slid down next to him and took the soft flesh into her mouth. She sucked until he had an erection, hearing his groans. He could not touch her as his hands were tied. He writhed and panted. She let him out of her mouth and untied his gag. He breathed deeply. Without more ado she placed her bottom over his face, circling her buttocks neatly just above his mouth. His tongue reached out to her. He flicked it into her peachy flesh, sliding into the red slit. She held herself just above him, then lowered herself on to his mouth. He sucked the fruit, tasting its fresh, virginal flavours and the sea taste of urchins and oysters. His teeth nibbled gently and his tongue explored her tunnel. She came several times like this, quietly, panting hard and sighing.

'Enough of that, Adam.' She deftly untied his ribbons

and freed him from the bondage of the corset strings, but he held the garment close to him.

'No, do not remove it completely, my little Trixie-Jane,' he said. 'I want to keep it on while I make love to you.'

And so we leave the Isle de Paradis, on a night where the waning moon still cuts a swathe, like rippling white velvet over the water. The palm trees sway and rattle their big feather-like branches on the hut roofs. Inside the island huts, all is joy and pleasure. At the Forbidden Apple there is a party. Jezebel is being thoroughly fucked by Samson and Bartolem. Tom is trying out new techniques with Sylva. Lana is whipping several heavily bound soldiers. Cherry-Ripe and Petite Gigi are busy.

Ric is at home with his wife, Gertrude, who has some new tricks she wishes to show him.

At the palace, King Aristide is happily being whipped by Queen Clementine who in turn is being sucked by Joshua. The handmaiden has been given the night off.

Angeline and Hari are wrapped in each other's arms, blissfully happy. Angeline wears a dildo and Hari wears a tutu.

And Adam has his paintbrushes in his hands once more and his muse is wearing a pink satin corset, which Queen Clementine has generously given her. She is lying back on the couch. He is leaning over her and painting her pussy lips a bright pink, the same shade, he hopes, as the corset.

'Did The Powerful One do dreadful things to you, Adam?' she whispered, not really wanting to know but fascinated by the stories she had heard.

'Oh, no, it was nothing really. I'll show you if you like.' He took a rubber band from his pocket and placed it over his soft penis and twisted it twice around the base. 'Watch this. Stroke my prick gently,' he said.

His model took the youthful weapon between her now

skilful fingers and rubbed. His prick grew while she watched. Her nipples felt sore as she watched the beloved cock grow in her tender hands. He kissed her hard and pressed her breasts under his palms. Her thighs opened to his touch and he slipped into her wetness. She was so ready for his caress that she came straight away. He carried on pushing into her, his cock going up to the hilt. She felt the strange rubber against her flesh. It felt nice. He fucked her hard and she came again, crying out in joy. He allowed her a moment's rest before he started caressing her again, pressing his palms on to her pudenda. Her swollen sex lips were like bruised peaches, yet she wanted more, and he gave it, because his erection stayed big and stiff, the rubber band holding back his orgasm.

After she had her pleasure five times she begged him to rest. He, of course, was still randy and eager. He wanted her touch on him; he needed her fleshy tunnel surrounding his rod. He kissed her passionately.

'I love you, Trixie-Jane,' he said.

'And I love you, Adam,' she said, and they both giggled.

Afterwards, when they held each other in their arms, the sound of waves in their ears, she thought of telling the queen about the rubber device. It would be an excellent method of keeping the king straight and stiff and making his womenfolk happy. She fell asleep, content that on the morrow she would be well rewarded for her 'invention'.

BLACK LACE NEW BOOKS

Published in November

THE STRANGER
Portia Da Costa

When a confused and mysterious young man stumbles into the life of the recently widowed Claudia, he becomes the catalyst that reignites her sleeping sensuality. But is the wistful and angelic Paul really as innocent as he looks or is he an accomplished trickster with a dark and depraved agenda? As an erotic obsession flowers between Paul and Claudia, his true identity no longer seems to matter.

ISBN 0 352 33211 5

ELENA'S DESTINY
Lisette Allen

The gentle convent-bred Elena, awakened to the joys of forbidden passion by the masterful knight Aimery le Sabrenn, has been forcibly separated from him by war. Although he still captivates Elena with his powerful masculinity, Aimery is no longer hers. She must fight a desperate battle for his affections with two formidable opponents: a wanton young heiress and his scheming former mistress, Isobel. Dangerous games of love and lust are played out amidst the increasing tension of a merciless siege.

ISBN 0 352 33218 2

Published in December

LAKE OF LOST LOVE
Mercedes Kelly

Princess Angeline lives on a paradise island in the South Seas. She has a life of sensual fulfilment which she shares with her hedonistic friends. When her husband's gorgeous young manservant, Adam, is kidnapped and taken to nearby Monkey Island, Angeline sets about planning his rescue. Adam is being held captive by The Powerful One – a woman of superhuman desires – who is using him as her sex slave. Can Angeline confront this fearful female and return Adam to the Île de Paradis?

ISBN 0 352 33220 4

CONTEST OF WILLS
Louisa Francis

Sydney, Australia – the late 1870s. Vivacious young Melanie marries a man old enough to be her grandfather. On a trip to England, their journey is cut short by his sudden death. Melanie inherits his entire fortune unaware that her late husband has a grandson in England who is planning to contest the will. The louche and hedonistic Ric Lidell and his promiscuous half-sister travel to Sydney in a bid to get their hands on the money. Concealing his true identity from Melanie, Ric uses his satanic good looks to try and charm her. But other suitors have designs on the highly-sexed young widow. Who will win Melanie's heart and their way to her fortune?

ISBN 0 352 33223 9

SUGAR AND SPICE
A Black Lace short story anthology
£6.99

This is the long-awaited first collection of original Black Lace short stories. The book contains 20 unique and arousing tales guaranteed to excite. With contributions from female authors from Europe, Australia and America, this compendium provides a variety of settings and themes. Explicitly sexual and highly entertaining, *Sugar and Spice* is a kaleidoscope of female fantasy. Only the most erotic stories get into Black Lace anthologies.

ISBN 0 352 33227 1

To be published in January

UNHALLOWED RITES
Martine Marquand

Allegra Vitali is bored with life in her guardian's Venetian palazzo until the day sexual curiosity draws her to look at the depraved illustrations he keeps in his private chamber. She tries to deny her new passion for flesh by submitting to the life of a nun. The strange order of the Convent of Santa Agnetha provides new tests and new temptations, encouraging her to perform ritual acts with men and women who inhabit the strange, cloistered world.

ISBN 0 352 33222 0

BY ANY MEANS
Cheryl Mildenhall

Francesca, Veronique and Taran are partners in Falconer Associates, a London-based advertising agency. The three women are good friends and they're not averse to taking their pleasure with certain male employees. When they put in a bid to win a design account for Fast Track sportswear they are pitched against the notorious Oscar Rage who will stop at nothing to get what he wants. Despite Francesca's efforts to resist Oscar's arrogant charm, she finds him impossible to ignore.

ISBN 0 352 3221 1

If you would like a complete list of plot summaries of Black Lace titles, please fill out the questionnaire overleaf or send a stamped addressed envelope to:-

Black Lace, 332 Ladbroke Grove, London W10 5AH

BLACK
lace

BLACK LACE BACKLIST

All books are priced £4.99 unless another price is given.

BLUE HOTEL	Cherri Pickford ISBN 0 352 32858 4	☐
CASSANDRA'S CONFLICT	Fredrica Alleyn ISBN 0 352 32859 2	☐
THE CAPTIVE FLESH	Cleo Cordell ISBN 0 352 32872 X	☐
PLEASURE HUNT	Sophie Danson ISBN 0 352 32880 0	☐
OUTLANDIA	Georgia Angelis ISBN 0 352 32883 5	☐
BLACK ORCHID	Roxanne Carr ISBN 0 352 32888 6	☐
ODALISQUE	Fleur Reynolds ISBN 0 352 32887 8	☐
THE SENSES BEJEWELLED	Cleo Cordell ISBN 0 352 32904 1	☐
VIRTUOSO	Katrina Vincenzi ISBN 0 352 32907 6	☐
FIONA'S FATE	Fredrica Alleyn ISBN 0 352 32913 0	☐
HANDMAIDEN OF PALMYRA	Fleur Reynolds ISBN 0 352 32919 X	☐
THE SILKEN CAGE	Sophie Danson ISBN 0 352 32928 9	☐
THE GIFT OF SHAME	Sarah Hope-Walker ISBN 0 352 32935 1	☐
SUMMER OF ENLIGHTENMENT	Cheryl Mildenhall ISBN 0 352 32937 8	☐
A BOUQUET OF BLACK ORCHIDS	Roxanne Carr ISBN 0 352 32939 4	☐
JULIET RISING	Cleo Cordell ISBN 0 352 32938 6	☐

- - - - - - ✂ - - - - - - - - - - - - - - - - - - -

Please send me the books I have ticked above.

Name ....

Address ....

....

....

.... Post Code ....

Send to: **Cash Sales, Black Lace Books, 332 Ladbroke Grove, London W10 5AH.**

Please enclose a cheque or postal order, made payable to **Virgin Publishing Ltd**, to the value of the books you have ordered plus postage and packing costs as follows:

UK and BFPO – £1.00 for the first book, 50p for each subsequent book.

Overseas (including Republic of Ireland) – £2.00 for the first book, £1.00 each subsequent book.

If you would prefer to pay by VISA or ACCESS/ MASTERCARD, please write your card number and expiry date here:

....

Please allow up to 28 days for delivery.

Signature ....

- - - - - - ✂ - - - - - - - - - - - - - - - - - - -

WE NEED YOUR HELP . . .
to plan the future of women's erotic fiction –

– and no stamp required!

Yours are the only opinions that matter.

Black Lace is the first series of books devoted to erotic fiction by women for women.

We intend to keep providing the best-written, sexiest books you can buy. And we'd appreciate your help and valued opinion of the books so far. Tell us what you want to read.

THE BLACK LACE QUESTIONNAIRE

SECTION ONE: ABOUT YOU

1.1 Sex (*we presume you are female, but so as not to discriminate*)
Are you?

Male	☐		
Female	☐		

1.2 Age

under 21	☐	21–30	☐
31–40	☐	41–50	☐
51–60	☐	over 60	☐

1.3 At what age did you leave full-time education?

still in education	☐	16 or younger	☐
17–19	☐	20 or older	☐

1.4 Occupation _____

1.5 Annual household income
    under £10,000   ☐   £10–£20,000   ☐
    £20–£30,000   ☐   £30–£40,000   ☐
    over £40,000   ☐

1.6 We are perfectly happy for you to remain anonymous;
but if you would like to receive information on other
publications available, please insert your name and
address

_____

_____

_____

_____

SECTION TWO: ABOUT BUYING BLACK LACE BOOKS

2.1 How did you acquire this copy of *The Lake of Lost Love*?
    I bought it myself   ☐   My partner bought it   ☐
    I borrowed/found it   ☐

2.2 How did you find out about Black Lace books?
    I saw them in a shop   ☐
    I saw them advertised in a magazine   ☐
    I saw the London Underground posters   ☐
    I read about them in _____
    Other _____

2.3 Please tick the following statements you agree with:
    I would be less embarrassed about buying Black
    Lace books if the cover pictures were less explicit   ☐
    I think that in general the pictures on Black
    Lace books are about right   ☐
    I think Black Lace cover pictures should be as
    explicit as possible   ☐

2.4 Would you read a Black Lace book in a public place – on
a train for instance?
    Yes   ☐   No   ☐

SECTION THREE: ABOUT THIS BLACK LACE BOOK

3.1 Do you think the sex content in this book is:
   - Too much ☐ About right ☐
   - Not enough ☐

3.2 Do you think the writing style in this book is:
   - Too unreal/escapist ☐ About right ☐
   - Too down to earth ☐

3.3 Do you think the story in this book is:
   - Too complicated ☐ About right ☐
   - Too boring/simple ☐

3.4 Do you think the cover of this book is:
   - Too explicit ☐ About right ☐
   - Not explicit enough ☐

Here's a space for any other comments:

SECTION FOUR: ABOUT OTHER BLACK LACE BOOKS

4.1 How many Black Lace books have you read? ☐

4.2 If more than one, which one did you prefer?

4.3 Why?

SECTION FIVE: ABOUT YOUR IDEAL EROTIC NOVEL

We want to publish the books you want to read – so this is
your chance to tell us exactly what your ideal erotic novel
would be like.

5.1 Using a scale of 1 to 5 (1 = no interest at all, 5 = your
     ideal), please rate the following possible settings for an
     erotic novel:

     Medieval/barbarian/sword 'n' sorcery   ☐
     Renaissance/Elizabethan/Restoration   ☐
     Victorian/Edwardian   ☐
     1920s & 1930s – the Jazz Age   ☐
     Present day   ☐
     Future/Science Fiction   ☐

5.2 Using the same scale of 1 to 5, please rate the following
     themes you may find in an erotic novel:

     Submissive male/dominant female   ☐
     Submissive female/dominant male   ☐
     Lesbianism   ☐
     Bondage/fetishism   ☐
     Romantic love   ☐
     Experimental sex e.g. anal/watersports/sex toys ☐
     Gay male sex   ☐
     Group sex   ☐

     Using the same scale of 1 to 5, please rate the following
     styles in which an erotic novel could be written:

     Realistic, down to earth, set in real life   ☐
     Escapist fantasy, but just about believable   ☐
     Completely unreal, impressionistic, dreamlike   ☐

5.3 Would you prefer your ideal erotic novel to be written
     from the viewpoint of the main male characters or the
     main female characters?

         Male   ☐   Female   ☐
         Both   ☐

5.4 What would your ideal Black Lace heroine be like? Tick as many as you like:

Dominant	☐	Glamorous	☐
Extroverted	☐	Contemporary	☐
Independent	☐	Bisexual	☐
Adventurous	☐	Naïve	☐
Intellectual	☐	Introverted	☐
Professional	☐	Kinky	☐
Submissive	☐	Anything else?	☐
Ordinary	☐	_____	

5.5 What would your ideal male lead character be like? Again, tick as many as you like:

Rugged	☐		
Athletic	☐	Caring	☐
Sophisticated	☐	Cruel	☐
Retiring	☐	Debonair	☐
Outdoor-type	☐	Naïve	☐
Executive-type	☐	Intellectual	☐
Ordinary	☐	Professional	☐
Kinky	☐	Romantic	☐
Hunky	☐		
Sexually dominant	☐	Anything else?	☐
Sexually submissive	☐	_____	

5.6 Is there one particular setting or subject matter that your ideal erotic novel would contain?

_____

SECTION SIX: LAST WORDS

6.1 What do you like best about Black Lace books?

_____

6.2 What do you most dislike about Black Lace books?

_____

6.3 In what way, if any, would you like to change Black Lace covers?

_____

6.4   Here's a space for any other comments:

_____

_____

_____

_____

Thank you for completing this questionnaire. Now tear it out of the book – carefully! – put it in an envelope and send it to:

> **Black Lace**
> **FREEPOST**
> **London**
> **W10 5BR**

No stamp is required if you are resident in the U.K.